Girl From The Oil Sands

J.L. Green

Copyright © 2022 I.L. Green

Cover design by: Neda Aria at NedaAria.Info, as featured in Outcast Press' second anthology, *Slut Vomit*

www.Outcast-Press.com

(e-book) ASIN: B0B6B264DH

(print) ISBN-13: 978-1-7379829-5-1

This a work of fiction. All characters, names, incidents, and dialogue, except for incidental references to public figures, historical events, businesses, and services are either products of the author's imagination or used in a fictitious manner not intended to refer to any living persons or to disparage any company's products or services.

Part 1:
Girl Behind The Silver

Chapter 1

I was so pissed. That piece-of-shit Nova picked the wrong time to die. Mid-river at the crest of the highway bridge. I couldn't walk the rest of the way into town 'cause that's where the police would come from. So I walked the opposite way toward nothing, but I had to get off the bridge. Cars were starting to line up, traffic-jam style, and it was so apparent that the skinny, twenty-something bean walking away was the owner of the stalled car. I hadn't traveled through the Midwest since 1980, and this was the nefarious beginning of a five-year reunion with my favorite part of the country.

"Hey, girl," someone shouted.

I kept walking with my head down.

"You there! What the fuck is going on?"

I looked up from the pavement. Green eyes magnified by giant plastic-framed glasses engaged me through the window of an old serial-killer van. I was cold though the temp was 40 degrees: the wind was blowing and the heater in the Nova hadn't worked since St. Louis.

"Stalled car," I shouted back at the big glasses.

"Fucking traffic isn't moving!"

I kept walking.

She hung her head out the window, dark locks blew in the breeze. "Hey, girl," she shouted at the back of my jacket. "Aren't you cold?"

Her van was the last vehicle before the start of the bridge. Sparse, leafless woodlands framed the highway and river on the bank, offering little resistance to the frigid breeze. Autumn announced her presence in this part of the country much sooner than when I first fired up the ghastly Nova in Florida. I turned and hurried back to her window. She looked to be my age and was alone—not that I was going to trust anyone, but I was cold.

"It's my car. I hafta get outta here before the cops come."

"You live in a cornfield? 'Cause that's all there is in the direction you're going."

"You need to shut up. You're drawing attention and I need to be outta sight quick."

"Intriguing," the dark-haired girl said. "I'm often trying to stay away from police. We're birds of a feather, you and I."

"That's sweet. Maybe we can be pen pals." I turned away again.

"You can get in," she offered. "I'm heading toward town."

I stopped walking.

"You know, *town*: food, shelter."

I turned back to approach the window. "You can get me over the bridge?"

"No one will even know you're in here."

"Why should I trust you?"

"Comrade, we're sisters-in-arms. Let me show off my police avoidance skills to you."

A spider tattoo decorated her forearm. Her eyes were set deep in too much dark shadow and lashes elongated by darker mascara. In normal circumstances, those wouldn't be signs to trust a person. But I didn't think we were going to have a bible study if I hid in her van. I was screwed anyway. The direction I was heading would lead to certain doom. Staying with the car would cause the same doom. I really had no choice 'cause I doubted any better offers would arise if I kept walking.

I opened the passenger side of the van.

She was opening a thermos. Steam rolled out of the top when she was finally successful. She poured some into its screw-on cup. "I'm Kira," she announced. "Black coffee." She handed the cup to me.

I gratefully accepted and took a long drink.

Kira stared at me like she was trying to decide something. She held a finger up for me to wait a second and silently moved to the back of the van, where she hunted through bags. Traffic was not moving. It looked like she was packed up and on the move. But there were only a couple bags and a few cardboard boxes in the back, which might even have been empty.

"Here," she said after returning to the driver's seat. Kira removed the screw-top on a dark bottle, which looked like it held some kind of medicine. She took the coffee cup and slowly poured liquid into it, carefully holding it in front of her face so she could judge the amount. "Elixir of terpin hydrate cough medicine laced with a little codeine," she explained as she watched the thin stream fall into the coffee. "It'll make you feel better and sweeten your coffee at the same time." She smiled as she handed back the cup.

I took a sip, then swallowed down the rest.

"So," Kira started, "what's the deal with you?"

"Just a gal trying to make a buck."

"Seems like you need a better car."

"The car is a piece of shit, but it's not mine."

"Did you steal it?"

"No, my boss gave it to me for the trip. He probably stole it."

"So. What's the gig?"

"I'm making a gold run."

"*Gold run?*"

"Yeah, running gold to Canada."

"Canada? For what purpose?"

"For me to make five grand. It's a quarter million in gold bullion for whatever reason. I was just told who to deliver it to and not to get caught with it."

"That's a lot of gold! Too heavy for the car?"

"It only weighs about 30 pounds. But he said not to get caught, so I'm leaving it."

Traffic moved slightly. Kira put the van in gear until having to stop again. She stared at me again, thinking. "How about a name?"

"Oh, you don't wanna know who this guy is. He's really hardcore. The less you know, the better."

"No," she laughed softly. "Your name."

"I'm Iris," I said, embarrassed.

"Iris. That's an older name. Pretty, though."

I didn't answer. I should have said thanks, but I suddenly noticed how relaxed I was becoming. Kira was right. Her magic elixir did make me feel better. My anxiety was melting away.

She seemed thoughtful. "Can we retrieve that gold?" We were inching close to the old Nova toward the top of the bridge.

I pointed ahead. The police were on their way from town.

"This is my *'Professional'* hat," Kira explained. "Put it on to kinda use as a disguise." She handed me her black-wool stocking cap. "*The Professional*," she explained. "Jean Reno, Gary Oldman, Danny Aiello."

"Natalie Portman!"

"Yeah, yeah. I fell in love with Reno. Mostly, I fell in love with his black cap. As soon as I could, I got me one. Wasn't an easy find."

"You want to be a hitman?"

"No."

"A killer for hire?"

"I can't even kill a spider. I'm just an admirer."

"Kinda want to be a bad gal?" I asked.

"I stole this van," Kira explained. "If I stop, there's a chance the police will run the plates and figure out I'm not the owner, and I'm two counties away from where I want to be."

"You some kind of criminal?"

"Just a gal trying to make a buck."

"Keep driving," I suggested.

She gradually accelerated along with the rest of the rubberneckers. Kira had the softest, most inviting green eyes I had ever seen. Her hair was long and dark, framing an oval face, her eyes alluring as she looked in my direction. She struck me in that moment as a kind of dark angel, or a friendly daemon. She had put a spell on me with a most congenial potion.

I smiled and looked into her eyes, searching for her purpose. I was rewarded with a large, heartwarming smile.

Her face lit up and her eyes sparkled as she turned forward to see the road ahead. She nodded.

"These bigger towns are the worst," Kira started after cresting the bridge. "Not quite a city and zero small-town charm. Small-town charm can get a girl pretty far. Stop in for a coffee at the local Dunkin' Donuts and someone is bound to strike up a conversation. Even the cops aren't afraid of a vagabond kiddo like me."

"You running scams?"

"I've some experience with grifts but not enough to work alone. I'm more of an opportunist."

"A user..."

"Everyone's a user, Iris. Ya can't go it alone. It's *misuse* that crosses the line."

"Says the girl driving a stolen van."

"Yeah, I could tell right away you're gonna be a hard nut to crack. My last gig, I was paid with a shovel full of amphetamines and phenobarbital, which doesn't translate into cash very easily. So maybe I misused my boss, but I felt pretty justified."

"What was the gig?"

"I'd rather not say, except it wasn't as clean as running gold."

"I've never been addicted to anything," I explained my feelings about the pills.

"Me either. Cigarettes, I can take or leave. Don't care much for the hooch. But I'm kind of a garbage-can drug enthusiast."

"A poly-pharmaceuticalist?"

"That's a big fucking word."

"It's been used to describe me in the past. Coke is my thing now."

"Ew." Kira put her oversized blue sunglasses on as we passed the cops. "We good?"

"Just fine..."

"Well, we need cash."

I closed my eyes. "Dammit!"

"What is it?" Kira asked.

"I left my cash in the car."

"Well, fuck me..."

"We need to go back."

"Bad idea."

"It was a lot of money."

"Money is easy to come by," Kira assured. "Gold bullion and cash, that's too incriminating."

"My tapes were in there, too."

"I have no music. And I'm hungry."

"Well, we're in a pickle."

Kira laughed. "No money, food, or tunes. You hooked your wagon to the wrong horse." She reached into the pocket of her leather jacket and removed a bottle. She poured some pills into her mouth without even looking. "You want some amphetamines?"

"How many you got?"

"I dunno. Few hundred."

"We could sell them."

Kira laughed. She turned toward me, glasses still on and mouth wide open in a glorious smile. "That might get us a hamburger! You want some?"

"Not right now."

"I have a few dollars. Nothing much, but enough."

"I appreciate that."

"Don't thank me yet," Kira laughed. "I have enough gas just to get us clear of this town."

At least we were able to get off the bridge and into town. And I felt an attraction to this girl. Like we were kin. The feeling came on quickly. Probably with the talk about food. But there was something else. A feeling or a vibe she was giving off. We were opposites in most ways, I could tell that already. In some way, though, that I couldn't put a finger on, we were alike.

"Camping," Kira announced after driving an hour.

"Are we far enough away?"

"They have no idea. Clueless, the authorities."

The large town on the river had disappeared long ago from the rearview, giving way to hilly and curvy country roads.

Kira assured me we were on a main route. "This is Illinois," she explained. The landscape was wooded and the last leaves were clinging to branches, unwilling to make way for the barren bleakness of winter.

Occasionally, the woods would give way to harvested cornfields, for which I was thankful. Allergies were my only complaint when it came to the Midwest. Fall in a deciduous forest was my favorite thing in the world. I'd been all over in my short life, following the money trail from the desert to the heart of New York City. There was no geographical region hospitable to me besides the center of the country with its constant variation in weather. I even looked forward to winter.

It was my hope anyway, to see the snow with enough cash to settle in for a bit. Relax and regroup. It had been a long time on the move with few moments of reflection or rest. Actual sleep was hard for me unless it was chemically induced.

"What if they dust for prints?" I asked.

"You have a criminal record?"

"No," I said.

"What the fuck? Just paranoid?"

"I might be hungry…"

"I saw a sign for a state park up ahead. Let's stop and see if we can camp the night."

If we were to keep traversing, I was close to accepting the speed Kira offered. But sleep was a more exciting prospect. The weather would be comfortable for outdoor slumbering.

When we got to the site, I said, "You just paid for a camping spot for the night and you have NO tent?"

"Don't have a tent. Got empty boxes."

"We're sleeping in empty boxes on the ground?"

"We're sleeping in empty boxes in the van."

"So what did we just pay for?"

"Firewood! It ain't camping without a fire."

In the pine forest, there was a metal fire pit and, indeed, a small pile of logs and kindling. We looked around at the empty sites.

"Guess it's late in the year for campers," I observed.

"Fine with me."

"Are we hunting for rabbits or something?"

Kira actually laughed. "I saw a crappy-looking diner back down the road. Let's see if we can rustle up a meatloaf or something."

"How much money you got?"

"That's about it. We eat, though, and I may want to finagle up some liquor."

By "finagle," Kira meant trading a handful of phenobarbital to a horny parking-lot grunger for a pint outside a shady liquor store. We didn't get to eat the meatloaf of our dreams, but the nearby diner had a nice thick burger on the cheap.

In the van, Kira rummaged through our plain paper bag that contained a couple colas and pint of Everclear.

"Wow," I commented. "That's hardcore."

"I feel like getting drunk, but not so much like drinking."

"Why not just keep doing barbs?"

"Not the same. I'm nervous. Hard to blow off steam with a sedative."

"Why so nervous?"

Kira hesitated for a few moments. She obviously didn't want to get into it. "Circumstances. Strangers."

"Me?"

"Well, you don't know me, I don't know you. Maybe after a little drinkie poo and a warm fire, I won't be so nervous."

So I was expected to open up some. I wasn't just hitching a ride. She was expecting more time from me than I wanted to invest. But then, everyone does. I wasn't as interested in her, further than a meal and a place to bunk. Was that a character flaw? I'd always done pretty well on my own. Kira could hardly be considered dead weight, though. And what did I have to lose, really? I was stuck and she offered more than breaking the law for fun and profit, or being raped.

"Need to clear my mind, too," Kira explained. "There's a lot going on all of a sudden."

"Tell me about it."

"You get anxious too?"

"I've been on the road for a bit. I just go with the flow, ya know? It's a survival technique. I don't get anxious 'til I sit still and relax a bit."

We pulled back into the camping area. Kira ripped one of her cardboard boxes apart to start the fire. She lit a cigarette with a lighter. I reached out for a drag and she gave me the cig. Smoking wasn't really my thing, but she made it clear it was time to warm up to each other. Sharing a smoke with her was more of an act to express friendliness.

She studied me as I handed it back. "I like your short hair," she said. "Not many girls pulling that off these days."

"Thanks. It's more for convenience than fashion."

"Are you gay?"

"I don't think so. At least, I've never had the opportunity, so I can't really say." There it was. And I wasn't going to lie to her, not at this point. My past was littered with sticky situations from leading people on. I rarely opened up, and when I did, it was often interpreted as coming on to them. I was finished with that. Easier to be honest up front. If I was nice to someone, I wanted them to know my intentions were simply kind. When I wanted sex, I was upfront about that too. Either way, situations never turned romantic. At least, not for me.

I didn't ask Kira. Seemed obvious at this point, so why pursue it? She was a gay girl and, so far, I wasn't. If I seemed interested in her sexuality, a familiar sticky situation might arise.

Kira seated herself beside the burning fire on one of the many large logs meant for that purpose. "We're safe here," she said.

"I don't think anyone's looking for us," I agreed.

"I mean *safe*." She took a long drag from the cigarette. "You and I are safe. Cool?"

"Cool."

Kira opened a bottle of cola, then the Everclear. She took a small swig of the booze and chased it with the soda. She handed me the unopened cola and strong spirit. I took a healthy shot and waved off the soft drink."

"Tough guy," she teased.

"I don't like a chaser. I've had a taste for liquor from my first drink. I'll take a cigarette, though."

She obliged and drank more Everclear. I lit up and took another drink. The fire was burning well and casted eerie dancing shadows off the bottom of the pines. The booze started affecting my head. It had been a while since my last binge, and I felt like I could finish the entire pint myself.

"It's nice here," Kira observed. "The breeze is making a whispering sound. Might not be bad sleeping outside after all."

"Enjoy it while you can."

"The breeze?"

"The peace."

"You have a sharp edge to you, woman."

I took another large gulp. "Just don't get much rest."

"A gal's gotta make a buck."

"Yeah."

"How did you get a gold-running gig in the first place?"

"Just a thing. I found out right away I couldn't punch a clock for a living. Been hustling one way or another most my life."

"Can't stand the daily grind?"

"I have times in my life when it's just plain hard to get out of bed."

"Times?"

"Weeks. Maybe longer. Just too hard to move, or even breathe."

Recognition shone in Kira's eyes. That should satisfy her a bit, I thought. She wanted to get to know me? Well, that was about it. But her demeanor changed. Her features softened a bit. She looked at me differently from that point on. It must have been a comfort to find she was traveling with someone like her. A kindred spirit. I didn't care to spend time with people exactly like me. I could tolerate Kira, but mostly I found misery does *not* like company.

"I have to keep moving," she said. "To stop is to, you know, *stop*."

"Yeah. Gotta keep things interesting. Right?"

Kira raised the pint in salute to my words. She downed a large swallow without a chaser and handed it to me. "We need an opportunity," Kira explained. "If one doesn't present itself, we'll just hafta make one ourselves."

"What you got in mind?" I asked.

"Nothing yet. Just listing priorities. Number one has to be money. Are you sure we can't go back and get into that car? Things must've cooled down with the authorities by now."

I shrugged. "The gold and money are stashed in the trunk in place of the spare tire. Guess it depends on if it's been searched yet."

"Maybe it got put off."

"We met in the evening, probably at shift change."

"People want to get home. Put things off 'til the next day."

"Maybe?"

Kira took another swallow and looked thoughtfully into the night. The fire cast flashes of orange across her face. Her hair was wild and her eyes reflected the snapping flames. They were still greenish in color, but lighter, almost gray.

I felt a surge of attraction. I suddenly wouldn't mind tagging along with her, even without knowing her destination. I'd never met anyone whose company I actually enjoyed. Maybe she was the friend I never had. I was never taught how to have a friend. I didn't know there was such an allure I could feel to any one person. I knew other people were able to bind themselves to another person. Look out for them, care for their well-being. But not me.

"Stop looking at me," Kira ordered, breaking my reverie.

"Oh! I wasn't really," I lied. "Just staring in your direction."

"Thinking about it?"

"What's that? The car?"

"No. Girls. Wondering what girls are like?"

"I think we're both getting drunk."

"We're drunk and about to spend the night together in a really small space."

"I'm okay."

"It could get cold in there."

"Whatever. I'm fine, really."

"You sound kinda like you wanna be here."

"Shut up and hand me the bottle."

"Oh fuck," Kira said with embarrassment. She handed it over. "How rude can I be?"

I smiled as I put the glass to my lips and made sure she saw me smile. "Getting to know each other was a good idea."

"Yeah..." Kira pondered before taking a drag from the cigarette.

"We have one thing going for us if we go back," I said.

"What's that?" Kira asked.

I reached into the pocket of my jeans and produced the keys to the Nova. "This might slow them down a bit."

💧 💧 💧

By morning, I awoke with Kira's arm draped over my breast with her fingers hooked onto my right shoulder. I always slept well with another person close by. And I considered that a sign that all was not lost. That I didn't hate all of humanity and it was possible for me to develop relationships with others. Even if I didn't like the person, if they were next to me at night, I could relax.

Something about warm breath on the back of my neck was the best sedative I could find. Booze usually kept me up at night, but this morning, I didn't even feel the leftover effects of grain alcohol. What I did feel was contented, and I made up my mind to go with this feeling. This knowing that Kira was going to be good for me.

What was uncommon about this morning was the silence. Kira carried herself with an easy confidence that had engulfed me in the night, leaving me with a silence in my head I had no memory of ever experiencing. The voice was quiet, the guy in my head who hates me so much, constantly telling me to hurt myself and filled with awful ideas that always ended poorly. He was silent and I wasn't alone.

Even if this ends up being a temporary arrangement, I'm sticking with Kira. My mind's made up.

Chapter 2

My heart was so guarded. Getting a good night's sleep wasn't really a basis for lifelong commitment. Getting something to eat after I woke up became a priority, making any warm fuzzy feelings background noise.

"Hungry," Kira announced, rubbing her eyes.

"Yeah."

"Let's check the car for loose change."

"Really?"

"You have any better suggestions? Unless you have a checkbook, we need to scrounge money for a McBreakfast."

"Checkbook?" I asked out loud. *Said*, actually. A statement that I put an upward inflection on because I knew I had checks—not mine. They would have to be forged. But maybe we could pull it off.

"You holding?"

I nodded and smiled. I knew Kira would approve, and somehow that made me happy.

"We need to clean up," she announced. "Or one of us. We won't pull this off dirty and smelly like we are."

Like a Boy Scout, always prepared, Kira produced another hat. It was green and knitted—bigger and more wintery than her wool cap, which I gave back to her. Washing in a gas station bathroom was easier than expected. Except for our hair, we silently cleaned the stink off with actual soap and warm water.

"Our jackets still smell like campfire," Kira said. "We'll have to not wear them in."

"We need something to purchase." I was ahead of her in planning the forgery at the grocery store.

"Something to drink. And more cigarettes."

"I want peanut butter." I hankered for the creamy ecstasy.

"Really?"

"Gods, yes. I fucking love peanut butter."

"Then we need bread, too." Kira was clearly nervous about our endeavor and fussing like a momma bear.

"I don't need bread, just a spoon."

Kira did a double take I pretended not to notice. I wasn't about to let her make me nervous.

"Inside the store," Kira spoke softly so only I could hear, "you want me to do the writing?"

"Doesn't matter," I said in my regular voice because I didn't want to attract attention.

"It does, actually. The person writing the check is guilty of the crime and the one who will be charged."

"I wasn't even thinking about that. So you want to go to jail?"

"I do not want to go to jail. I just don't want you to."

"I hate when people overthink crime. Don't worry about it. Neither of us are going to jail. If I get arrested, I'll be back on the road by nightfall. I'll sweet-talk the court-appointed lawyer. Give him a little pro bono of my own."

"What if *he's* a *she*?"

"Where do you think we are, California? Sure! Maybe you should write the check..."

"Discouraging..." Kira went from a bundle of nerves to a bundle of confusion.

"How's that? You offered and I'm taking you up on it."

"Your opinion of female attorneys."

"I do better with what I'm familiar with," I explained.

"Suit yourself."

"I will, thank you."

The crime went off without a hitch. Most crimes did, at least the ones I committed. The thing with the Nova didn't count because I was working for someone who told me what vehicle to use. Anyway, we were on our way to rectify that. Very quickly. Small towns were dangerous to people like us—young, disheveled women on their own, smelling like a campfire. It was suspicious, or unseemly, whatever triggers those white folks. I hated backtracking, though. Made me feel incompetent. Should have been moving forward, not cleaning up the past.

We returned to the town on the river pretty early so we had a picnic along the water. Made a meal of cold, grocery fried chicken and salty potato chips. The weather was cool and the force of the wind made a lot of chop on the river. We didn't talk much. The taste of the chicken grease reminded us how hungry we were. But I watched when Kira wasn't looking. She was a meticulously clean eater, which might have caused our lack of conversation. Her mindfulness was almost irritating, especially after I caught myself wiping grease on my jeans. Kira didn't touch any part of her body without wiping each finger on a paper napkin. She must have thought I was a pig.

"I used to dance," I announced for no reason at all.

Kira turned to me, licking her fingers.

I shrugged. "We didn't really get to know each other last night. Isn't that what you wanted? Have some alcohol and get to know each other? 'Cause I don't think that's what we did. At least, I didn't feel like I did my part."

"Well, what kind?"

"Started with ballet. Then did other stuff. Mostly jazz."

"So you were taught," she clarified.

"From about eight-years-old."

"So you had parents? They put you in classes?"

"That's irrelevant," I said.

"Gotcha."

"I mean, obviously I didn't have that kinda money at that age."

"I didn't know, know if you were raised by Daddy Warbucks or whatever."

"That wouldn't have been bad."

Kira wiped the fingertips she just sucked clean. She smiled, seemingly happy with the little bit she got from me. "I play guitar," she admitted.

"Cool. How long?"

"Long as I could remember. Been a while, though."

"Did it bore you?"

"No. I don't have my guitar anymore. Had the same one all my life. Then I lost it. Never replaced it. Don't know if I could."

"You can't play a different guitar?"

Kira shook her head. There was more to that story, but I wasn't going to press it.

"We're gonna lose sunlight," Kira insisted.

"Police station?"

"Why?"

"I have no idea where the impound yard is."

"Right…"

Chapter 3

Vic was coming to town and I was scared. I didn't make delivery, and it was worth him making the trip. After all, the car belonged to him. It must have been reported stolen at the impounding yard. I was suddenly in a hurry; Kira was self-possessed with that damn confidence permeating her being. The yard manager said Vic had to talk to the police, but the car was right over there. No one around to open it.

"Can I try?" Kira asked.

"Well, the owner is coming to town to claim it."

"Yeah, Vic. He's my boyfriend. I have the key. He sent me to get the registration out of the glove box to take to the police station." Which worked. In minutes, we found ourselves unsupervised over the open trunk of the Nova.

The cash was in one of those cloth zipper-bags made for holding bills. It was right next to the box of gold Kira couldn't help but open.

"No. Fuck the gold," I swore. I never said that word and yet it jumped out of my mouth like it was a daily occurrence. "I was told not to get caught with the gold. The cash we can explain away. Everyone finds a way to get cash. No one sets out to obtain gold bars. Especially this many."

"Shit." Kira stared into the box with wide, lustful eyes.

"Where the fuck would you exchange them?" There I went again.

"Can't be that hard," she whispered.

I closed the lid and slid the box back into the wheel well. "We can't have them. You gotta trust me." I slammed the trunk, but not before throwing the keys in. "Taking those is automatic jail. Not getting caught with them, but taking them with you right now, will put you in jail as sure as the sun will come up tomorrow."

Kira turned and walked out of the yard. Hadn't said a word but clearly wanted to get away from me. I generally didn't care if people were mad at me. It didn't really bother me that Kira was angry, but she was walking away with the money.

My only consolation was that I had her cigarettes. I lit one, took a couple long drags until it occurred to me to leave the yard also. Was Kira merely being prudent? Standing there in the open, clearly connected to the Nova and its contents might be a bad idea after all. The van was a couple blocks away, parked on the street. It was still there, locked, and I didn't have the key. I lit another cigarette for spite and sat on the bumper.

The sun was setting when the lights of a Volkswagen Beetle approached me. The vehicle parked behind the van a yard from my feet. I wasn't surprised when Kira exited the driver's side. She hurried to the van, key in hand, with the Beetle still running.

"Gotta get our shit," she explained.

"Where the fuck did you go?"

"We gotta ditch the van. Stolen, remember? We've already been in one place too long." Kira exited with our jackets and the groceries from earlier. She also took a gas can from the back after throwing the key inside and slamming the doors locked.

"You planning arson?"

"Get in," she ordered.

"You got the money?" I asked inside.

She lurched the manual shift into gear and smoked the front tires while driving away. "Been a while since I handled a clutch."

"Strange choice of car to steal then."

"The door was open and it was on a hill. No keys but I got it rolling and popped the clutch. That's why we need the gas can. Turning the car off to fill up is problematic." Kira pulled the zipper pouch from her jeans and plopped it on my lap. "We have most of the cash."

"What did you buy?"

"Look inside."

I pulled the zipper, and inside was a plastic bag of white powder along with the rest of the cash.

"You're shootin' up?" I asked.

"Fuck no! That's coke."

"That's a lot of coke!"

"It was a bargain."

"How the fuck did you find street drugs so fast?"

"I have a sense for such things."

"A sense..."

"Some people have an intuitive sense of direction..."

"You have a sense for drugs? Like a Spidey sense?"

"Exactly!"

"How do you know it's not laundry detergent?"

"'Cause I'm so fucked up right now." The car lurched again as Kira found third gear. She was lying to me.

"You weren't gone very long."

Kira didn't reply.

"Like a half hour."

"We gotta get back to the freeway," she offered. She was quiet until the Beetle left the city. Oddly contemplative for someone "speeding on coke."

"Okay, we have all of the money," I observed. "So, where did all the coke come from?"

"Can we not talk about it right now?"

"But you lied to me."

"I'm sorry for lying. I've never said that to another person, ever. So that's something. Just trust me, we need to keep moving."

"Did you kill somebody?" I was beside myself with anxiety.

"Today?"

"Yes. Just now!"

"I didn't. But I don't want to talk about it right this minute. I'm concentrating on maintaining the speed limit."

"But something happened."

"Something," she agreed, turning her head to me, "*happened.*"

Kira was shaken. I couldn't trust her, but I saw in her face that something occurred she wanted to get away from quickly. It obviously involved the coke, which she wasn't traumatized enough to part with.

"I want to use the coke," I said.

"I was hoping so."

"I want to know about this 'something' later."

"Later…" she reiterated.

"That's fine."

"No hurry."

"I'm never in a hurry." I felt Kira stalling for time though.

"Well, I am. Time to get outta this shitty little town."

I took a hit from the back of my hand, successfully, even with Kira popping the clutch so often. It felt good to have the cash back. It felt good having Kira back. I never got used to the letdown of people exiting my life on a whim. In a way, I was sure I'd never see Kira again. But she surprised me. I didn't have to deal with the shame and sadness today.

The drug kicked in. I turned in her direction, but she was too busy trying to drive to notice. Suddenly, I wanted more booze. More food would be a good idea, too. It would have to wait. Kira was in the zone and heading out of town.

"Are we in a hurry?" I asked 'cause I felt out of the loop. Kira was being a clique of one.

"We left a stolen van at a crime scene, I'm driving a stolen car, we have a bag of stolen coke and more cash than we can explain. We're sorta in a hurry."

"Who's after us?"

"No one yet."

"But we can get busted for all those things no matter where we are."

"That's why I'm not driving too fast." Kira took a long, cleansing breath to clear her head.

"We're escaping something."

She clammed up.

"I'm sorry. I remember, *later*."

"Sorry."

"Can we hang at that campsite again?" I asked.

"We have to be farther than that."

As long as I didn't talk, she stayed quiet. I hadn't known her long enough to learn her tells. I fondled the cash bag on my lap and turned my attention to myself. I hated doing that. My life was a constant struggle to distract from myself. I not only became anxious but scared when I considered the amount of coke in my possession. "Fuck," I breathed.

"I knew you'd figure it out soon."

"Vic carries this much coke. All the time."

"And this is his fucked-up car. That guy has no mechanical sense."

"He buys throwaways."

"I feel guilty, like I put you in danger," Kira said.

"Tell me what happened."

"One of his goons pulled up. I was on the sidewalk. I got in."

"Is he still alive?"

"Unfortunately. He said he was from Chicago and knew everything that happened to your car from Vic, and he had gone to the impound yard."

"So you just go off with anyone?" I was astonished.

"Gal's gotta make a buck."

"When you found out he was bent on revenge, you came back to me? Like I'm sloppy seconds?"

"I fucking told you I wouldn't dump you. I don't promise that, to anybody, ever."

"So you were planning on picking me back up?" I was furious.

"I was curious. He wasn't being threatening. I wanted to see if there was some angle I could exploit."

"The cash just wasn't enough."

"I was still pissed about the gold, I guess."

"No," I disagreed. "No. The cash is not enough for you. I'm not enough. The gold and Vic's business was just too attractive to you."

Kira started crying. "That's not true."

"I'm not sure I trust you."

"Do you know how to drive a stick?"

"No," I admitted.

"Then you have to shut up 'cause I can't drive and cry at the same time."

"I've never fucked Vic, ya know."

"I don't fuck men," Kira said.

That finally shut me up. I forgot that Kira wasn't a boy-crazy girl looking for the next free ride. She really wanted to exploit Vic's Neanderthal henchman and, apparently, she was successful. We had his car and his coke. What was he going to do? Even if he got the Nova back without the cops finding the gold, it wouldn't go very far. The head was most likely cracked.

Kira pulled the Bug onto a side street to park. "He'll think we're heading north. He thinks you still have the gold and that you're going north. He's gonna think you're finishing the job."

I stayed quiet. My anxiety was subsiding, but I still needed to catch my breath and collect my thoughts. "He has no transportation."

Kira turned in my direction. She was still sniffling, her eyes puffy and red from crying. "But we're actually heading that way. He can make a phone call. I didn't actually kill him."

"What happened? It's officially 'later.'"

"I may have been flirty. He got out with the keys to remove his pants."

"What happened?" I was amazed again.

Kira gestured with her hand to show the inside of the car. "The coke was sitting on the dash."

"So you know what's more important to me than being dumped?"

"I won't lie again." Like she read my mind. "To you."

"What about how you feel about me?" I asked, thinking I could get more than my due.

Kira kicked the car back into gear. "You already know that."

I shut up. Let myself get lost in the confusion. I'm sure she ran into my type all the time. Confused. Wanting to be nice. Be girly. Just not sure.

"We're going west," she announced. "I've never seen the Mississippi."

"Ducks," I finally said when she was on the interstate.

"What about them?"

"They'll be on the river this time of year, eating. Mostly, all you see are their butts while they look for food."

"Duck butts?"

"Yup."

"Isn't it too cold? I thought they went south."

"It's warming up. They're on the move."

"Does Vic know about your duck-butt obsession?"

"I developed it before running into him. It just came to mind. Haven't been to the river in years."

"It's decided then." Kira softly giggled.

I started disassociating. This hadn't happened in a while and seemed to be triggered by remembering the past. In a few moments, I'd be tranced out.

"Food," I managed to say to her.

"Yes."

"Booze."

"Okay."

"Tampons."

"Right."

Waning cognition...

Chapter 4

*I'm that portion
you were told did not exist
I'm the awareness
they want you to resist
But you found far too early
I wasn't an intruder
And when we became lovers
you discovered the selfishness
to be true after all*

"They're onto us."

"Kira?" I mumbled.

"Wake the fuck up. We gotta move."

"Who? Where?"

"Remember where we were going?" Kira asked.

"Duck butts?"

"Well, we have cops instead. Get outta the car now."

We were still in the Bug. I must have fallen asleep, passed out. Or zoned out. I could tell by how I felt that I didn't get any booze, food, or tampons. Kira came around to the passenger door and yanked me from the car.

"I don't understand."

"Of course not. You've been sundowning for the past day."

"Shit." We were parked at the river's edge. The Mississippi, I assumed.

Kira walked to a small dock, opened the bag of coke, and let it fall into the water.

I screamed.

She glared at me. "You wanna go to jail? That's a lot of fucking drugs."

"Vic called the cops!"

"That's what I was guessing."

"Sorry," I said as I watched the last of the coke dissolve into the rolling water.

"What for?"

"Getting you into this. Vic's my problem, not yours."

"I made a choice," Kira explained. She turned to me. The fact that she was still with me had a sudden meaning. This sort of thing never happened to me. Her look burned into my soul. I was out. She had the drugs and the cash. Abandonment would be the obvious choice. Yet here she was, green eyes with a subtle longing and determination.

"I'm not sure you made a good decision."

"Doesn't matter..."

I shook myself away from Kira's truth-burning gaze and turned to the water in time to see the ass feathers of a Mallard drift up to the dock.

The duck flipped and his head appeared. He let out a loud *squawk* of disapproval, then floated under the dock.

"Hey," Kira exclaimed. "Mission accomplished."

It was windy again, much like at Illinois River. Less chop on the water, though. The area was cultivated into a park, aesthetically pleasing even with the overcast of autumn. Kira and I seemed magnetically attracted to rivers. Moving water as opposed to lakes or ponds that went nowhere. Rivers were always on the move, washing impurities southward from the cold and pure sky.

"Cute little fucker."

"Looking for fish?"

"Or maybe he's a coke fiend."

Red-and-blue flashing lights reflected off muddy water.

"Where's the cash?" I asked.

"In the Bug."

"Shit..."

"So we have to start over. I've done it before," Kira said.

"Vic's a guy, and the police are guys, so you know where we are headed."

"But Vic's a criminal."

"He's more of a corrupt asshole than a criminal."

"So why would the police be on his side?"

I rolled my eyes in an exaggerated fashion. The police cars pulled up the river's edge.

Kira looked thoughtful. "I don't want to be separated." For the first time since I met her, she seemed at a loss.

Two officers exited the squad car, hands on their holsters. They seemed to think we possessed drugs, so those two were going to want to search us. That never ended well. I felt the need to be diplomatic for Kira's sake. At the same time, I wasn't in the mood to go to jail or be raped.

They obviously had a description of Kira: short with dark hair, bright green eyes, stupid big glasses, and a black-wool cap. Without a word, they went at her with their clubs, hitting her in the gut, knees, felled her with a strike to the back of the head. We were in it deep. Vic *paid* these fuckers to retrieve his cash. He was a coward, and so were these cops.

But they were men, bigger than me, and armed. Kira laid unconscious on the pavement, a puddle of blood oozing from her mouth, nose, and ears. A normal person would have asked for the money first. But these thugs were hired to strong-arm us. There was not a name I could think of to describe a cop who beat an unarmed woman unconscious. Perhaps one had not been invented yet.

"She breathing?" one of them asked. I named him Jethro and imagined he played banjo and drank White Lightning in his off time.

"Can't tell," the other answered.

Before they remembered or were aware of me, I was behind them, peeking for a glimpse of Kira. She seemed bad, probably wouldn't recover well, so I knew the instructionally abusive voice would soon return to my thoughts.

The advantage of being such a small bean, is that I am quiet and quick. In a split-second, I had both guns out of their holsters and a barrel crammed into my mouth. The other, I pressed against my temple. I was trying to be fast, and it was my downfall. While I squeezed the triggers with no result, the cop was able to retrieve them.

Though the safeties were on, they were loaded, which was the legal reason I stayed behind so long at Illinois' Watertown State Hospital after Kira was released.

Chapter 5

Group therapy at Watertown State Hospital was weekly in institutionalized life. The hospital itself wasn't aesthetically detestable. The rooms were well-lit, paint on the walls. Light and fresh. The temperature was always comfortable. We were just trapped with the smell of laundered blankets and floor polish. There was no out-of-doors, except what could be gleaned through steel-reinforced windows.

Our life consisted of fold-out chairs, hallways, and cafeteria tables. Kira didn't change outwardly after the beating from the cops. What changed was her personality, and it was subtle yet fraught with a dissociative darkness grounded in depression.

"I can't buy a gun," Kira explained. "'cause I'm crazy. I come up on background checks. But I can buy an antique percussion pistol kit. Or even an antique pistol. Just for looks, right? Fucking .50-caliber lead projectiles. Blow your fucking brains right outta your head. Walk into a gun shop with cash and walk out loaded for bear."

"Such plans you have," I'd exhorted.

"I'm not vain, and I don't want to suffer."

"Suicide never solved anything," the group leader espoused.

Group leaders and therapists were not always the same. Therefore, we experienced a lack of consistency. There could be as many as 30 people to a group, or a group as little as Kira and myself.

"That's bullshit," Kira retorted. "Of course it does."

"The problems don't change. It fixes nothing."

"I don't care. I'll be dead. I won't have any concept of what happens after I die, 'cause I'll be dead."

"So that's it. When you die, everything ends. Problem solved."

"Are you going to try to convince me of an afterlife? 'Cause there is none. Not for me anyway. Maybe there's some reward after death for someone like you. But not me."

"So there's an afterlife for me and not you? That's delusional."

"Is that your diagnosis? That I'm delusional? I don't believe in some sophomoric tale about God and bodies rising from the dead, so that makes me delusional? If you believe in this fairy tale, then it has to occur to you that I'm not included. Just look at me! Look at what I've been through in my short life. This God you believe in doesn't believe in me. I exist to be robbed, raped, and beaten. That's my contribution to society. Your God does not include me in his plans. Now or in the future. There's nothing for me after. That's my fucking reward. That's what I have to look forward to. And I do. I desire it with every cell in my body. I can't wait! I just want to be nothing!"

"You sound angry."

"Not really."

"Why not?"

"Doesn't really matter."

"It doesn't matter? Or *you* don't matter? I've heard a lot of frustration from you. But you typically fail to get angry."

"It's a waste of time."

"Being angry? Everyone gets angry at some point. Everyone has a tipping point. Being slow to anger may be a virtue, but denying anger is dangerous. Sometimes, that anger is a spark or part of a spark. That thing that keeps us alive. That little flicker of light that defends us against an illness that's trying to end our life."

"So by that logic, Iris doesn't have this spark you're talking about."

"Maybe, in her case, you were that spark."

Kira lowered her eyes in shame. She knew she had played her part in my demise. Her infatuation was a motivation for her intrusion into my life.

"Kira, you're not a guest here. You were brought here from the hospital after..." The therapist flipped through her notes, trying to find the correct thing to say. "After it was determined you were suicidal and severely depressed."

"A knock to the skull will do that to a gal," Kira quipped.

"A fractured skull is nothing to joke about. You could have had brain damage. In fact, your file says you're still under scrutiny for signs of that exact thing."

"Maybe I'm just avoiding the police," Kira offered.

The therapist went back to flipping through notes. "Police? There's no mention of an arrest or police. Oh! Police found you injured and called an ambulance."

Kira turned back in my direction. *Wow*, she mouthed while rolling her eyes.

🜆 🜆 🜆

I said my goodbye to Kira long ago. The last time I'd seen her at the mental hospital. Back when it was a mental hospital, before they gave us all the boot.

We had shared a room. We were bunkmates and friends. But there was something different with the relationship I had with Kira that I'd never experienced with anyone before. It started the last night, not much different than any other night. Kira could get desperately sad and, when she did, she would wake me up. It was always in the middle of the night. That was the hardest time for her.

I'd had plenty of girl friends growing up, and we'd occasionally disrobed in front of each other. But nothing had prepared me to see Kira sitting shirtless on the edge of my bed. I turned on the bedside light as she softly sobbed. She had a second tattoo. I'd never met anyone with a tattoo before, much less two, though I'd often wanted one myself. It had large block lettering. Nothing fancy, just three words: **Bite Down Bitch**. I had no idea what that meant, but it gave me a strong, fearful feeling. I didn't get a chance to ask about it because she continued to sob. And then she turned to me, which caused me to forget the whole thing. That green-eyed goddess was the most beautiful half-dressed creature I'd ever seen. Her tits were smaller than mine, but she tapered, from her white shoulders to her muscular stomach. It was hard to comprehend that a woman of such beauty and appeal could exist, much less be perched on the edge of my bed in the middle of the night. I wanted to reach out and wrap myself around her as I had never with anyone. I stopped though, because of the tears dripping from her cheeks, and the red swollenness of her eyes.

Kira turned away and that's when I reached out, touched her back, let my fingers slide up and down her soft, pale skin. I stroked softly and her sobbing subsided. My hand slid to her lower back. I wasn't about to feign comfort. This was a different touch. An exploration. She straightened and I lingered, squeezing a bit harder. She responded with the slightest of movements. Perhaps this was of some comfort. If she felt someone loved her. Depression was extreme loneliness, when we wanted to be withdrawn but lavish any sign of affection from a caring soul. She didn't leave my side. Something I was afraid of. Reaching out was always a gamble and a thrill.

It was a minimal gamble, considering that she came to me. Kira wanted something of me so I was obligated to respond. We were roommates after all, in a fucking mental hospital. Being on each other's side was essential, for survival. Somebody needed to have your back. And I had hers, literally. She still had not moved. I rubbed her lower back as sympathetically as possible while still enjoying the feel of her flesh against my fingers. I resisted the urge to act on my still flourishing desire to wrap myself around her. "I get so scared," I admitted.

Kira nodded.

"Scared of living. Scared of dying. Scared of you."

"Don't be afraid of dying. Or me. I won't hurt you. I'm on your side, and I won't dump you."

"Sounds like your mind is made up."

"I do that. I make a decision and get pretty stuck on it."

"I admire your resolve."

"I'm resolved to not living. Is that admirable? We're alike that way. Afraid of living."

"We're alive now."

"No, we're not. We're here, locked up."

"Not really. There's no locks. We can leave if we want."

"See, there. That's the thing. I know that. Yet in my mind, I'm locked in here. To go beyond those doors is to seek life. Staying in here is to exist in safety. Out there, I'm scared to death."

It was my turn to cry. I knew exactly what she meant. My sobs were silent and I stopped caressing Kira's skin. She wiggled her shoulders a bit for me to continue. When I didn't, she caught me crying.

Kira whispered, "When was your first time?"

Most people would think she was talking about sex. It would normally be a confusing question, but I knew exactly what she asked. "I drove my car off a cliff," I answered. I didn't make eye contact.

"So that didn't work..."

"My car landed in the tree tops. It was a sharp drop. I expected to crash to the ground. But trees were everywhere. I didn't expect them to hold the weight of a whole car."

Kira smiled. It embarrassed me.

It was disappointing, waking up alive. Embarrassing at worst. It was a stupid idea and the park district was footing the bill to get my car out of the trees. I always wanted to be dead before I started drinking, but it was just a feeling. The action didn't take place until I was well into a fifth of Jack and became brave as Hell. Brave as Hell to do stupid shit, like drive my old Camaro off a cliff only to land soft on the canopy below. This was attempt number seven and the dumbest of the bunch. Landed me in the damn psych ward, but first I had to talk to the police.

"A doctor told me a long time ago, 'If I was meant to die, I would have,'" Kira said.

"That's rather philosophical."

"Docs get that way when they have no scientific explanation."

"Okay. The story behind that is...?"

Kira looked away. It was her turn not to make eye contact. "Asphyxiation."

"Yow!"

"Not if you breathe in charcoal. Lethal. Foolproof. Any idiot can do it."

I was glad it didn't work.

"I fell asleep," Kira explained. "I slept for a long time. When I woke up, the bathroom was clear and the coals had burned out."

"So it just wasn't meant to be..."

Kira turned back. "Fuck that. There's no such thing as miracles. The doctors are stupid." She hung her head. "I just fucked it up somehow."

"You know about rehearsing?" I asked Kira.

Her eyes studied her bare knees. She nodded.

"I had an incident during a trial run. I just wanted to know what it looked like, how it felt. You know, to have the rope around my neck."

"Rope? This sounds like it has a bad ending."

"Actually, clothesline."

"Efficient."

"Leaves no mark." I blanked out for a few moments, remembering the incident.

Kira returned to studying her knees.

"The box I was standing on broke," I continued, "with the cord around my neck. It was tied off."

Kira didn't look up.

"Amazingly, the first thing to happen was all of the air left my lungs, completely."

"Were you stoned?"

"Of course..."

"Doesn't seem to have worked."

"My toes just touched the floor. Enough to keep breathing."

"A predicament. What's a gal to do?"

"That's right. Lots of things ran through my head. First, was surprised panic. I struggled a lot."

"What room were you in?"

"Garage."

"Parents?"

"Not worth talking about. In fact, how 'bout never."

"No one there to save you then..."

"Like I said, let's not go there."

"My ol' man was a real piece of work," Kira explained.

"Drunk?"

"No, a prude. Straight as an arrow."

"Mom?"

"Dead."

"Sorry..."

"Fuck her."

"I was just in the garage, standing on a box and it broke. Nobody but me. Wouldn't be found 'til morning. I really didn't mean for it to happen. Just a try-out, you know? Get a feel for the actual thing."

"It's sexy," Kira said.

I just looked at her blankly.

"Oh, come on. You know it is. It's a rush. A sexy rush. Gets your blood flowing."

I really wanted Kira to like me as much as I liked her, so I smiled, even though I had no idea what she was talking about. I guess there was something. The anticipation of that first slice with a razor. Now, that was sexy. But I couldn't bring it up to Kira. I didn't know if she was a cutter. I didn't want her to hate me if she wasn't.

"I still need to know," Kira said.

"I spent a lot of time getting free, mostly 'cause I had to decide if I wanted to. At one point, I just let my weight hang, then panic set in. When the panic had me, I was able to pull myself up enough with one arm and untie the cable."

"Did it hurt?'

"Not until after, for weeks, my neck and back. I had to get a ladder to untie the cable from the rafters."

"Did you use a ladder to tie it off?"

"No. Just tossed it over."

"How did you knot it?"

"I don't remember. Wasn't hard though."

"Why did you take it down?"

I wouldn't address this. And it was kind of a trigger because Kira was fishing. Wanting me to open up about home. She had to stick around a long time before I talked about that.

"It wasn't my garage," I answered.

"You know how they say, 'Don't trust anyone over 30,'" Kira quipped.

"I don't want to be 30. That's like the end."

"My birthday will be March 19th. I'll fucking be 30."
"I'll be 28."
"Then the 18th."

I was solemn considering the implications of this arrangement. It must have shown on my face.

"Are you thinking about it?" Kira asked. "Are you in?"

"Are we doing this together?"

"I'm leaving today, Iris. They're kicking me out. I don't know if they're doing the same to you."

"Then how will we know?"

"You'll know, 'cause I'm doing it. March 18th I'll be done. Guess it kinda depends on if you get outta here."

"I promise. One way or another."

Kira grasped my shoulders. It was the first time I'd seen her smile in here. Saw a sparkle in those dark eyes. She pulled me close and rested her face on my neck.

It was glorious. I meant my promise, at the time. And I trusted her to go through with her end. I wasn't afraid. I was done, too. This was enough.

"I'm so sorry," Kira said.

"For what?"

"That you have to be the strong one."

Me, strong? Strength wasn't on my attribution list. But Kira saw it. So I had to reconsider. I had to take all of her thoughts into consideration. I fucking loved her. If I loved her, then what she said, what she stood for, had to mean something to me. Me, strong? It took a bit to consider.

Leaving. Kira was leaving me in this shit hole. But as shitholes went, this wasn't too bad. I could be *working* in a shit hole. I was just a resident. Fed daily and had a soft cot. I could be out using, getting used nightly for a line of coke. What I wouldn't do. Sickness, addiction, and rape was preferred to the big empty. The loud darkness that incessantly called to me.

If I learned anything from Kira, it was to give in. The dark was a friend. It was an end. The stopping place where I no longer had to feel—anything. Mostly the pain. Even joy was a form of pain. That was hard for most people to believe. Kira understood. Pain was in everything.

Chapter 6

I wasn't unfamiliar with firearms. My expertise was restricted to pistols and shotguns, though. In the spirit of a gal trying to make a buck, I experienced a situation after Watertown that swore me off guns. It was a job, but different from any other. I was attracted to the big payouts that led me to people like Vic, and this guy. Didn't even know his name, just a voice in the dark, and a paper bag full of dope. I did lots of different work, from waitressing to welding, but those weren't quick scores. They didn't get me from point A to point B as soon as I wanted.

I parked my old, snow-covered Ford Fairlane in front of Ritz Crown Mobile Estate Park. After removing a grocery sack from the trunk, I stepped through the front door as silently as I could, walked to the kitchen table, and forcefully set down the paper bag of horse. I announced, "There it fucking is." I turned a chair and sat on it backward, lit a cigarette, and crossed my arms on the back of the chair. I took a long drag and blew the smoke out, looking at the others seated around the table.

"It's about fucking time, Iris," said Woody as he eyed the bag. "You're a bit late."

I ignored him and kept smoking. I had the upper hand and did the leg work on this one. I had a say in how it went. Out of everyone at the round kitchen table, I was the most intimate with the details.

"Good work," said Shorty. He was ironically nicknamed and the lead man on the job. He got his orders from the bosses, hired me, told me I was a live wire, but also a professional.

Woody reached for the bag, and Don grabbed him by the wrist. "We're waiting for Sal."

"Fuck off, cocksucker," Woody barked as he shook his wrist free.

"Waiting for Sal?" I asked Woody.

"Yeah," said Don.

"Guess I'm not late then, asshole."

"You talkin' to me?" Woody asked.

"Shit yeah, you ugly bastard. You said I was late."

"You are fucking late."

"But no one is doin' nothin' 'til Sal gets here."

"We waited a long fucking time."

I took another long drag. "That doesn't make me late."

"Fuck it don't," Woody answered. "You were supposed to have your bitch ass here a long time ago."

"We ain't doin' shit 'til Sal gets here," I reiterated.

We all looked across the table at each other. In the background, Sal's girlfriend, Lisa, was doing dishes. She was a quiet woman with long, blonde hair. She wore her usual T-shirt and jeans.

"When does Sal get home?" Shorty asked over his shoulder.

"Any time now," Lisa answered. "You want a beer?"

"But when does he get off work?" Woody asked.

"Half an hour ago," she answered.

"Fucking late," Woody said to me.

I ignored him, nervously chain-smoking.

"I'll take a beer," said Don.

Lisa pulled a cold bottle from the fridge and served it.

"Well, there's the thing," Woody started. "We got the bag here in front of us, and this broad bringing it late, and we have no word from the guy."

"It don't matter," Shorty said. "Sal ain't even home yet."

"Ya know," I said, "it's fucking Sal who's late, not me."

"You were supposed to be here," Woody complained.

"But I'm here now. And we're waitin' on Sal."

"It happens," Lisa said. "Sometimes, he gets late tryin' to leave the shop. Sometimes, he stops for a beer." She went back to her cleaning. The kitchen really wasn't dirty. And she rarely paid this much attention to it. She probably hoped Sal would come home soon because she didn't want to be left alone with these creeps.

Lisa hated me and seemed frightened every minute I was in her home. But, after that night, we'd all live high on the hog and never have to see each other again. The score was that big, and everyone was that much more on edge.

"But we got the fucking package," Woody cried.

"The guy ain't ready yet," I said.

"Why all the fucking secrecy?"

"Ain't no secret," I said. "It's just a thing. Just the way it worked out. And I ain't late."

"The fuck you ain't," Woody said.

"Just shut the fuck up," Shorty said. "There's no reason for any of this shit. Let's just keep cool 'til Sal gets here."

"But the guy," Woody said.

"It's just a thing," I repeated.

"Your thing."

"You got that right."

"What the fuck do you mean?" Woody asked.

"Just what she fucking said," shouted Don. "I'm getting sick of both of your shit. We gotta stick together on this."

"Don's right," said Shorty. "We gotta see it through. It's not just the guy, but the bosses too. They got their thing."

"And we got ours," cried Woody.

"And we got ours," repeated Shorty. "And ain't a thing we can do 'til it's all ready. And it ain't gonna be ready 'til Sal gets here."

"So where the fuck is Sal?" asked Woody.

I snuck a peek, and Lisa was crying. She wiped her face with dishwater, probably hoping the moisture would cover her emotional state.

"Hey, Lisa," I said, "I'll take a beer too. Or even something stronger."

She went to the refrigerator and got me a beer. I knew she was repulsed being hospitable to someone she never would have allowed in the room. She walked to me and set the cold bottle down. My hand shot out and wrapped around Lisa's still on the bottle, clenching with a vise grip.

"Hope Sal didn't run into some emergency," I said.

"He can handle himself," Lisa said as she jerked her hand away.

"I want a look," Woody said.

"No one looks at shit," I ordered. "We ain't doin' shit 'til Sal gets home."

The phone rang. It was wall-mounted right above Shorty's head.

"Yeah," he answered. He sat listening a few minutes. "It's Sal," he finally announced. "There's a change of plans."

I jumped from my seat, grabbed the bag, and shouted, "No, there hasn't been any fucking change!"

Woody sprang up, pulled a pistol from his boot. He leaned across the table, pointed it at me, and shouted, "Put the motherfucking bag down, now!"

I reached in my coat and pulled out a 9milimeter, pointing it at Shorty. "The thing is now. We do it now!"

"Put the bag down, cunt, or I'm blowin' you away," Woody shouted.

Lisa slipped out without anyone else noticing.

Don reached for Woody's hand, startling him. He pistol-whipped Don until his limp body fell to the ground. When he raised his hand again to point the gun at me, it was dripping with blood.

My mouth dropped open and I looked incredulously at Don. "You kill him?" I asked.

"Shut the fuck up and put the bag back down now!"

Shorty stiffened as someone pressed a gun into the back of his neck. He slowly turned face-to-face with Lisa's shotgun barrel.

"You give me the fucking phone right now, you son of a bitch, or I'm blowin' your head off," she ordered.

"No need to be going off half-cocked now," Shorty said.

"You sayin' that to me?" she asked. "Look down on the floor next to ya. I think he was a partner a few seconds ago."

"Now look, Lisa. There's lots of people interested in this thing. Sal here on the phone has business. We got a guy to see."

"Right," Woody agreed. "So let's get fucking cunt-face here to drop the bag."

"Gimme the goddamned phone, Shorty!"

I swung around and pointed my gun at Woody. "Drop it now, you piece of shit!"

"You drop the bag, cunt!" Woody answered.

Lisa jabbed Shorty with the end of her barrel.

"I'll hang it up," Shorty threatened.

"Put the bag down," Woody ordered.

"You drop the fucking piece," I demanded.

I saw it coming and hit the deck. The *crack* of gunfire was deafening, but not as offensive as the smell. I hated the smell because it reminded me of factory work. Oil and fire reminded me of hot metal and three-digit temperatures in a dusty building that resembled a cave more than a place for human habitation.

Leaving the brown paper bag, I slithered along the floor like a snake until I was safe to get out the door and back to my car. The only person I saw leaving was Lisa. She ran to a car without the paper bag. I waited after she left. Curious if anyone else would show their face, but not enough to go back in to look for survivors.

I felt sorry for Lisa. She was screwed by her boyfriend and every asshole in that run-down trailer. Dead or alive, she deserved to get away. I was sorry to see her empty-handed. But I sure wasn't interested in retrieving the dope myself.

Chapter 7

I wanted to get as far away from the trailer park as possible, but the going was slow. The roads were already snow-packed and large flakes were falling again. The Fairlane drove like a tank, but wind and visibility called for caution.

Lisa's headlights shone from the side of the road. It seemed like a mile before I could stop. There was so much ground cover, at least six inches of snowfall, and the roads were packed. It was no wonder a car would go off. And Lisa's in particular. She was scared and on the run, though everyone she was afraid of laid dead in the mobile park behind us.

This was a stretch of country road between towns. And the drop off was deep over the edge. A car could get lost on a night like this. I could be the only person for hours. It was my duty to stop.

I cautiously backed up, my lights barely cutting through the dark. But the lights from the spun-out car were visible. Like a surreal moment from a scary movie. Bright beams pointed up into the heavy-falling snow.

I parked. The wind howled from the storm. Music played in the distance. Probably from the car over the hill. That gave me a bad feeling. Whoever was in the car might be unable to turn off the radio. I left the engine running and walked toward the lights.

I had a moment of doubt or an instant of clarity. My instincts told me to get back in the Ford and drive off. The dope, the guns, the killing; Lisa and I were the only link to what had occurred miles back. No one was looking for us, and in blizzard-like conditions, it would be slow-going. Was I to leave Lisa to her peril after all I had just gone through? All I had gone through and still penniless. That really pissed me off.

"Hello," I shouted when the car lights shone over the hill. Deep tracks had cut into the snow where tires had slid, the car turning around before falling backward over the edge.

"Down here," a voice said feebly. It was a treacherous walk to get down the hill to the car. I didn't want to go there if I didn't have to. Actually, I wanted to leave.

"Are you okay?"

"I'm bleeding," the voice said. It was faint and sounded like Lisa. I was in for a night. It would be a trick trekking down the hill without sliding, getting wet or avalanched with snow, and painfully cold. I went back to my car. I turned off the engine. Grabbed gloves and an extra blanket from the back seat. After thinking for a moment, I grabbed the first aid kit from the trunk. A few tools laid about the bottom of the trunk. I tried to decide what to throw into my pocket, settled on pliers, a hammer, and vise grips.

The walk down the slope was as ominous as it looked. And I did exactly as I thought. Slipped and slid the rest of the way to the car. My feet stopped against the front of the vehicle.

"Help," her little voice cried from behind headlights. I was blinded by the high beams, feeling my way along the front of the car.

At the edge of the bumper, the car was bottomed out in a ditch and would fall no further. Crawling across the front of the vehicle, I imagined a deep ravine, the car about to fall into a cold abyss, me with it.

As it was, I had a hard time maneuvering to see in the passenger side. When I did, I found her alone.

Disco played on the radio. She was belted in and trapped behind the steering wheel. The car was bashed in on that side. "Iris?"

"What's the situation, Lisa?"

"I think I'm bleeding," she said.

"Bad?"

"I can't tell. What are your intentions?"

"How long have you been down here?"

"Maybe 10 minutes?" Her voice was soft like she was tired. Her eyes weren't visible, face shadowed from the light.

I slowly entered the car and assessed the situation. The front window was smashed. "I come in peace," I assured her.

Someone shouted from above.

"There's been an accident," I yelled back.

"I have a phone!" someone shouted. "Calling for help." It was a male voice, getting closer.

"A what?"

"It's cellular." He put the receiver to my ear. I heard a woman's voice: "What's going on?"

Lisa groaned, and I was shocked back into the moment. For a second, I felt like an alien, or someone traveling from the past. *What the fuck is a cellular phone?*

"She's conscious," I said to the responder on the phone.

"Is she hurt?' the woman asked.

"Bleeding. She says she's been here 10 minutes."

"Unbuckle her and try to find the laceration. Be careful, though. You don't want to make the bleeding worse."

I looked at the futurist with the cellular phone. "I'm out," I announced. "You take over."

"No way, man. I'll just throw up and then pass out."

"I'm leaving. This is way above my pay grade."

"If you leave, she's going to die," came the mystery voice in my ear. I shook my head to get the vile device away from me. But the man was relentless.

I removed my keys from my pocket. A penlight was hooked to the key ring. I aimed it at Lisa.

She held up her left hand. It had blood on it.

"I'm supposed to see how bad it is," I explained.

I unbuckled her and peered over her lap. Her dark coat was wet with blood, but not soaked. I couldn't see what was causing the injury. I leaned back and turned off the radio. "I can't see anything," I said into the phone. "She has on a thick coat. It's zero degrees out here."

"That might be a good thing," she said.

I shone the light at Lisa's face. "Sorry," I said. Her eyes looked glassy and distant like drugged. Probably in shock. "Feeling okay?" I asked.

"Tired. Numb."

"Numb?" asked the voice on the phone.

"Yeah."

"Try to look under the coat. Carefully."

"I have to look again," I explained.

"Want me to move?"

"I think that's a bad idea."

"I'll just scoot over a little."

"Don't let her move," the woman on the phone said.

"Don't move," I said.

But it was too late. Lisa had stretched away from the steering column and scooted a few inches toward me. "Ouch."

"What is it?" the responder asked.

"I don't know. She moved."

Lisa's face was pale.

"Is anyone coming?" I asked the mouthpiece.

"A few minutes out," she answered.

"That hurt," Lisa said softly.

I started unbuttoning her coat. It was easy enough since she moved. I was able to quickly undo it and look underneath.

Lisa looked at her lap. "Oh." She looked up at me with half a smile. "My mirror."

"There's an injury to her left leg," I said to the woman on the phone. I looked out the front window and up the hill. I doubted I could get myself up to the road, much less myself and Lisa.

She was bleeding a bit more from the wound. I suspected it was because she moved. Steam was rising from her lap, fogging the window.

"Dammit," I said. I reached to clear the condensation from Lisa's warm blood. It was a creepy feeling.

"What is it?" the woman asked.

"Appears to be a small, square mirror lodged in her thigh."

"In the front or side?" the woman asked.

I turned to look and Lisa was holding the mirror in her hand. Blood spurted from her leg.

"Shit," I said with an exasperated sigh.

"Now what?" the voice asked.

"She removed the mirror!"

"She shouldn't have done that."

"Lisa!"

She was holding up the bloody piece of glass, studying it. She was unaware of the blood spurting from her lap.

"There's a problem," I said into the phone.

"Blood spurting?" she asked.

"How did you guess?"

"Just seems the next logical step." I could hear her talking to someone on another line.

"How far out is the ambulance?" I asked.

"Hard to tell in the snowstorm," she answered. "A few minutes."

"You said that a few minutes ago."

"What's your name?" she asked.

"Iris."

"Iris," she started, "you need to help Lisa." More talking off-line. "She's going to bleed out quickly if we don't stop it."

"How much time do we have?"

"Only a few minutes. You have to act fast."

"Shit."

"What is she wearing on her legs?"

"Blue jeans."

"You have to get them off quick."

"I'm gonna throw up," Lisa warned when she finally noticed her leg.

"Do it out the window while I get your pants off!" Which was exactly what happened. I had to use my pocket knife to cut them most of the way off.

"Pants off," I announced into the phone. "The blood is spurting, like every time her heart beats."

Lisa looked at the fountain of blood coming from her leg, spurting straight up.

"Has Lisa passed out yet?"

"Surprisingly, no."

"Apply pressure on the wound to stop the bleeding. It's the most important thing." She spoke off-line again.

I ripped off more of Lisa's jeans and pressed on the gash left by the sharp mirror. The blood continued, gushing between my fingers. I pushed harder. Tried to squeeze her flesh in hopes of closing up the wound. I could smell the copper fluid. Steam filled the inside of the car, fogging my glasses.

Lisa screamed.

"Ignore her," the voice said in my ear. "Keep trying."

"It's not working."

"The artery is severed!" The woman sounded panicked for the first time.

"You have the EMTs on the phone."

"They're en route," she assured.

"It's cold," Lisa said.

"Your coat and pants are off," I said.

"No," the voice said in my ear. "She is losing blood fast, that's making her cold. You have to stop the bleeding."

"How the fuck do I do that?"

"Listen carefully. You have to lay her out and clamp off the artery."

"Impossible."

"No, it isn't!"

"I'm no doctor."

"You don't have to be. Just do what I say. It'll be easy."

"This is fucking hopeless. How about a tourniquet? People always do tourniquets!"

"Won't work in this situation, Iris. The artery is slippery and loose. It will pull in and you will lose it. You can tie her off, but she will still hemorrhage. You can't give up or Lisa will die. It's not hopeless. Lay her down flat."

"I can't. The gear shift is in the way."

"Pull her out of the car now!"

I did. She screamed louder: "What are you doing?"

"I have to get you flat."

"I'm freezing!"

"That's good. When you stop freezing, then we have problems."

Blood covered my arms. It was warm but froze fast in the night air. I let her drop into the snow. She had a look of horror. Blood still poured. Each spurt exhaled a puff of steam. I couldn't believe she was still conscious.

I bent close and shone my flashlight into the injury. "Hell," I said into the phone. "I can see the artery."

"Good," she said over the phone. "Any way you can just squeeze it?"

I tried.

Lisa let out a spine-rattling shriek.

The artery was in my hand, and then it slipped away, disappeared into her leg. It was wet, slippery. Completely severed.

Lisa was tensing and screaming. Blood was all over me. Covering the ground and melting the snow around her legs.

"Where are the EMTs?" I asked.

"Close," the voice replied.

I noticed the phone in my hand. The stranger had abandoned me. Probably off throwing up somewhere. "They need to be here now." I fished around my coat pocket and found the vise grips from the car. They were small needle noses. Perfect for Lisa's spewing artery. Dirty, but there was no time to think of being sterile.

"They are doing the best they can," the woman said.

"They have to do better than that."

She was talking to someone. Probably the ambulance driver.

"It's desperation time," I said. "They have to be heroes. Do better than what they are capable. This girl is dying."

There was silence on the other end.

Lisa was sobbing. She heard me, I was sure of it. That news, the pain, the cold, it had to be more than she could handle. What a horrible place to die. That was the stuff you read about, heroic people rising above in a desperate situation, interviewed in hospitals, all warm and cozy. An IV in their arm and loved ones by their sides. "I just thank Jesus I survived," was what they always said.

Who would Lisa thank? She was slipping fast. Making less noise. The spurts were less powerful and farther apart. It coated my arms. My coat was drenched. I was only aware of the cold in my fingers. The rest of my adrenaline-charged body had no clue what the weather was like.

"This isn't happening," Lisa said softly.

"What's that?"

"This has to be a dream. I want to wake up."

I started crying. Her voice was melodic. Even in the midst of trauma, she sounded like a songbird on a summer morning. I needed to come up with something, some way to stop crying so I could see to continue. A way to refocus us.

I took my watch off and put it on her wrist. "Look, Lisa. This watch is mine. It's my most favorite thing in the world and I'm giving it to you. It's from Sweden and it's called an Axcent. My mom gave it to me, and I'm giving it to you."

Lisa looked at my watch on her wrist.

"This watch represents reality. No matter how desperate you feel when you look at this watch, just remember what's really happening, right now, and you're not alone. We're gonna get through this together."

Lisa nodded. Closed her eyes. Hopefully to be present.

I flexed my fingers to get some feeling back. I wiped my coat to remove blood and adjusted the vise grips so I could close them all the way. With one hand, I gripped the tool. The other pulled back the gash in Lisa's leg.

She made a weak protest. It had to hurt. Was worthy of the scream she had been making before. Only, she was losing energy. Probably had no more screams left.

The penlight was in my mouth. I shone it into the wound and searched for the leaking artery. I had to pull the skin apart farther than it had been. It ripped a bit.

Lisa's back arched. Her other leg kicked in the snow. She tried to push away but lacked sufficient strength.

The blood still squirted. I followed the stream. Just barely located the end of the artery. I reached in with the tool and grabbed it. The end of the needle nose clamped and held.

I breathed, probably for the first time in minutes. I tugged on the artery and it came back into the night air.

Lisa managed a little scream.

With some kind of superhuman precision, I grasped the end of the slippery artery, folded it over, and clamped it off with the vise grips. The bleeding stopped. I really had no confidence that I could have done that. It completely surprised me that I not only did it, but did it in one try.

I collapsed, drained, prostrate across Lisa's lap.

Lisa's stomach rose and fell with her breathing. I just wanted to lie there and feel that. Do nothing else. Consider my evening done and relish in the feel of her still functioning body.

The cold crept in, though. My rush wore off and I became acutely aware of the weather's icy sting. Couldn't imagine what it might be doing to her.

Lights appeared from above. The rescue truck. I heard voices.

"Down here," I desperately shouted. "We're down here!"

Lisa coughed. I stood and looked at her. She was breathing heavily and coughing some more. Trying to catch her breath. Her body started convulsing.

"Lisa!" I bent to study her face.

Her eyes bulged and her mouth gasped for breath.

"Get down here now," I shouted. "I'm losing her!"

The lights flickered and moved randomly as rescue workers slid down the hill. They were probably trying to decide how to get down and back until they heard my voice. Then dived over, into the snow. I hoped they remembered to leave someone on top to pull the rest of us up.

I held Lisa by the shoulders. Tried to reassure her. Her eyes still bulged and her breathing was becoming more sporadic. She looked me in the eyes, grabbed me by the shoulders, and pulled herself into my blood-soaked coat. She coughed. Her arms tightened around me.

I put my arms around her and held, trying to restrain her convulsions.

Suddenly, she stopped moving. Still held me tight. Coughed a couple more times. Took a couple deep breaths, and then her arms went limp. She stopped breathing and her head fell back.

"Lisa," I called.

She didn't answer. Didn't take another breath.

I held her tight in the cold. For the first time, I noticed the snow had stopped falling. Some stars shone in the crisp, night sky. The voices and light got closer. I let her body down into the snow. Her mouth was open as well as her eyes. Her face racked with pain.

I stood as the EMTs arrived. They went right to work. Bags and equipment. Lights and shouting. I couldn't catch my breath. I walked over and leaned against the front of the car.

The lights were still on. Engine purring. Lisa was dead. The moment was still there. The world was still going on, and she wasn't. She laid there in the freezing cold. Breathless. Rescuers worked on her. It looked like slow-motion. I disassociated from the whole scene.

Lisa was dead and I was far away.

I became hot. Sweaty. Had trouble breathing and seeing. I was pounding on the hood of the car. Blood was everywhere, but it wasn't mine. I was frozen but not hurt. It was her blood seeping from my sleeves. Splashed on the hood of the car as I pounded. All I could see in my head was Kira, bleeding on the dock, two police officers with snide smirks doing nothing, hoping she would die.

They called it ruminating, the people with degrees who would later poke and prod my thoughts to cure my PTSD. But the tape would keep playing on repeat, with Kira bleeding from her head, not moving on the wet boards of the dock.

A voice was calling to me. "Lady? Lady, are you okay?"

I couldn't answer. All I could do was pound my fists and then my head. I heard nothing, saw red. That was the last I remembered of that night.

♦ ♦ ♦

My cognition returned with me institutionalized again. McKinley Park Residential Home, where I was alone, or mostly alone. Everything after Kira was alone, and I got stuck with Lisa, whom I detested. The silver door to the kitchen was open. Kira was inside with the other employees, working on dinner. A spider tattoo showed as she opened industrial-size cans with a tabletop crank can-opener. She looked too small for it, but handled the task easily. She did it every day. Day after day. I didn't know how. They all did. The kitchen was full of workers, mostly men with hairnets. Kira looked better in hers.

I pulled up a chair and watched her work through the open window. It was a stainless-steel countertop where food was served, place settings reserved for washing. Kira spied me watching her. She smirked and winked at me. I smiled.

My mind drifted off to a place where Kira didn't exist. I drifted off to a place of blood and snow. Steam and freezing cold. Pain felt ten times worse in the freezing cold. Screams were ten times louder. That's where I went. My doctor gave me thousands of dollars' worth of advice that I never followed. So many tricks to get out and get away. Escape from Lisa and the snow. *She screams, and the cold.* I just stayed there. I stayed in it. The screams were distant in the back of my head as I watched Kira.

I remembered. Like it was that morning or moments before. The redness, glowing, radiating. It filled the cold air, lighting the night with its life force. Lisa's life force. She breathed so heavily. Gurgling like she was drowning in her own life force. Eyes bulging from the panic and fear. The pain. There was a lot of pain and screaming.

Chapter 8

The buzzer kept sounding at McKinley Park Residential, echoing down the hall because someone had opened the front door and hadn't found the **OFF** switch to quiet the halls. I was having coffee after lunch while the regular crowd shuffled out. Old Rose was wheeling herself around, looking for her coffee cup.

"I didn't take it," I snapped at her. I was in a bad mood and couldn't figure out why. It had been a bland morning. Something inside of me was like a cold piece of angry steel lodged in my chest. Old Rose was grating on me. All of them were. Rose wheeled herself around, lost, in circles. Some idiot had taken her cup, I was sure. But, like the rest of us, I was sure she was attached to the one she had. "Scoot off, you crazy old hag," I told her.

She looked at me with a mean eye. Spun off in her chair. I didn't have it after all.

What did I care about her coffee cup? I could get a cup any time I wanted. And so could she.

The girl behind the silver door, who worked in the kitchen... she always had coffee cups. The cute, short brunette with sad green eyes—not always sad, sometimes happy. Her crow's feet smiled when she smiled, beautiful little lines that showed years of happiness, a face accustomed to smiling.

"Old Rose, get the hell away from me."

She snorted and rode off down the hall.

The buzzer started up again. I'd been there over a year and still, that buzzer went off every day at random. That was no way to live. Sugar Bobby whisked up from behind me and sat down in the next chair. Sugar Bobby was huge. A gigantic man with big teeth that shone when he smiled, which was what he was doing right then. He opened his sweatshirt to reveal Old Rose's coffee cup. It was a big plastic deal, a travel mug. They all had travel mugs and traveled all over the building with them. I used regular glass mugs.

"I hate that bitch." Sugar Bob was smiling ear to ear, his pearly whites beaming.

"What did she ever do to you?" I asked.

"I just get sick of listening to her."

She was across the room, parked at a table in the corner of the cafeteria. The cafeteria was large enough to hold eight restaurant-style round tables. She had no idea what we were doing on our end.

"I was a person," I said to Bob.

"That's right," he answered. "You were a big guy around town before you came here. We were all somebody before we came here. Then life took a shit on us, and now we are here. And here we sit, with the buzzer forever buzzing and me amusing myself by stealing travel mugs from an old, defenseless woman."

"I sit here and listen to your shit," I said. "Day after day. And I was a person before."

He just smiled. "That's right. And you're a person."

"You mocking me?"

"*Patronizing*, child. An intelligent girl should know the difference."

I turned in Rose's direction and raised my hand. When I didn't get her attention, I started waving it back and forth. "Rose," I shouted.

Her wrinkled head whipped around in my direction.

I pointed at Sugar Bob. "Your coffee cup!"

She snapped the brake off her wheelchair and sped in the direction of Sugar Bob.

"You sure turn on a friend fast," he said to me in the face of the coming onslaught.

"You cocksucker," Old Rose shouted.

"Just set the cup on the table, friend," I instructed. "It's the only way to get out of this unscathed."

"I'll talk to you later, asshole," Sugar said. He stood and did as I said before heading off down the hallway.

Old Rose looked at me as if I was the Antichrist when she arrived at my table.

"I saved it for you, Rose," I pleaded. "You saw the whole thing."

"Cocksucker," she said to me.

I picked up the cup and held it over her head. "Tell me you love me, Rose. You know you do. You have a soft spot for me. I'm your favorite gal."

She reached her frail arms up at the cup above her head. "Cocksucker," she said again.

I gave in quickly. I knew I would only be referred to by the same obscene name until I did.

She was satisfied. Set the cup on her lap and rode off in the opposite direction of Sugar Bob. Leaving me alone, again with only my thoughts.

♦ ♦ ♦

Phil Stone, another residential acquaintance. Hell, he was a friend—he and Sugar Bob were the only friends I had there. This was my world. The confines of the building. The darkened hallways, cafeteria, nurse station. The nurses were friendly enough, but they were hard to talk to about certain things. They had to maintain a professional demeanor.

Phil didn't have a demeanor to keep up. He talked about all kinds of stuff. Sometimes, I lost track of his talking. Just heard his voice, like a song on the radio. On and on, he could go.

"Phenobarbital," he said one day. We were seated in the common room—an open room with chairs and tables like the cafeteria. Except there was a television and windows. I could see outside. It was a cold, autumn afternoon. The trees had lost most of their colorful leaves. The scene was familiar. But it was warm inside and I was comfortable.

And Phil was talking: "I loved that stuff. They don't sell it much here in the States. They use it in developing countries. It's only used here for epileptics to prevent seizures. We have new stuff here in the States. You can buy it mail-order, though. Places like India, they make it and distribute it. Illegal, though." Phil was convinced that drugs drove him insane and that was why he was there. He seemed to know a lot about drug abuse, so he could be right.

He was much shorter than Sugar Bob, or myself. Cropped dark hair, always neatly combed first thing in the morning. I could look half-asleep, walking out for coffee and breakfast, and Phil would be there eating already. Fresh as a spring morning, every hair in place and his clothes perfectly pressed to his body.

"Poppy pods," he started again, "now that's the way to go."

"Do we go outside?" I interrupted.

Phil stopped and looked at me thoughtfully. "Out there on the grounds?"

"Yeah."

"I don't fucking go out there. I hate it out there. Are you crazy? You can go out there, though. Anyone can. You could use some phenobarbital..." Phil thought everyone needed drugs. "They're legal. You can buy them at craft stores."

"What's that?" I asked.

"The poppy pods. You buy dried poppy pods. The kind they get the opium from. There's still opium in them. But that's not what people use them for. Not everyone. Or at least that's what the people selling them say. They are used in flower arrangements. People use them for art. That's fine with the Feds. Though it might be hard to explain needing 600 of them. But they sell them like that. 600 or a thousand. Or 20. You buy them and they get boxed up and sent to your house Priority Mail. It's all fine and legal unless you grind them up, then it's a federal offense. The ground pods still have opium in them, so you make a tea with a percolator. It's great. I never bought too many of them. Got me paranoid. But nothing ever happened. No one ever knocked on my door to take me away."

I wondered often if Phil was full of shit. No one ever gossiped about him. Either we all took his word at face value, or people didn't have the energy to question him. Sometimes, denial was an easier course than disbelief.

Chapter 9: *Lisa*

Lisa's bags had been packed for many months while she waited for Iris to become sane. It was more than Lisa could take. Her fiancé, Robert, had been waiting in the wings for so long, hoping to get their lives underway while Lisa kept putting him off. "We can make it another day," he would say on several occasions. "If you were dead, you wouldn't be impatient at all. We never would have met. And we wouldn't be getting married. You're an angel, Lisa, making sure this girl snaps out of her delusion and can have a normal life."

It wasn't the truth. Lisa was a murderer, not an angel, but it wasn't like anyone cared. The police investigated the bloody scene at the trailer, shrugged their shoulders, and closed the case. Sal was the one who had to answer for the death scene in his trailer. No one knew who the fuck Lisa was, except Iris.

"She saved my life, Robert. I can never repay that debt. The least I can do is be a friendly face while she's under the state's care. It can't be easy for her being lovelorn and confused." Lisa's real motivation was self-preservation. Would Iris spill the beans? In her present mind or after waking up from her fugue state, she was a dangerous girl as the only one who knew who pulled the trigger. She either had to be brought around, or become another victim of that fateful day at Ritz Crown Mobile Estate Park.

Iris being so dangerous did not negate the fact that she did indeed save Lisa's life, so she hesitated to pull the trigger on her until she could be sure.

In another life, Lisa and Iris could be friends. In the world of *Them vs. Me*, Lisa was certain it would be her. So she was biding her time but becoming impatient, mostly due to anxiety. She was ready to get the fuck out of the Midwest, marry Robert, and start the life she always wanted. Maybe finish school and become a marine biologist. Washington was the perfect state to peruse such a dream and, with Robert splitting time between a first-class hospital and private practice, she could breeze through school with few worries.

"Look," Robert said, "even if I have to go out there by myself, we'll still make it work. You can travel back and check on Iris, or stick around for a while until I have us settled in with the job and a nice living space."

"That's not fair to you."

"It's not fair to you either, but it's not that girl's fault. She's sick and needs some time."

Robert lived in a rundown studio apartment, the same one he spent his school career in. It came with ripped and stained furniture, no TV, and appliances that only worked half the time. He never complained because rent was cheap and the time he spent there was always occupied studying. Medical students in residency had little room for a life. It was on a rare respite from his studies when he looked up and noticed Lisa as the barista of his favorite coffee shop.

When their eyes met, Lisa saw a future where she could be the person she always wanted, instead of the poor trailer park girl hoping against hope Sal could make a final score that would be her ticket out of the Illinois cornfield.

"What if she never comes around?"

"That will be sad," Robert said. "But in time she will learn to live with her disability. She doesn't need you for that. And in time, you will realize you've done all you can do. There's a point where your constant involvement just becomes redundant, or maybe even harmful."

This was why Lisa wanted to marry Robert. His concern and kindness would help him as a doctor.

But it wasn't Lisa's style. In her mind, Iris needed a shakedown.

Chapter 10

"Iris?"

An evening *knock* on the door. I wasn't prepared. Bob Barker was on the old television. It was dark and I was dirty. Hadn't bathed and my clothes were dirty. I probably stank. The room was lonely. Just the way I liked it. I didn't want it disturbed. Didn't want light. No laughing, or that friendly feeling. Smiles and jokes. Old stories.

It was her. Lisa was at the door. No one else ever knocked, at this hour. I had no friends who ever visited. No one who ever cared. Most of the time, I liked it that way.

The *knock* again.

"Go away, Lisa," I shouted. It was her. Couldn't be anyone else.

"No," said a soft voice from behind the door.

"I'm watching television."

"I'm not leaving."

I stood and opened the door. She was crying. Not sobbing—just sniffling, tears running down her face.

"Let's go out," Lisa said. She wiped the tears. Pulled herself together. "I'm hungry. Let's go where there are people." She stepped up closer. I could feel her breath on my neck, it was a summer breeze of sanity. I felt like myself again, maybe gayer than I thought. It made me feel warm all over.

She unhooked my jacket from the wall, put it around me. Buttoned it up and held onto the collar. She stopped mid-thought. Lisa was always so serious. It was my fault she was so sad around me. She maybe laughed and had fun with her friends. "I just want dinner, Iris," she said. "Come on." She pulled me along by my sleeve.

We walked down the darkened corridor. It was silent, must have been late. I thought Bob Barker was on early.

We passed the closed kitchen doors. Stepped into the cafeteria, where a thought nagged me. I stopped to look at the room, the big, stainless-steel door was shut. I continued following Lisa. She looked forlorn with those eyes. Like the girl behind the silver door. Why so many people around me were sad, I didn't know. Was it something about me? I wished Sugar Bob was there, or Phil. They weren't so sad. Maybe it was just the women in my life. Did I break all their hearts somehow? Was I a bad person?

Lisa had long, blonde hair. She was cute when she smiled, which wasn't often enough. Pretty otherwise. A longer face than most. Oval and coming to a point at her chin. Age lines ran up and down, framing her smile, though I didn't think she was really that old. In my mind, she was in her twenties, yet something was etched into her face. Worry? Sadness?

We went to a nice place. No cheesy family place or fast food joint. "I want to buy you a good meal," Lisa said. "You must get sick of that institutional shit."

"I don't know the difference," I answered.

We were seated at a table for two in the middle of the restaurant. The food was nice, but the place wasn't so fancy that I needed to dress up. Lisa had, though: a yellow, floral dress, bright and happy. Sometimes, in the home, I was able to get up at a reasonable hour, shower and dress. Slacks and a button-up shirt. Long sleeves, no matter what time of year. Guess it was good enough. Lisa didn't tell me to change.

There were days, though, sometimes weeks, when I would wear sweats. A T-shirt and sneakers. Just lounge around. I didn't know what happened in those days. Eventually, I would snap out of it. Last time, Doctor Dave had to order me outside. That's when he initiated the evening walks. At least I would have to get dressed for that. Then with time, in the mornings again.

"I'm glad you brought me here," I said to Lisa. "It's nice."

"I'm glad you like it." She smiled and took a sip from her spoon. She was having French onion soup and a salad. I could smell it from her bowl. I almost regretted not ordering it. "Is your fish good?" she asked.

"Wonderful," I answered.

The waiter approached and Lisa slipped him her card.

She looked at me thoughtfully. "I'm moving. I'm getting married and I have to follow my husband to his new job on the West Coast. He's a doctor."

"I could swear you were dead," I informed her, as I had countless times in the past.

"No, Iris, I'm okay. I am okay now. You just didn't see. Your mind snapped before I was revived. You can't be blamed for not seeing my eyes open. You saved my life, Iris. Do you understand? You traded in your sanity for me to live."

I couldn't reply...

The waiter returned with Lisa's credit card. She signed the receipt. He smiled and left us. She dropped her card into her purse. "At least tell me you liked the food, Iris."

"It was good," I said.

Lisa silently drove me back. She seemed angry. I was questioning everything. Reality was taking on some kind of new meaning. It had a bite and an edge to it. I was in a car, being driven by a ghost. Was this really the way home?

"Every time I come by, I hope you are different," she said. "I have to go soon. I have to move away, Iris. I won't be able to see you as often."

"Good," I said. "I want you to go. You're dead. You're supposed to go. Go away to wherever it is people go when they die. Heaven or Nirvana or something. Go get reincarnated. Become a higher being. Live on a distant planet."

"I'm not dead."

"Oh God," I shouted. "You are! You are dead!"

The streetlights blurred by as Lisa drove. It was mesmerizing. It was like she was moving too fast. Or we were standing still. The world rushing past us.

"What are you doing to me?" I asked.

"Trying to bring you back."

"You feel guilty. That's it. You feel guilty about what happened."

"I do. Of course, I do. But I deal with that. I'm dealing with it now."

I felt dizzy. My head was starting to spin. It felt like the car was spinning on ice. I remembered that feeling from when I was young. My father would take me out on the frozen lakes in Minnesota. The ice was thick enough to hold his old van. After a day of ice fishing, he would let me sit on his lap as he operated the pedals. I would turn the wheel as he accelerated. "Turn sharp," he would instruct.

I would and he'd step on the brake. The van would spin in the darkness. Like lost souls, he and I. Spinning free in the universe. No control over where we were heading or what we might run into. Of course, he knew where we were all the time. He was used to it. Fished those lakes all his life. To me, it was just a dark carnival ride. And if it was snowing, all the better. Spinning wildly into the snow and darkness.

This was what Lisa was doing to me. Spinning me into the darkness, like the tunnel of love at the fair. Dark and scary. Not knowing where we might end up. Spinning and swirling. When would it stop? I felt sick and I wanted to be home, wanted to wake up in my bed. Tomorrow would be a day for sweats and stocking feet. Sugar Bob and I would pick on poor Old Rose. Pester her until she called us the names we wanted to hear. Maybe place bets.

"I'll be the first cocksucker," I would say to Sugar Bob.

"You're on." He would laugh and show those big teeth of his. A comforting smile. And in my sweats, all cozy and warm, I would be secure.

The spinning now dropped into my belly, where it skid full force. Like a tornado in my stomach. "I'm getting sick."

Lisa was on the phone. The spinning stopped. She was looking directly at me. "Iris," she shouted. It was hard to hear her, though, like she was far away, calling long distance. Lisa calling from the South Pole. The cell phone was at her ear and she was looking at me. The swirling stopped in my gut. Outside the car, lights stopped trailing off. We were in space. The stars were red and white and green. Comets flew by with regularity. I didn't know how Lisa kept track of them all. Surely, one would hit us soon. She spoke softly into the phone, looking at me, her eyes panicky.

💧 💧 💧

The silver door. I loved the silver door. Every time it went up, it meant the start of the day. Because the day started with food. Food and coffee. I was just an organism, taking up space at the home. Waiting to get my next bowl of soup, feeling special at the next taco night. I was just like a kid in school, wanting for everyone to wait on me, make dinner for me, make my bed, bring me drinks, and clean my clothes. There had to have been a time when this wasn't so. I vaguely remembered. I was childlike. And I lived in the world of grownups. I wore pajamas and the women wore skirts. They had lunches and drank cocktails. Talked about important stuff. And somewhere, there was the girl behind the silver door. And when the door went up, I was happy again. Something of me would come back when the door opened. A piece of myself returned and I was a full-grown woman again. Able to care for myself. As I looked at Lisa, I knew this was a paradox but still my life.

"I'm sorry," I heard myself say. "I'm so sorry for that night. It must have been so cold and painful. I'm sorry for every scream. I'm sorry for every bit of pain. Every labored breath. All I wanted was for you to be okay. I barely knew you. I'm so sorry. So sorry you died. That last breathe just took everything out of me. I know I should have gotten up the next day. I know I should have done it for you. That it was an insult to a beautiful dead person. But you have no idea what I went through. What you were like. What the last breath was like. It just hit me like a sledge."

Her hand dropped from her ear, the phone still in her palm. A tear escaped from her eye and fell down her face. "Iris," she whispered. Her face had sadness in it. She was caught in something, and she was so brave. She would see it through to the end, no matter what. She was going to be right there with me all the way to the end.

"Iris," Lisa said softly. She reached over and looked me in the eye. She whispered in my ear, "Feel this." Her hand was on mine and she was moving it up her leg, under her dress. There was nothing but the feel of her skin. The universe stopped the moment my hand touched her. It was like she was an angel and we were floating in space, on our way up into the firmament. White light framed her small face. She pulled and tugged, inched my hand farther up her thigh.

"Feel it," she whispered.

There was something there. Her soft skin had an imperfection. It felt like a knot of hard skin on her thigh. It was somehow familiar, even though I had never felt it. It was rough under my hand. Bigger than anything should have been on her thigh, in that spot. Lights were flashing outside. I sensed them first, then saw them. Bright lights, green and red and white. Some blue hues. Red and yellow flashing lights from all directions. I reached down and pulled up the hem of Lisa's dress. I had to see. I had to know. If I was about to become whatever it was people became. If I was about to enter into the nethers, I wanted to know. I had to know what had become of that night. I pulled, and Lisa let me. I saw her leg thicken as the dress inched farther. Her skin was flawless until I reached that point. The place where she made me feel the knot. It was the scar. I knew that scar. I knew what it was.

I remembered when it was a huge, gaping gash. And blood was pouring out everywhere. The snow was stained with Lisa's blood. The night was foggy with her steam. And she screamed, but there was nothing I could do. She was going to scream, but she was also going to die. And all of the work and screams and crying was for nothing. In the end, she'd grabbed me, looked up at me with pleading eyes, and breathed out her last breath. That was the end. I remembered so little after that. Woke up with Sugar Bob and Phil Stone. Making fun of Old Rose, talking about taking drugs and playing Spades.

She put her hand on mine, pushed down hard. "Goddammit, Iris. Feel that." Her mouth was next to my ear and she wasn't speaking softly. "It's real, Iris. I made it okay. Because of you, I'm okay. I'm so sorry I screamed so loud. I don't remember much. All I know is that I'm here. We had dinner tonight. I'm going to be married. I get to continue breathing and wake up in the morning." She pressed hard again. The knot of skin bulged under my hand.

The door behind me opened. I was going to fall out and away, into the night of mystery. Away from all this. Away from Lisa and having to remember.

She wrapped her arms around me tight and held me close. Her lips still in my ear: "Iris, there is no Kira! There's just some nice girl working in the kitchen. It's an easy mistake for you to make. She's not Kira!"

It was like falling from an airplane. Other hands were on me from behind. Strong hands. And a separate set of hands pulled at my shoulders. Tugged firmly. Lisa held on, not wanting to let go, but she did.

After a tug or two, she let go—voluntarily. Gave up on me and let me fall off into space. Out into the night with its flashing light and cold air. I could hear nothing. It was dead silent, or I was deaf. But I had heard Lisa. Saw her in the car as I fell away. Weightless into the beyond, I heard no other sound. It was a mystery, whoever was pulling me away or where I was going. Maybe they were angels. Everything went dark and I couldn't feel any more movements or hands or cold night air. Only wonderful darkness wrapping itself around me, cradling me like a child. Like I was floating in the ocean, riding the gentle waves without a care in the world.

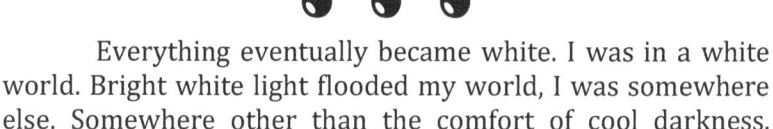

◆ ◆ ◆

Everything eventually became white. I was in a white world. Bright white light flooded my world, I was somewhere else. Somewhere other than the comfort of cool darkness. There was nothing other than the light. It was still cool, though, and I found that comforting. I wasn't with Lisa, or anyone. Just myself in this new bright world. I felt gravity again, so I was in the real world still, maybe. Or maybe I was in Heaven or dreaming.

I came to in a hospital room. Everything was sterile and stainless steel, like the door in the kitchen.

A nurse noticed me wake and smiled. I was restrained with leather straps. "Iris?" she asked. "How are you doing?"

"I don't know where I am," I said.

"County hospital. You had a psychotic episode, like before. Are you okay to take off your restraints?"

"I've never needed them before."

"Standard procedure, I'm afraid." She started removing them from my wrists and ankles. Her name tag said, **Mildred**. She appeared about my age, curly brown hair in a ponytail. Freckles and a warm smile. Brown, reassuring eyes.

I rubbed my raw wrists as she undid the ankle straps. "Is my doctor here?" I asked.

"He will be in the morning. We're going to run some tests tonight."

I started crying like a baby. I didn't want to be in the hospital with no control over what was happening to me.

"Your friend Lisa went home."

"She's not my friend."

"Well, she seemed pretty concerned about you."

"She's a ghost."

Mildred laughed.

"What's so funny?" I sat up and rubbed my ankles. It felt good to move even though I was a bit dizzy.

"She's quite alive." She pressed two fingers against my chest to push me back down with a bit of attitude.

"She looks that way, but she is very dead."

"I beg to differ," she said with a smirk. "I was here when they brought her in long ago. Big gash in her leg. Femoral artery cut right in two. It was a miracle she survived. What a night that was, zero degrees in the middle of a blizzard."

Doctor Dave had explained before that when I blitz out, my eyes roll up in my head and I start foaming at the mouth. It'd happened a couple times at the residential home. It was how I wound up with the leather straps, and that was what Nurse Mildred was struggling with now, trying to restrain me. Shock and concern on her face. I must have foamed again.

"Some help in here," she shouted. She looked determined, yet frazzled. The room filled up quickly with other determined faces. The straps were soon secure.

A prick in the arm, and I faded into the black again.

My next memory was that of a shadowy woman in the corner of my room. I could scarcely make out her face. I was strapped to the bed again. Uncomfortable yet relaxed, a living paradox.

"Why are you here, Kira?" I asked.

"Because I'm supposed to. It's what I do."

"You work for Doctor Dave?" I asked softly.

She didn't answer.

Mildred was soon back at the side of my bed. "Let's get you fed without another occurrence," she suggested.

That sounded fair. I didn't want to get foamy again. "It's upsetting that Doctor Dave isn't here," I said.

"Guess you're stuck with me," Mildred answered. She started unstrapping me. "You gonna be a good girl this time?"

"I can try."

"*Shhh...*" came from Kira's darkened corner.

Mildred had a serious look. She didn't acknowledge Kira's shadowy presence. Our eyes met and she smiled.

"Sorry about before," I offered.

"Not necessary," she said. "You weren't doing anything wrong. It's not a bad thing. There is just something that you need fixed. That's why we are all here." The straps came off and Mildred turned to hurry to her next patient.

"Have a good night," I offered.

"This is the neuro ward, Iris," Mildred said quietly. "Not the loony floor."

"Oh, thank you," I said.

"Don't thank me," she said. She looked suspiciously to the corner where I saw Kira, then turned to leave.

"Are you my guardian angel?" I asked when we were alone.

"I'm tired, Iris," Kira said. She had a blanket pulled up to her shoulders and closed her eyes.

I didn't understand. Why was Kira there, much less keeping watch or falling asleep? Her eyes didn't open back up. I watched for almost an hour. I was exhausted and the sedative was still in my system. I drifted, eyes barely open. Her breathing filled the room. Before succumbing to sleep, I had a vision of Kira: her face lifeless lying in bloody snow. Hair wet with blood against the white snow. Blood everywhere, and the copper-smelling steam. Her eyes closed and body motionless. Was she breathing? Was my love really gone?

Chapter 11

Seemed any time I spent in a hospital bed, I also spent with Lisa. It became difficult to find anywhere to spend time alone. This hospital bed felt different though, free of anxiety. A light shone at the end of a lonely tunnel where I'd spent so much time without myself, the one and only person I could depend on. Outside the tunnel was freedom, and the conclusion of this skinny love affair with Lisa.

I woke up to harsh voices: "I wish you had never found me," said an angry voice.

I turned and saw Lisa's ghost standing on the side of my bed. Her hands rested on the railing, the same way Mildred's had the night before.

"I'm so fucking tired of fighting with you."

I turned to the other side of the bed. It was Kira.

It was Kira.

I knew it was her. I remembered. This was odd, the two of them together. Revelations were occurring hourly.

"Could you guys do this somewhere else?" I asked, then noticed a tray of food in front of me. With hot coffee.

"You guys?" Lisa repeated. "Who all is in the room, Iris?"

I turned to Lisa.

"What's going on?" She pointed at the tray, an annoyed look on her face.

I picked up the coffee and started drinking.

"I wish..." Lisa started, "I wish I really were dead."

Kira stared back at her. She was determined about something. I took another drink of coffee. I felt a hand on the back of my neck. I glanced up to discover it was Lisa's. Kira was examining something on her nails.

"I feel kinda good this morning," I said to no one in particular. Then became interested in what else might be on the tray. "Must have had a good night's sleep."

Kira caught my attention. She looked up very thoughtfully, studying Lisa's gaze. They glanced in each other's direction. Lisa gave the back of my neck a squeeze and then removed her hand. She turned and walked out of the room.

"Ghost gone," I said.

Kira sat back down. She had a cup of coffee on the window ledge by her chair. "I'm glad you are feeling better."

"Are you going to go home soon?"

She turned and gave me the most serious look ever. "I am home, Iris."

"You don't live here."

"Wherever you're at is my home."

Lisa returned with a cold can of diet soda.

"I'm sorry," I said.

"About what?" Lisa asked.

"That you wish you were dead."

"I don't really. It would just be easier." She pulled up her sweater sleeve up to check the time.

"She has a hot date?" Kira asked.

"That's my watch."

"Getting hungry. It's past lunch." Lisa was distractedly blasé. She held up her wrist so I could see.

"That's my watch."

"It's past time," Kira announced. "I'm leaving now."

She's leaving now...

I didn't need the announcement, but Kira gave one anyway. My attention was on Lisa's possession of my watch.

"My watch," I repeated a third time. "That's my fucking watch, goddammit!"

"I'm not giving it back."

"No? Hey! You and I have secrets!" Lisa holding a shotgun at Ritz Crown Mobile Estate Park flooded my memory. My belly on the cheap laminate of Lisa's trailer. The deafening gunfire left to ring in my ears.

"We're in the clear." Lisa touched the side of her nose to acknowledge the shady past of our relationship.

"*We?*"

"No investigation," she whispered. "No cops."

"Who ended up with the money?"

Lisa shushed me with an index finger on her lips.

I grabbed the front of her jacket and yanked her so we were nose to nose. "Where's the dope?"

"Fucking Sal for all I know. Or nobody. I fired the shotgun until it was empty. I dunno who shot who, but I got outta there in a hurry. I couldn't even breathe or see straight."

"Didn't have presence of mind to grab the bag?"

"That was your fucking deal, sister, not mine." Lisa was gritting her teeth.

I let go of her jacket and let my head fall back to the pillow. It was a fact I wasn't in jail, and she was here instead of far away. I couldn't judge her for a lack of backbone. "You're okay?"

"That's what I've been trying to tell you!"

"And Kira's okay!"

"I don't know. I haven't seen any Kira."

💧 💧 💧

Sugar Bob was not only my best friend but my Spades partner. That says a lot, because Spades partners have a certain connection. They share strategy and an intuition that others know nothing about.

We had daily tournament play. Twelve players usually showed. Six teams of two, which meant we started with three games to 500 points until the last two teams. By that time, the side bets were in full swing. People put up everything from potato chips to hydrocodone. Seemed like it was always the schizos against the manic-depressives. The major depressives didn't have the staying power and the anxiety-sufferers didn't have the attention span to count tricks. I paired up with Sugar Bob. He knew the game, built our strategy, and consistently knew how much trump I had in my hand.

Bob was staring at me with his best poker face. It was Wednesday and we hadn't made it to the championship game in weeks. He usually had trazodone by 2 o'clock and was fast asleep by 2:30. But there we sat, inquiring eyes peeking over the top of our cards. All my spades on the left of the hand, per usual. And he was eying me up, ascertaining the trump I held. By the twinkle in his eye, he was holding pretty heavy too.

"13," Bob announced. A bold move since we had bid first.

"By yourself?"

"Together."

I shake my head. The manic-depressives would need one trick to set us. I didn't care for that strategy.

"That's enough table talk," warned one of the women from the other team. A young woman, a girl actually. Bright green hair with a pierced nose. "Just bid."

Sometimes, it took up to six hours to get the tournament concluded. A few times until sundown. There were always a couple who wigged out by that time from lack of PRNs. But that was the rule and we all abided by it. Better to play wonked out than to be under the influence. Everyone agreed to stay frosty, suck cigarettes, or drink all of the Mountain Dew required to finish up the tournament. Sleep was for the evening.

If the state lackeys ever walked in at two in the afternoon, they might've been very surprised. But what could they say about a group of card-playing mental misfits not watching TV? We weren't up dropping acid and hitting each other with hammers. It was a card game, nothing more. It was Spades, and it was everything.

"Five," I said. I held seven.

"Eight," Bob added. So he meant to go through with this strategy. He took the first trick with the ace of clubs. I took the next one with the king. A smirk curled up at the ends of his mouth. I stopped doubting.

I wasn't going to stay at the residential hall any longer. I'd never play Spades with Sugar Bob again, but the memory of that game would stay with me for the rest of my life. I'd be confused about Kira or even my own existence, but my one and only perfect 13 trick game made a lasting impression.

Before Lisa left for her adventure in marital bliss, we exchanged stories, hugs, and vows of silence. Her only thought to impart was not to go looking for that Kira girl. Advice that would become repetitive in all my future friendships.

Chapter 12: Kira

Zach had disappeared, coward that he was. Kira laid on the bed in her Monterey, California, apartment hands painfully zip-tied behind her back with a bloody nose to teach her a lesson about stealing from a drug dealer's stash.

"You read too much," said the obese, dark-haired man examining Kira's copy of *The Picture of Dorian Grey*.

"You want I should watch *Gilligan's Island*?"

"Too much thinking and not enough action," the man explained. "You American youth think you're so enlightened but you know nothing of the real world."

"My arms hurt like this," Kira complained.

"My name is Tino," the man ignored. "See, *bebita*, in the real world, stealing from a drug dealer may put you at the bottom of the ocean, tied to a bag of quick cement. But you won't be alone, I have a collection of bandits down there, all with their own bags of cement."

"Where I come from, stealing from a drug dealer shows initiative."

"Ah-ha! Are you turning this into a job interview?" Tino laughed a bit too loud, overcome by Kira's audacity.

"I could use a job."

"Can you handle a boat, *bebita*?"

"I can handle anything."

"You say this now to stay alive." Tino's tone had a serious edge. He was taking her seriously, glared at her a few long minutes while the gears turned in his head. Tino was accustomed to recruiting employees for his drug smuggling business in this manner. Employees who were grateful to be alive were loyal employees, and the money was pretty good. "An associate of mine will be along soon to take care of business," Tino explained before abruptly turning to leave the apartment.

Kira had no idea what this meant. Was she getting a job, or getting the axe? She strained against the plastic zip-ties but that only made her hands and wrists hurt more. Hours before, she had been walking along the beach, minding her own business. A short, orange summer dress bustled about her thighs as she enjoyed the sand and fading sun sinking into the horizon. The color of her long hair lightened in the sun and salty air since arriving in Monterey.

She'd known for a long time this wasn't her final destination, but her progress had been halted while she secretly waited, hoping one day Iris would catch up to her. Kira's obsession with the girl could become tedious so she often occupied her time feeding her head illicit drugs. This time, boredom got her hand caught in Tino's stash.

Eventually, a tall, dark, muscular man silently entered Kira's room. He expertly produced a switchblade in one hand and flipped Kira over with the other. After cutting the zip-ties loose, he pulled her to a sitting position.

"So I got the job?" she asked.

"I'm Tino's son, Larry," he announced. "I'm your boss from now on."

"Larry?" Kira chuckled. "That's a sorta bland name."

"Our business requires blandness. And don't say anything racist. Unlike my father, I'm a United States citizen with an American name."

"Sorry. I joke when I'm scared."

"Don't worry. I'm taking you home. Don't talk to my wife and kids. Just do what I say and do it well, you'll be fine."

"And if I'm not fine?" Kira was still scared.

Larry answered by flipping his butterfly knife before grinning and returning the weapon to his pocket. "You'll be fine. I see the outlaw in your eyes."

Kira grabbed her notebook and penned a quick message for Zach, warning to keep Iris alive. She showed it to Larry just to be safe.

"Love," Larry commented. "Come, we have piles of money to make. You'll return to this shithole of a town soon enough."

Chapter 13

I woke up to the memory of Kira's arm around me. Holding on and greeting my morning with a connection I'd never felt before. Waking up optimistic, even though I'm not a morning person. Just like that first morning in the van, and after, every morning, over and over again, she was there holding me close. Resting against me, like a promise to always be fulfilled. Like I could somehow be better. In a skanky motel, under a park bench, or beneath a freeway bridge. She stayed with me everywhere. Woke with me each morning. Feeling her chest expanding and contracting, her breath on the back of my neck, the soft sound she made while breathing. Early in the morning before she awoke, I could hear it. I thought I could hear her heart beating, but I wasn't sure. I could feel it against my spine.

I remembered when I thought I was alone and Kira had left. Then I never wanted to wake up. I remembered being out in the elements, behind a bush in some small-town park. It was just before sunrise and I knew I had to leave. But I couldn't. I was frozen with tears in my eyes, wishing I never had to awaken again. That's when I was alone in the world with absolutely no one. There was not a single person on the entire planet I could claim was on my side.

Then I'd learned where Kira was and I was never alone again. I was so pitiful, traveling aimlessly, taking food where I could, and not having cigarettes for weeks on end. It was so much better once I found her.

In a moment of clarity, I looked to pick up the trail of my life's love at the last place I saw her: Watertown. Some guy was casting a shadow in the only room with a light on. I was uncomfortable, of course. This was no place for me to be with a healthy mind. The door was locked. I tapped on the guy's window. What was I doing? How was this important? He came to the window. Young. I was expecting an older guy. The window was jammed and he couldn't open it. I gestured with my finger in the direction of the front door. Reluctantly, subtly, in case he was stupid and might not get my meaning. He proved his intelligence, though, as he pushed the door open.

"Thanks," I said. "I used to live here."

"A patient?" he asked.

"Yeah. I'm looking for someone. A roommate who also lived here."

"Good luck. This place is a barren wasteland of information."

"I was just curious."

"Come in. No one's guarding the place. I'd rather let you in than have another broken window."

He walked me to his office. The place was deserted and dark, cold, haunted. His light was the only except for the windows.

I experienced a bout of panic. This was really no place for me to be. Why the stop? I was on my way, focused on a healthy destination. "Two years ago, I was here with my friend. Little over two years."

"They let you room with a friend?"

"Not at first, but we switched."

"Different times. Different rules."

"Trying to pick up her trail..."

"There aren't any records from then," he explained.

"She was here. We both were. 1987, they let me out."

"Kicked you out."

"I was released."

"The state ran out of money to support institutions like this. Everyone was released. Not all at once. In small groups, but no more housing for mentally ill patients."

"Where do patients go now?"

"Jail. Prison."

"You're the only one here?"

"For now. I don't know what's gonna happen. Maybe they'll tear the place down."

The guy told me where the unlocked entrance was so I could walk around and reminisce. I went for a look. Nothing changed. It was like everyone just disappeared, raptured to Heaven or stolen by aliens. Maybe an apocalyptic virus. My imagination ran wild. The tall chain-link fences remained. No barbed wire, but not an open campus. If someone found their way there, they had to earn their way out.

Our room. We were roommates. It was like I could feel her fingers on the back of my neck. Her breath in my ear, whispering secrets. Making deals, love pacts. I realized that now. Pacts weren't made between two people for any other reason than love. I loved her, we were in love. I knelt to the floor, my eyes welling with a revelation. The loose corner-brick we hid our medications. Still loose, frozen in time. No one thought to check. Too busy making notations on crazy people.

I removed it and nothing was behind. No magic note telling me what to do, or where Kira had gone. No instructions on how to spend the rest of my pathetic life. Not even a leftover trazodone. It wasn't until I looked at the back of the brick to judge how it should be replaced that I noticed the scratches. Numbers, an infamous date: **3/18/89**.

It was February and the sun hadn't shone in 22 days. Even traveling all this way, I hadn't experienced a moment of sunlight. I was so sensitive to this cloud cover. So sick of the fucking rain. It crept in a little deeper every dark day. Dark days and lonely nights with nobody to love, except a dreamy memory of someone whose lips I never even felt.

Fucking Reagan and fucking Ortega Saavedra. Goddamn crooks with their guns and dope. That's all I'd heard about during my trip 'cause I had no music. The tapes I gave Kira. I comforted myself by thinking that they were with her, to the end. It got so she couldn't exist without Patti Smith every day.

The beds were still there. Obviously, exactly the way we left them. No one had been in there to replace me or Kira. The indents on the mattresses were ours. The sheets still soiled with our sweat. None of it was reclaimed. They were just going to bulldoze it all down. I sat on her cot and put my hand on her tear-stained pillow. She was gone. I knew in that moment, she was gone.

My hand on her pillow, sitting on her mattress, my resolve renewed. I could be strong too. I could tell the world to fuck off and jump ship. I didn't care what anyone said after, 'cause no one was saying anything now. No one ever said anything except Kira. Only she understood what it was like. The darkness and the voices, calling to me. Always calling me to come home. She heard them. She answered. She was unafraid.

I flipped the pillow. A distant memory made me reach inside, not even considering spiders or roach infestations. It was there. Kira's black-wool stocking cap and, goddamn, if it didn't smell like her. Her face was faded in my memory, her picture wrinkled in my head, scratched and blemished like an ancient Polaroid. And yet fierce green eyes flashed like neon light in a snowstorm. Something was amiss and I could feel it in my soul. Faraway, her memory had become. Almost out of reach. This wasn't about her anymore. That was the itch in my soul. Somehow, I already knew it was too late. My days with her were over, but my redemption was closing in.

"I found you!"

I jumped out of my skin. It was the desk guy. What a mean trick, being so loud in this place haunted by so many memories.

"I came across some records. I may have a lead on your friend. Somebody wrote a short note on her discharge papers. Seems a bus ticket was bought for her."

"1985?"

"Yup, destination Denver, Colorado."

"Who bought the ticket?"

"Some social worker, I'm sure. It doesn't say, but that was their job. Get patients connected like that. Get them home or somewhere safe."

Nowhere was safe for Kira.

"The state usually footed the bill," he explained.

"The government bought her a bus ticket?"

"Yeah. You know if she has family in Denver? Probably where she went."

Kira had no family. I was her fucking family. And I might be her only survivor. "I think I have an idea..." I didn't really. But I wanted this guy to think I did. Maybe believe that Kira had a family. That some social worker did the right thing after all, so many years ago. My guess would actually be that she wanted the maximum distance allowed by law.

"There's a note," he added.

"From her?"

"The social worker, probably. Just a file note from someone after a session."

"A session?"

"Maybe a therapist." He gave it to me. "It's of no use to the state now. Program closed, building empty, and patient long gone. It's just paper now."

Patient was alert and oriented X4. Patient thought pattern was linear and future-oriented. Patient mood was congruent. Patient denied SI/HI. Final session included story about stealing guitar from neighbor during childhood years in Arkansas and desire to make amends. "Neighbor currently resides in California." The writer advised against making the trip from here. Bus ticket obtained for patient.

"I'm going to California," Kira announced, voice echoing in my reverie from our tragic past.

"When?" I had asked.

"Before I die," she had replied.

This was the memory my brain chose to resurface. A good cry, puffy red eyes, and a chance at redemption. I couldn't choose to ignore this. It wasn't a delusional memory that I just created. Before 3/18/89. Her birthday in 1989. Sometime before then, she traveled to California. Goddamn, Kira said what she meant and kept her word, always. I couldn't count on her to weasel out in any fashion.

"I've never seen the ocean," Kira had observed. "I hear the saltwater is cleansing."

"Me either... Why not go east?" I had asked. "There's an ocean on that side too."

"East sucks. West is the promise land."

"Ocean is an ocean."

"I don't want to die in a shitty place."

"Doesn't matter to me." I had shrugged. "Just depends on who I'm with, or not with."

"I won't dump you," Kira reiterated.

This made me smile. "Geography doesn't excite me."

"You're not very romantic, are you?"

I lowered my eyes and shook my head. She was right, I wasn't. Not with people or places. I didn't have a story to live. No backstory to guide me, or quests to undertake. Like the walking dead, viewing life through zombie eyes. "Maybe Canada," I offered.

"Canada?"

"Alberta. Jasper."

"Fucking cold!"

"The cold is cleansing, I hear."

"That's so specific," Kira teased.

"You get around on horseback. I guess that's why Jasper. I mean, I guess you can get around in a car. It's not like there are no roads. But to really get anywhere, you need a horse."

"What's anywhere?"

"The mountains…"

"You're a pioneer woman," Kira observed.

"Pioneers pushed into the frontier. There's no frontier anymore," I said.

"There's fresh air, all that bullshit."

"It's not like a fresh start or anything. Just a place I want to go."

"There's a story there I'll probably never hear."

I had been silent. And I looked away because Kira could make serious eye contact. Ever since that night at the campsite, she had acted like she had an in. Perhaps I was paranoid because she spilled the beans. Told her wish to me, what her amorous intentions were. It was paranoia, maybe homophobic. She said I was safe and I believed that. Just those green eyes were piercing, probing, like a can opener trying for a peek inside. She knew she wasn't my type since she had no penis. But still, there was desire in her stare.

She wanted salt in the air and I required icy breezes. My mind searched for a middle ground. An ocean shore located north. Motorcycles instead of horses. "You were on your way there," Kira realized. "Heading north."

I was found out. "I'm always heading north," I explained. "My adventures somehow turn me around, though. Gal's gotta make a living."

Chapter 14: Denver, Colorado

Hitching was my main mode of transportation, but not without the chance of falling victim to many highway evils and those who contributed to them. It got to where I only accepted rides with professional truckers. They were too busy making time to be distracted by raping little women.

My attempt to pick up Kira's trail had led me to a shady strip club by process of elimination. People like Kira and I stuck close to the shadowy parts of town, so I didn't have to search all of Denver, just the places where a drink could buy a whisper of sightings of a pretty transient girl with green eyes.

"She said she needed quick money..."

"Saw her hustling some rube..."

"Almost killed that coke dealer..."

"Saw her dancing..."

I presented my scratchy, black-and-white picture while walking around the room. I showed it to each girl, most of whom looked away, except a few who turned toward where a young, black woman sat alone at a mirror, bare-chested and holding a tube of whore-red lipstick. I walked to her and held the picture for her to see.

She looked angry. "Good ol' Green Eyes."

"Where is she?"

"She's long gone. Couldn't make it in this business."

"If ya got tits and hips, you can make it in this business," I countered, mirroring her attitude.

The woman stood. She was much taller than me and her face became even fiercer.

I suddenly figured out it was not me she was mad at.

"You can't be a real person and expect to keep working as a dancer. I told her that. Green Eyes could act like a stripper, but she had nothing to hide behind."

I completely understood. I knew what it was like to look into Kira's eyes. She was always there, all the time. "Where did she go?"

"Get the hell out of my dressing room."

"I just need to know..."

"Aw. Is little Skinny Legs in love?"

I didn't answer, but I didn't look away in shame either. I was tired of feeling guilty.

"You're looking for something that doesn't exist."

"It's more complicated than that," I explained.

The woman's eyes widened with revelation. "I know who you are. I know what you're doing, chasing after death like it's a cat in heat, you sick little bitch. I'm telling you, for the last time, to get out of my dressing room. I can get a bouncer in here post-haste, but I don't really need one. I can throw your ass out myself."

I left, all the way to the street. It was dark and rain started to fall. So I cried. The door suddenly opened and light flooded the sidewalk. Out stepped the tall woman, bare tits and all. She walked right up to me and got in my face.

"Look, Skinny Legs. We all fall in love. And everyone fell in love with Green Eyes. Just take your little schemes and your stupid white ass home."

"It's not me you're mad at," I proclaimed.

The woman was silent. Her face softened.

"Just say California. You'll never see me again."

"Florida," the mostly naked woman said.

"I know that's not true. And I'm going to do whatever the hell I want, no matter how demeaning you are."

"Monterey," she said softly. "You fucking twisted bitch. Fucking crazy cunt. You shouldn't even be allowed to walk the streets alone."

Stares fell on us from the open door to the club.

"Why is it always the talented ones?" she asked, not really making eye contact. Looking through me to someone else. The same someone she was in love with, same as me. "Always the smart, gifted ones. The ones who know better. It ain't that hard to just keep goin'. Focus on other things. Pleasant things. The little things."

My hair and clothes were getting soaked. My night was about staying dry and surviving. Not talking philosophy with some stripper who obviously didn't understand. Just another in a long line of lovers with no comprehension. She told me where to go and I appreciated that. But fuck her, I needed to get moving.

"See you in Hell, Skinny Legs," she sobbed as I turned away. "Fucking selfish, little white girl looking for a dream. It's gone, Skinny Legs. It's gone."

Sleeping under a bridge was the same in every city in any state. I was becoming an expert. An aficionado of sorts, traveling via thumb, having never perfected freight train travel. Being caught in a train yard was against the law and required talking to police, after getting a beating, or worse, from the yard boss. Police merely ordered vagrants to move along. The streets might *belong* to the police but were *home* to the vagrants. Police understood that better than the yard bosses who were one step away from vagrancy themselves.

The overpasses and viaducts were hotel rooms for the homeless, which I technically was, even though I considered myself to be traveling. But this sleeping space was cold and I had nothing dry to find comfort in. The information I'd gotten about Green Eyes was valuable, but Monterey was a long ways away. It seemed like paradise to me that night. I shouldn't have been shivering under that bridge. The information was worthless if I didn't survive. If I didn't make it to the West Coast to find out if Kira still lived, which was highly unlikely, in which case…

I played the waiting game, though. If the rain let up, I would venture out into the city once again. Find shelter for the night. A place that took the homeless, a laundromat, or a damn dumpster in an alley. I was heading to the end, the bottom. I didn't care how I lived and had no pride in myself. The bleaker the circumstance, the happier I was. But I needed to breathe long enough to get farther west.

I slept. In my dreams, Kira rode a motorcycle. A big, roaring Harley. Her eyes were shielded by large, round mirror-glasses. Dark hair flowed behind her like a demon's veil. A cigarette in her teeth and thick, sensuous lips were covered in bright red lipstick. A sawed-off shotgun was strapped to the back of her black leather jacket and a revolver hung at her hip. She was being followed by many state troopers with flashing lights but no sirens. Only the sound of the Harley. Kira's face was decorated by the most enormous smile I'd ever seen. She braked and spun so she was facing the oncoming police cars. The shotgun found its way into her hands, and she pumped it to the ready. Aimed forward with her left arm and started the Harley forward with the right. I turned away, not wanting to watch. What I could see was the ocean and a red sunset over a serene beach. The roar of the motorcycle suddenly stopped.

I woke up crying. Angry at the fact I was under a bridge with zero dignity, trying to sleep in the deep wet cold. This was not right. This was not how Kira would do things. And I should've been honoring her on this trek across the country. I wasn't a transient. I was Iris, Kira's friend and confidant. It was time to get up, brush off, act like the woman I really was, and steal a car.

🜂 🜂 🜂

John Steinbeck wrote about Monterey, a lot. That was the extent of my knowledge of my destination. I did read at one time, trashy novels and otherwise. I had always been a fan of the legendary Ed Ricketts. At least, the way he was written by Steinbeck. There was a spark of excitement at the prospect. I was so motivated that I stole a nice new truck, a Chevy with the keys in the ignition, open beer in the cup-holder. The owner was inside the gas station where I had paper-toweled myself a bath in the locked restroom. This was how it was going to be then. A cakewalk across the west to a favorite Ricketts hometown.

I picked up the open beer and threw it out the window while maneuvering the pickup to lower elevations. I had nothing against beer. Ricketts would stop at cheap diners for beer with lunch, ignoring the waitress telling him not to drink and drive. I didn't trust whoever had opened it and winced at the thought of the can being full of tobacco spit.

At the next small town, I pulled over. Was there money in the glove box? No. A gun. Figures, matched the open beer can. Was it loaded? Of course, it was loaded. I held the pistol in my hand. Felt the weight. Everything could all end so quickly and violently. I couldn't keep my eyes off of it. Couldn't turn away. One second was all it would take. The pull of a trigger. A flash, then the darkness. Right there on the side of the road in the middle of Nowhere, Colorado. I wouldn't have to drive anymore. Care anymore. Feel anymore. Breathe anymore. No psych wards. No hospitals. No Monterey.

The West Coast. I knew Kira was dead, I could feel it in my bones. I knew she was true to her word. More than I was, or could ever be. But what if? If I was wrong, this ended like a tragic Shakespearean play, leaving her alone. I could see her, tucked away in some corner of a hospital. Or in a dreary studio apartment, waiting for me. Hoping. Either way, I couldn't let her down. I had to know for sure. But I also couldn't leave a loaded gun out on the street or keep it with me. With complete concentration, I figured how to pop the clip, empty the chamber. With tears running down my cheeks, I managed to chuck the ammo out the window and drive on, the empty gun in the seat next to me. At the next town, I'd dispose of it in a dumpster behind a 7-Eleven. I should've been done sobbing by then.

But Monterey sucked more than Steinbeck ever let on. What was going through Kira's mind? I knew she favored the West Coast and wanted to see the ocean. But this town was horrible. A rotten place to die.

Chapter 15

"This was her room," he said. "This was where she stayed. She was found dead over there, under the window."

Kira would stick out in a town like Monterey. I knew she would have a bit of cash and want to be near the ocean, near enough to walk barefoot in the sand if she chose. A bit of cash was different than a lot of cash, which eliminated housing on a level normal people were accustomed to. Again, I found where she stayed by process of elimination, knocking on the doors of establishments in her price range, in my price range, the places only the lost could afford.

She was looking out the window. Then crumpled into a pile of dead bones onto the floor. I put my back against the wall and started sobbing. Streams of tears ran down my face, dripping from my chin. I slid down the wall and buried my face between my knees. Was I delusional, to imagine she was looking out the window for me? Hoping at the last minute, after waiting so long? I felt like a coward. I'd let her down. I was so caught up in my obsession with her that it never occurred to me that the feeling might be mutual. Maybe she favored me the same way. Maybe she felt exactly as I did, maybe she even loved me.

I lifted my head and slowly scanned the room, looking for some trace. Under the bed was a small package. Winstons. I reached for them. Could barely snatch them with my fingertips. It wasn't empty, and I had a lighter. I smoked. It felt so good. I felt alive, attached to this place and time. The smoke filled my lungs and the space above my head. My fingers ran across a bump in the package. In the cellophane. Two little white pills with crosses on them. Kira's amphetamines. So these were hers. Left behind and overlooked. I smoked and sobbed. And I sat there with my back against the wall for the rest of the day.

When the sun set, I was still there, in the spot where Kira died. Still crying and smoking. It was horrifically sacred.

"Hey," a voice broke my reverie. "You can't stay here."

"What's your name?" I asked.

"Zach."

"Zach. Did you fuck my friend?"

His eyes bugged from the shock of blindsiding him. "She was gay," he answered. "Very gay. Not part gay. Not bi-curious. She was fucking gay."

"So you tried?"

"Of course. I'm a red-blooded, horny American boy. It's always worth a shot."

"You haven't given me a shot."

"You're sitting on the floor in a dark room, crying. Kind of a turn-off." He smiled at his joke. "Plus, I'm assuming you're super gay too."

"I've never even kissed another girl."

"You like guys?"

"I always thought so."

"Just because you love another woman doesn't mean you're gay."

"Oh, thanks. That clears up the confusion."

"It's just love. People love each other. It happens. Can't label plain ol' love."

"Who said anything about love?"

"Guess I was assuming again."

"Maybe she was my sister."

"Was she?"

"No..."

"Are you afraid of being gay?"

"I wasn't brought up that way," I answered.

"What way?"

"To be gay!"

"So you're hetero because you think it's the right thing to do? Yet the love of your life passed and you never even kissed her."

"That's not right? It's not normal?" I asked.

"The love of your life dying is not right. Loving her and not loving her, that's not normal."

"Sex isn't necessary in a love relationship."

"It's not," he said. "But you're a young woman in good physical health. Unless you have issues, maybe you should have fucked her."

"Well, I didn't," I answered so loud that I shocked myself. Yes, of course, I should have kissed her. And deeply for all eternity. I should have taken my clothes off and offered myself on the altar of Kira. I should've worshipped her and ravaged her. Let her have and own me. But I didn't. I didn't. All I ever had were boyfriends and the thought never occurred to make advances on her. It never occurred to me. I never really went all the way to get what I wanted. Or even what I needed. I had needed Kira! I needed her now. Yes, I should have offered. She might still be here if I had. "I didn't."

"Sorry. I pressed when I shouldn't have. It was obvious and I should have known."

"No. Obvious to you. I just found out... I'm a coward."

"I didn't mean to..."

"I know. Just hush for a minute."

By some magnificent miracle, he did. I let my mind wander until I visualized Kira, standing barefoot in the ocean. A rocky place, not a beach. Somewhere Ed Ricketts might have seen as he searched for marine life. Starfish and whatnot. "I hope she went to the ocean," I said, finally breaking the silence.

"You can't help that in this town. Have you been out yet?"

"I've only been here."

"You wanna go see the ocean?"

"Fuck the ocean."

"Well, then we're back to you not staying here."

"Sorry. I'll go find a rock to crawl under."

"It's just that I'm supposed to manage this place."

"You have a renter for this room?" I asked.

"Not tonight."

"What the fuck?!"

"I can't just leave you here alone."

I glanced at the bed. "Then don't."

"I'm not sleeping with you."

"You will."

"No."

"I need you to."

"Need?"

"I need you to have sex with me, not leave me alone, and help me in the morning."

"Too weird. You can come stay at my place."

"I have to stay here tonight. I can't go anywhere else."

"Go ahead and stay then," he said.

"Not alone. I can't do this alone."

"You don't even know me."

"I will after I fuck you."

He sighed. "Want some coke?"

"I have a couple speeders."

He reached into his pocket and produced a small baggie with the powder inside. I gave him a pill and he gave me a snort. It was the most alert I'd been in years.

"How do I know this really happened?" I began an existential crisis.

"That I just gave you coke?"

"Kira. I don't even know if she was real anymore."

"I met her..."

"You might be full of shit. Maybe you just want sex."

"With you, of course."

"Yeah. Yeah with me. You're a guy. Fuck me, and then tell me about Kira. Something I'll recognize. Something true."

"I can do that now."

"Just fuck me and get it out of the way. Then you won't be manipulating me for sex."

"Not all men are manipulative."

"You're not attracted to me?"

"It's not fair to get high with me and have this conversation."

"Just fuck me, Zach. I need some truth." I sauntered into his personal space. Pushed myself as close as I dared. "Is this real? Was Kira actually here?"

"There's proof," he offered with a shaky voice. "A police report. Just a couple blocks away is the town hall and office of records."

"They're not open 'til morning. What will I do 'til then, chew my fingernails?" I lightly pressed against him. I was making him nervous. I went too far again, but I was really lost and needed an anchor. Just as I was about to give up, he placed a hand on my shoulder. Then the other on the other shoulder.

"I'm not her," he said. "Whatever happened between you two, I can't fix. She's really dead, man. That ship has sailed. If for some reason it will help if I fuck you, then I'm here. If you want to not torture yourself, we can go to my place for a drink and I'll feed you."

I kissed him. He was trying to be so noble. Maybe he actually was. But before he helped, or strung me along, by God, he was gonna fuck me.

I decided to at least act like I was there. Bend my knees up. Move a little. He was already in me, but timid. I lifted my feet and wrapped my legs around his waist, pulling him in. He got the idea. All I could think of was how much I hated his hair. The hair on his head, his arms, legs, ass, face. It wasn't him, and the experience wasn't unpleasant. I enjoyed how he was getting into me. Loving my body. Caressing my skin. Looking into my eyes. His ecstasy heightened with every thrust.

While I was acting that I was there, my mind was on Kira. My mind was on Kira so much that I worried about how real she actually was. How much was I adding to this mythology? Somewhere between ecstasy and suicidal depression, Zack finished with me. And I wasn't high anymore. I started to want that drink he had offered.

"You believe in Jesus?" I asked.

"Sure."

"So you think Jesus loves a drug-addict whore?"

"What the fuck? You take a lot of drugs, but you ain't no whore."

"I just had sex with you for coke." I didn't mean for that to slip out.

"Really? That's why you fucked me? Just to get high?"

"No. Because I want you to stay. But you did give me the coke."

"So technically that makes you a coke whore?"

"I think so, yes."

"Well, bust my buttons." He smiled. "No. If you fucked me for drugs, then Jesus doesn't love you. If you fucked me just because, you should be okay and make it into Heaven."

"I'm kinda serious."

"Jesus loves you and you're going to Heaven," he said sardonically.

"What if I died of an overdose? What if I killed myself?"

"You're still going to Heaven."

"What makes you so sure?"

"Some people are just going to Heaven. No matter what they do or what happens to them, they're going to Heaven."

"That's not what the bible says."

"You read the bible?"

"Not really."

"You ever watch foreign movies?"

"Of course the fuck not," I answered.

"Some people think they're weird, lots of subtle symbolism." He pulled his shirtsleeve up. "You see this tattoo?"

"A rose tattoo?"

"It's a blue rose. The blue rose is symbolic."

"What's it stand for?"

"It stands for an innocent heart. An innocent heart in a fucked-up world where anything can happen to anybody. And things that happen cause reactions in lots of different directions. A young woman gets fucked by her dad as a child, grows up, starts on the drugs and drinking 'cause it shuts the feelings down. Kills the voice in her head. Soon, she's trying to please that abusive son of a bitch in every man she can find. So she thinks she's a whore, but her heart is still innocent. 'Cause it wasn't her fault. She didn't choose that shit. It happened and caused a reaction in her life. She apologizes constantly but did nothing wrong."

That was why I fucked him.

"You're a blue rose, Iris. You're goin' to Heaven."

"An iris being a rose. That makes no sense."

"Kinda poetic."

"So, friends and family, they wait a long time in Heaven."

"For what?" he asked.

"For a reunion."

"If you believe in the absurdity of linear time, maybe."

"Linear time? They gotta wait, right?"

"We're all together right now. If you believe in Heaven, then there's no wait. Time is different than what we're stuck with on this planet, in this life."

"Not sure I get it."

"Time is circular," he said. "We're born small and helpless, grow up, then grow old when we become small and helpless again. When we die, we can go anywhere we want, any time we want, and see anyone we want."

"That's Heaven?"

"That's paradise. It's got nothing to do with streets paved in gold. The real treasure is no sense of loss. You're with everyone right now. You're alive in this body at this time in this plane, but if there's an afterlife, you're somewhere else. With everyone you ever loved. That's the reward for living a good life. For loving as many people as you can."

"I'm in two places at once?"

"I hadn't thought of that, but yeah. Omniscient, like God. No one is waiting for you to die. They were with you immediately after they died."

I had a hard time wrapping my head around that and went into space zone. I disassociated until he wasn't there anymore. I couldn't connect with anything. There was no anchor to hold me in place. But somehow she was there. Kira, with all of her faults and bullshit disbelief. She was with me in the space zone and I wondered if I would ever return. If this time I was gone forever. Being sucked into that space and time my lover spoke of without having to lift a finger. Without going to the hardware store and slipping the rope around my neck.

I smoked another Winston and felt tired. Crawled in bed and pressed against Zach until I crashed. Thankful that he stayed. Grateful that at least this night I didn't have to be alone.

I had another dream about Kira. We were on an unfamiliar street and she was taking me to a bar. The street was more like an alley. A dark alley. The door was nondescript and steel. In fact, I would have walked past it without noticing if she hadn't took me by the hand and led me. Inside was like any bar on any street. Brick wall exposed as some kind of decorative space. It was crowded. Very crowded. People did more drinking than talking. I lost Kira to the crowd, but there was an open stool at the bar. I ordered a Chivas on ice. It was perfect, just the way I loved it. The bartender was a pretty girl with an expressionless face.

I sat on the stool, very comfortable. Like this place was meant for me. Maybe even made for me. People talked a lot, but not to me. The way I liked it. My favorite pastime was listening in to conversations. Yes, I realized this meant I spent a lot of time alone. I liked alone. I liked listening in. Maybe I should have been a writer. Writers spent lots of time alone and listening in when they shouldn't. Someday, listening in would be normal. Somewhere in the future, people would become part-time voyeurs.

I had no idea why I knew this. There was barely a thing like mass voyeurism, except in science fiction books. But in this place, I felt a connection to the future, but more to the past. Kira was my past, but she was gone. I was drinking, and drinking. The bartender kept filling me up and not expecting payment. This was a clue. I wasn't anywhere on Earth. Nowhere I was accustomed to. So I knew. I knew. This was on Kira's turf. She lived there. This was purgatory.

I drank and realized I was dreaming. Yet I was being introduced to my future. I found Kira and she was dancing. Not with a boy. Another girl. A girl in a black leather jacket with a wool cap. Just like me. A girl like me. Or was it actually me? Kira dancing with me. The music was electronic and fast. We were moving in sync with movements of beauty.

Then the music changed up and we were slow dancing. "Alone in this together," the voice echoed in the bar hall. She clung to me. Pulled on me to get closer to her body. Her hips and thighs slowly moved with the rhythm of the music. I couldn't give in. What was wrong with me? What a strange question. If Kira was a boy, there would be nothing wrong. But she was female. Petite. Her hips the most pronounced feature of her otherwise boyish figure. Her hair long and dark. Green eyes, nose completely regular, lips like a siren. Lips shaped like no one I had ever met.

That was it! Her lips. I wanted to let go. Have her pull me in against those inviting hips and feel the press of her movie-star lips. Those luscious lips. Bare, yet shaped and full in a way that drove me wild. Was anything more passionately personal than a deep kiss? Always, I had kissed boys. But this moment, I wanted to kiss Kira. Deep and open, forever. Our eyes met, and I woke up. I knew I had been in Hell. That Kira had clearly shown me where she was, and how to reach her.

I'd never loved anyone in my life. A person who could extract caring and longing from me did not exist. I was not kind to myself or any other person on the planet, except Kira. It was sad actually, that this was so foreign to me. The only feelings I'd ever had for others were suspicion or contempt. She confused me. The most confusing being that she was a girl. It was so shocking that I came to terms with it in stages. The first was a violent distrust of the emotions I projected on her. Only then could I accept my feelings and, in so doing, myself. And I realized she was my reason for living, then for dying.

♦ ♦ ♦

In the morning, Zach took me to the town hall to find Kira's death certificate. Our path didn't take us near the ocean, but I could smell it. The salt in the air was nauseating. He offered more coke and I took it. Why not? What was my deal anyway? No drugs or drinking, no sex, no homosexuality. I was disgusted at my spinelessness. My past was catching up with me, and I realized my lack of living was leading to my death.

The clerk handed me a paper over the bright, nondescript counter. Zach put his hand on my back and I flinched. I shouldn't have, and he didn't remove it. I stared at the document a long time. Kira's name listed so formally. So direct and final. "So that's it," I said. "It's over. She's gone."

"Whatcha gonna do?"

"Is that room still vacant?"

"Just for tonight."

I bent my head to study my shoes. I didn't wanna talk or move. I wanted to shut it all down. "Fair enough," I whispered.

After we returned to the room, Zach observed that I didn't even look at the ocean. I didn't answer. There was no ocean, or salt air, or Ed Ricketts. Just the sun going down.

"You got any money?" Zach asked. "For the room."

"I have a few bucks."

"Fuck it. Just don't let anyone know you're in here."

I didn't respond. I wasn't there.

"I have to go home. I need to sleep in my own bed." His eyes appeared anxious. "You wanna come with me?"

"I can't," I whispered.

"You gonna be okay?"

"No..."

"Should I be worried?"

"It's fine..."

"If you head north, stick to the shore. Your traveling will be easier."

"Thanks."

"I wish I knew for sure, one way or the other..."

"I'm good," I answered. It wasn't a lie. I was fine, finally, after such a long time. Zach hated me. Which was okay. I hated me too.

After Zach left, I felt in my pants pocket to make sure my wad of cash was still there. It was. I had means. The window called to me again, drew me closer. I stared out at the twilight, red and smoky. Losing track of time, or disassociating again, the scene turned dark. The sun had set. Night fell and surprised me. I had a clue how long I had been standing there, based on the ache in my leg muscles.

After this meditation, a long-lost reverie, it dawned on me that I was grieving. Logic told me all along that Kira was gone. But it was just sinking in. And like a moment of clarity, I realized that I wished she wasn't. That I would have had a chance to change her mind. Break the pact. Feel those lips against mine and hold her against me so tightly that she would change her mind and choose to stay with me.

Grief, despair, and love drove me out into the night. Zach knew what he would find in the morning, and in doing so, he had made a judgment about me. But I was in love. In my life, I'd loved one person, and all I wanted was to be with her.

Chapter 16

You keep calling...
I know,
just a drink,
let's catch up
and not tough it out.

It's such a long trip
and we've bottomed out
at different times
with the dense fog
so thick between us.

How about a nice rainy night?
A cool bar stool
in a dark tavern,
a couple laughs,
one last game?

    There are secrets the soul knows that the mind doesn't comprehend. This was the miracle that put me in a meadow in Jasper, Alberta with a tent, a horse, and the night filled with glorious stars. I finally allowed myself to fall in love with Kira, and by doing so, with myself. I was alone and in love, mostly because I no longer needed an environmental guide. I was finished being an intern, I now belonged to the mountains. Cold Canadian nights were my shelter. I danced to the music of a crackling fire and sang the song of the wind through the trees. The wolf's howl became my heartbeat and the rapid flow of a sparkling stream instructed my spirit.

    I was practiced at living and staying alive. The itch never returned with enough strength to demand a scratch, although depression and her cousin anxiety still visited... and probably always would. I became an accomplishment junkie, measuring my recovery by how far I'd make it. Being this far north was the largest achievement so far, beyond becoming a junior Canadian conservationist. I obviously had to make a choice to break the pact. In the spirit of my love for Kira, it was deemed necessary to try this instead of death. She hardly followed the rules in any situation and, in doing the same, I honored my love for her, holding a cherished ideal of her being in her right mind and best self.

I wasn't able to cast off her memory, but, as the Makyo proverb went, The only way to shake off the demon was when Milarepa put his whole head into its mouth. I ran out of ways to fight the darkness. I became defenseless against the demon who I named Kira; yet I found no freedom without her, not until I gave in with all of my being.

After all, it was her who promised, "I will never dump you." And that was my great epiphany, not that I'd fallen in love with a girl, but, more importantly, that she loved me.

🝆 🝆 🝆

During Zach's watch, I disassociated, as I was so prone to do. I'd come home that night from the hardware store to my room where no one was around and no one knew me. Where no one knocked on the door, expecting me to answer. Where a short girl like myself had to stand on a box to reach the hangers in the closet. I knew it was March, and that the sun would come out eventually. I also knew I wanted to redeem myself from cowardice.

And I believed what Zach had told me. That I was with Kira right at that moment and I wasn't 30 years old. We were together somewhere and I wanted to be there to hear her voice. I wanted to finally feel the softness of her lips pressed against mine. In my disillusionment, I felt her breath in my ear. "I love you," she whispered, the heat of her breath settling on my neck. Making me hot all over. I was on fire. Kira had found the magic spot on my body that caused me to feel alive again.

My neck! My neck! I wanted her to just bite down once and for all.

I ran away under the cover of the night and found that Zach was right; travel was much easier along the coastline.

♦ ♦ ♦

"I'm never going back to California," that's what I told myself. Whether it took begging, borrowing, or stealing, maybe even murder, I never wanted another taste of hot Pacific beach again. My route was north along that very seaside and I was nearing Eureka on Route 101, that's when the decision came to me. To return would mean despair and agony.

I had enough suffering, so being on the move was the best thing for me. Hitching mostly, or scrounging enough scratch for bus tickets. At the moment, I was on the highway with my thumb out and being triggered by a beat-up blue Chevy slowing down to check me out. I stereotyped people, which was a personality flaw, but this guy looked creepy and his old truck advertised serial killer.

He stopped and hand-rolled the passenger window. "Where ya heading?"

"North."

"How far? I'm only going to Eureka."

"I think I'll walk," I hesitated.

"That's a long way."

"I'll catch a bus."

"Suit yourself," he said and started rolling the window back up. Playing hard to get intrigued me, and I could smell fresh cigarettes from the cab. I hadn't had a smoke in a long while and decided it might be worth a ride for a bit of nicotine.

"Wait," I pleaded. "Eureka sounds perfect."

"Jump on in, little lady."

Little lady, like he was John Wayne. That should have registered as a red flag, but my peripheral was blinded by my tobacco craving. And, even though my status as a lady might've been questionable, I was indeed little. It was a struggle stepping up into the Chevy and took a couple tries.

"Want some jerky?"

Did that mean sex?

He kicked the truck into gear and started off.

"Jerky?" I asked.

"Got a bag of venison jerky." He held up a wrinkled paper bag for me to see.

"I'll try some. You got a smoke?"

"Aren't you a little young for cigs, darlin'?"

Darlin'? "I'm short but on the 30 side of my 20-somethings."

He inspected me with squinting eyes. "Guess you look about that old." He handed me a pack of Camel Filters and I greedily yanked one out.

I took the paper bag and inspected the contents. A savory-smelling dried meat. I bit off a small piece. "You got a light?" I asked between chews.

"Want me to smoke it for you too?" A joke from school play yards.

I managed a muffled giggle, which produced the man's Zippo. I lit up and cracked the window. I inspected my driver while he concentrated on the road. Heavy set and scruffy but clean. He was tall, dark, and creepy. His whiskers were a couple days old and the bags under his eyes hinted at as long without sleep. I hoped he wasn't speeding. I'd just crashed from my own session since Monterey and recalled the chaotic thinking that accompanied those days. Nonetheless, I'd start another at the drop of a hat. "You take drugs?" I ventured. "You look a little wired."

"Do you ever bathe? You smell a little dirty."

"I've been on the road for a bit," I answered with a hint of embarrassment.

"Well, me too. But I know which truck stops have showers."

"I'm new to the road."

"I have a bit of weed but I'm saving it for a special occasion."

"It was just a question, man. Not really leading anywhere. I'm not big on weed."

"What are you into?"

"Booze and pills, sometimes."

"Those are introverted drugs."

"What?"

"Central nervous system depressants are for introverted personalities. Opium, coke, speed, booze: those are inward soothing highs. The personalities of people using those substances cause them to want to feel better inside and they don't care so much about the outward expressions of the world."

"Whatever you say, dude. I'll buy it, I guess."

"Well, you have to 'cause it's based in fact."

"There's facts about personalities?"

"Of course. Now, take weed, or LSD, those are hallucinogens. They tend to attract the more extroverted personalities. People who want a better way to engage with the world around them instead of the world inside them."

"That's interesting as fuck, man. Does this radio work?"

He turned off the highway and started down a gravel two-track toward a heavily wooded area.

"Short cut?"

"Naw, shorty. We're gonna try an experiment."

"Not interested. Stop the truck."

"Don't worry, little lady. I'll get ya to Eureka. I just wanna have you try some of my weed."

"Am I a special occasion?"

"Sure thing. We're gonna get those sad eyes happy, you'll see."

"Look, mister, this isn't really my kinda thing. Told ya I didn't do weed so just turn your redneck truck around and head back to the highway."

"Loosen up, darlin'. It's okay, you can trust me."

I kicked the passenger door open and jumped into the tall grass. Having never tried a stunt like that meant I didn't know how to land, but learned it wasn't on my feet. My legs crumpled under and I laid, unable to move, for a few precious moments. The sound of the truck turning around roused me into action and I stood in pain, started hobbling down the two-track back to the highway. In hindsight, I probably should have headed into the tall grass, but it wouldn't have mattered.

"C'mon, sweetheart," he shouted as he grabbed me around the waist with one arm. He carried me like a bag of potatoes and plopped me back in the truck. There was little I could do with so much pain in my feet and knees. He knew that and didn't bother locking me into the cab.

Sweetheart! He intended to rape me, and probably worse. I'd been raped before, mostly by family. I had no delusions of getting out of it. I had not experienced dying though, what with it being a one-time thing and all. But I'd be damned if I was going to die *today*. So I bent my intention on finding a way to kill this bastard, no matter what he did to me.

"So, I guess I'll be smoking some dope after all," I said.

"Oh, we're gonna party, honey. I can guarantee that."

We drove in silence for nearly 30 minutes across the field and into the woods. Night was going to fall and I could see we were quickly rising in elevation. "Heading up the mountains?" I inquired.

"Shut the fuck up."

"Just making conversation."

"Then let's converse about you running away. You ain't doin' it again. We're gonna party pretty hearty and you're gonna participate. I got a cabin up in these hills all stocked up and comfy."

"Sounds good, Earl. I'm totally game for a party."

"My name ain't Earl, you little hussy."

"Well, you never told me so I just guessed at one. I'm Iris by the way. We might as well get to know one another since we're going to share close quarters and all."

"Okay, so my name is Earl. You guessed right."

The sky grew dark and the trees became shadowy haunts. The sun was almost down and there was no sign of the moon. It was going to be a desperate night for me. Earl turned on the headlights and kept the tires on the two-track through the terrible forest he called home. I wasn't scared, somehow I saw success before morning. But my nerves were getting to me. I planned to use that nervousness to keep my edge. Stress can be handy in certain situations.

"Long driveway," I offered. "I hope you plan on giving me a ride back, seeing how I can't walk and all."

"You don't need to worry about that none."

I heard history in that sentence. He didn't just have a plan for me. Earl was recreating nights from his past. These woods could be dotted with unmarked graves of girls like me. Lured by the smell of tobacco or weed into an escape-proof situation where they lost more than just their innocence. "You got any more of those Camels?"

"Right on the seat next to you. The lighter too."

I thoughtfully puffed as he kept driving the bumpy trail. The sunlight was gone and all I could see was the gravel ahead of us. I was going to kill this man, just not in the truck.

The cabin was as much a wreck on the inside as it was on the outside. It was tiny but had a wooden porch with a swing in the front. The roof was metal and it had windows looking out the front. This is what I saw before Earl shut off the headlights. He opened my door and forced me to hobble in front of him to the cabin door, which was unlocked. Earl lit an oil lamp which clued me into the fact that there was no electricity to this shack.

"There's soap and water in the bathroom basin. Get the fuck in there and clean yourself off!"

I didn't look him in the face. There was only one door in the dark cabin so I assumed that was the bathroom. I took the lamp without asking and followed his command. He didn't complain so I assumed it was the right thing to do. The inside of the bathroom was small and cold. There was no roof, and no stool for shitting, only a shelf with a roll of toilet paper and a couple towels. So excrement was apparently deposited somewhere outside. The metal basin was filled with cold water and a bar of soap sat next to it. Above that, on the wall, was an 18-inch green-handled machete on a display shelf.

"You're shitting me. Really?" I said out loud. I grabbed the handle and it easily came loose. I grasped it in my hand, testing the weight. This was going to be easier than I thought.

"What's your fucking problem?" Earl asked from the other side of the door.

"You're a fucking dipshit, Earl. That's the problem." I remembered that the door opened into the bathroom so I stood against the wall and waited for his arm to appear on my right. When his arm appeared, I struck with a cumbersome one-handed chop. It created a large, bloody gash down to the bone but was not a disabling strike. I froze instead of striking again as he yelled.

"You fucker," Earl shouted.

I panicked and swung wildly as he entered the room, my blade finding no purchase. I felt a kick to my kidney I didn't see coming. It knocked the breath out of me.

Earl grabbed my forearm with his good hand and smashed it against the wall.

I dropped the machete. He bent for the weapon and I turned to run without the ability to breathe. I searched the room and found nothing that might help me save my life. The kitchen? Were there knives? What good would they do against the machete blade?

Then I saw it. A baseball bat leaning against the wall by the front door. My breath was back, though the pain in my side was substantial. I reached it and had the handle in both hands as Earl entered the room.

Before I could raise it, he was on me. The machete was brought down on me from my collar bone, through my left breast, across my belly and out, but did not penetrate my rib cage. Like me, Earl had swung in the dark to no avail. Yet blood flowed through my jacket and onto my blue jeans, joining Earl's gush of fluid from his arm onto the wooden floor.

I wanted to own that machete so badly that concern of my own well-being took second fiddle to the strong desire. I wanted to live to fight another day, yet, if Earl lived or died was of no concern compared to whether or not I had ownership of that fucking machete.

I swung the bat at his head. I knew how to swing from grade school. At recess, we often played softball in the dusty field behind the school. Mr. Sullivan monitored it twice a week and I always looked forward to it, because he always pitched at least one low ball to hit a home run.

That's what happened to Earl. After slashing me, he was bent over laughing to himself. His head was a low one that became a home run. It was pretty fucking messy but I watched anyway as his head exploded.

He dropped my machete and fell to the floor.

"Gonna rape me now, motherfucker?" I asked as I picked up the machete.

Earl didn't answer 'cause his head was bashed in and his mouth was nearly nonexistent on his stupid face.

I used the bat to steady myself like a crutch, but, as the adrenaline wore off, I fell into the puddle of my own blood on the wooden floor. I concentrated on my breathing until it came easily. When I could once again breathe, I felt better. My left tit was fucked and would never be the same. Before passing out, I thought about my lost love Kira, and any love that may come after this.

Would the girls in my future find my fucked-up tit repulsive? I hoped against hope that I would get laid again, by a pretty girl with dark eyes and thick lips who cared little about what one of my tits looked like.

Part 2: Woman of the Oil Sands

"Take the first aid kit," the pilot shouted. He was a large, muscular, brave man trapped in the open cockpit while bleeding out under his steering column.

I frantically searched until I found the familiar red cross on a white box.

"Hey," he shouted. "What's your name?" He must have hit his head and damaged his hearing.

"Iris."

"Iris, the flare gun!"

I saw where he pointed and grabbed the fat pistol. "Is there morphine in here?" I showcased the first aid kit.

"Has no effect on me."

"Alcohol?"

"Sure. Please."

I ran back to the kitchen area and searched the cabinets until I came across an unopened bottle of vodka.

"Are you injured?" he asked before taking a long pull.

"I wasn't on the plane."

"You're just up here in the mountains?"

"Yes, sir."

"Iris, I need you to look for survivors."

"There are none," I reported. "Just you."

"And I'm not going to last long."

"What happened?"

"Doesn't matter now. I'm almost bled out. Tell them, would you?"

"Tell ya what I'll do: I'll get all the identification I can from the passengers and take it down to the flats with me."

"Good girl." He reached into his back pocket and produced his wallet. "The cash is yours."

Frowning, I took the wallet in both hands. "No need for cash up here. Just a machete and a good horse."

"Who the hell are you?"

"Just a child of the mountains heading home. What are your last words, mister?"

He took a deep breath. "Check for survivors again, please." He exhaled and closed his eyes.

Chapter 17

The front door to the cabin was kicked open. It woke me but not with a start. I was weak from blood loss. I saw a tall, bald goddess in the threshold. She was so beautiful that I knew I was saved, yet I clutched my machete to my side.

The woman was wearing what looked like black pajamas and brandishing a katana half her size: curved, shining silver sharp on one side. She held it with both hands, dull edge forward, above her head. Her anticipation changed to confusion at the sight of the bloody room. She looked at my helpless body on the floor and elegantly sheathed the blade. If she had hair, I guessed it would be blonde, judging by her light eyebrows. She knelt and studied my chest wound. "Damn," she spat before standing again. The monster was a lifeless crumple in the middle of the room. With one hand on the blade handle, she reached out and felt for the man's pulse. She stood and relaxed her stance, seemingly reflecting on his corpse.

"I'm so sorry," she said like this was somehow her fault. She knelt again at my side. "I'm Janet." She had kicked the door in, dressed as a bald ninja ready for martial arts action, and her name is just *Janet*? A curious savior of the American Rockies, who stealthily hunted a bizarre serial killer who had me in his grips, is named Janet? "Your wound is big but it's only on the flesh. You'll survive with some rest and care. I'm taking you back with me."

"Back?"

"It's not far," Janet assured. She pulled a rug next to me. "I'm going to cover you from behind with this and gently cradle you out of here." She took the handle of the machete to remove it before moving me.

"Hell no," I informed with a raspy voice. "This machete is never leaving my side."

"Just for now. I'll give it back to you."

"You'll let go or die."

Janet laughed softly. "Have it your way. If you impale yourself, it won't be my fault."

Chapter 18

I passed out from pain and exhaustion. When I awoke, my first words were, "What the hell is this place?" I was on a cot in a communal cabin exclusively housing women. My old jeans were still on but I was shirtless, probably because the article had been sliced apart, blood-stained and useless. "What happened?"

"You're okay," said an unfamiliar voice. "I'm Dahlia. I'll be your caretaker until you recover. You were brought to us by the Sensei, and in a pretty messy state. But you'll be fine." Dahlia had strong, broad shoulders, porcelain skin, short auburn hair, thick sensual lips, and the softest brown eyes I'd ever seen; I trusted her because of that color. She was tall and strong like Janet, with a round face and exceptional jawline ending in a chin shaped like waves against a warm beach.

I had tried to get a bearing but could only keep my head up long enough to make out Dahlia and the inside of the bunkhouse. Fatigue overcame me, caused blurred vision and nausea. Must have been the excitement and hemorrhaging. I was a murderer. I killed that man and had no idea how this Janet person was going to handle it. "Where's my machete?"

"In your hand, my dear."

It was, and I somehow became her dear, which comforted me while I fell back to sleep, holding tight to the machete's green handle. I dreamed, and not in fragments, dreams I would remember. They were not about Kira, or a horrid history of childhood abuse. I dreamed of a brown-eyed angel named Dahlia, which included petaled flowers of various vibrant colors from which the name was derived. Dahlia's concerned smile and the summer sunshine mixed with the fragrance of a meadow decorated with sunflowers and spindly forest beauties.

I awoke later to Dahlia fondling my breasts. When I gazed at my new crush, she looked focused, like she was trying to solve an algebra problem. "Is this what they call second base?" I asked.

Dahlia smirked but didn't break her gaze. "I'm trying to judge the extent of your wound. I don't see any difference between the two breasts, but, without a plastic surgeon, there's going to be a nasty scar."

"How about the other damage?"

"The same. It all looks clean, I think we beat any chance of infection. At least the scars will look cool! I just hope you'll still have an attractive chest. Sexy curves are important to some gals."

"So what's the prognosis, Doc?"

"I'd do ya," Dahlia announced with a wink. She looked up into my eyes and I knew she was like me.

"Well, that's all I need to know. If you're not grossed out, then I still stand a chance with the gals."

She playfully patted my nipples before covering them with a sheet. "How's the pain?"

"Surprisingly none."

"That's good news."

"You got me medicated?"

She shook her head. "No, ma'am. Just clean and dressed. So, I know how this happened. We all feel so bad."

"*We all?* I'd like to talk about 'we all.' The air feels thin, so I know we're still in the elevation where Earl met his fate. Can you clue me in?"

"This is a school. A karate school."

"Karate?"

"I suppose a karate school run by a woman up in the mountains is surprising. But that's where you are, and more directly *why* you are."

"I don't understand."

"Earl was kind of a rogue student," Dahlia explained.

"Rogue as in an asshole?"

"Exactly. He started as good, but as soon as he learned some skills, he went a bit crazy on the girls here, which are in the majority. Eventually, he got his ass kicked and left. Sensei has been looking for him ever since hearing of perverse stories from the locals."

"Is this some kind of cult or something?"

"No! We're legit. Sensei wanted to teach up here in the mountains, which is hard to get to, so students stay for extended periods of time. Some have to go home and come back again to keep jobs and relationships going."

"I may be one of those extended stay patrons..."

"I doubt Sensei will let you go until she thinks you're over Earl, and probably not without teaching you some self-defense."

"Could we go back to you touching my tits?"

"In a few hours," Dahlia said through a chuckle. "We have a request, though."

"*We?*"

"Sensei, the other students, and me."

"Sensei? Is that Janet?"

"One and the same. We just have one problem: We don't know your damn name!"

"Oh! It's damn Iris."

"Iris? Oh my God, how cute! I love it."

"Ya think that's cute?"

"It's perfect for you. We were calling you Titmouse."

"Oh, good God."

Dahlia laughed loud, a brilliant laugh with a stunning smile punctuated by deep dimples on either side. "We will compose odes to Iris' tit!" With that, she walked off, leaving me alone to my dreams.

💧 💧 💧

The next time I awoke was to Janet kneeling next to my cot. Her expression was stoic, even though I knew her concern was real. I hadn't the ability to search my surroundings yet, but had the impression many other women filled this building. Quiet talk and sly shuffling about by students who tried to be unnecessarily careful of Titmouse recovering on her cot. The air was a mix of fragrant wild blooms and the bodies of warriors fresh from practice battles. The building must have had openings much like Earl's roofless bathroom.

"You're recovering well," Janet noticed.

"Thanks to you. I don't know whether to call you Janet or Sensei."

"I'm Janet for the time being. I wish to extend my teachings to you for your future benefit though. If you accept, after a full recovery, you can address me as Sensei."

"Well, I guess that all depends on the police," I contemplated.

"Police?"

"I murdered that man. Remember?"

"I remember very little, except a small woman escaping from the clutches of a serial rapist, but not without injury."

"You didn't call the cops?"

"Why do the police need to be involved? It's not like you're at the hospital in town."

"But what happens when someone goes looking for him?"

Janet laughed. "No one wants Earl. No one comes up here, not even when a cabin burns down. And anyone who stumbles upon that place will only find ashes. Ashes that only two people in the entire world know anything about."

Janet had not only saved me but destroyed evidence! Evidence of my murder and her failure. I didn't even care if the whole school knew, it would be Earl's word against mine and he wasn't exactly talking.

"What does Dahlia know?" I asked, assuming she would be curious about my backstory. I also wanted to know about the person who'd be spending her time on my recovery.

"Dahlia knows nothing that can be proven in a court of law."

That was a relief. I couldn't say I was worried that I'd become a murderer, I just didn't want to be a convicted one. I breathed easy for the first time since waking up on this cot. I had no idea what I was up against, if these women were friends or foes. But I knew I felt pretty decent besides tires, thanks to their help. And I knew I wanted to see Dahlia again. "I won't wait for a full recovery, Sensei. I accept your offer now."

"Very well, Titmouse. It will be many weeks before training can take place. I'll modify my weapon instructions to include this thing." She poked the machete still at my side.

"I forget about this," I said.

"It's well that your weapon becomes such a familiar extension of yourself. When you feel safe with us though, you may want to store it under your cot."

"Can you set it down for me?" I asked, holding the machete up for her.

"Ah, lesson one, and you're still on your back."

I was confused.

"Always present a weapon to another warrior with both hands, palms up. This is an expression of trust and safety for the receiver."

I did so and stoic Sensei smiled as she slightly bowed her head to receive my blade in her upturned palms. She placed it under the cot. "You have no need here for weapons except to practice. I promise you safety among your sisters. And the brethren of this place, though they are few. There are certainly no other Earls."

"Thank you, Sensei."

"So, may I ask what your destination was before the detour with Earl?"

"Eureka," I lied.

"Ah. That's not far. You have family."

I was immediately remorseful for lying. Eureka wasn't technically a lie, but it was not my final destination. I reached into the back pocket of my jeans and produced a pamphlet I'd acquired shortly after leaving Monterey. I handed it to Janet.

"Canada," she remarked. "A very comprehensive conservationist intern program. Don't you have to be a citizen?"

I rolled my head back and forth, knowing I only had to be an enrolled student.

Janet's expression softened as she studied my face. "I see it took a lot for you to divulge this information to me, even with it being such a noble undertaking."

Noble? When did selfishness become noble? I nodded slowly and broke eye contact.

"It's so cold in Alberta," she informed.

"You've been?"

This time it was Janet's turn to nod. "A personal goal then. I will have you Alberta-ready before the date on this brochure. I know the way to Jasper and I'll take you there myself. I'll consider my debt to you for ridding me of Earl paid in full at that time."

I started crying softly.

"Go easy on yourself, Titmouse. Because in the coming weeks, I won't be."

I nodded, sniffling.

"Say, 'Yes, Sensei.'"

"Yes, Sensei."

At this, Janet stood and left me.

🝆 🝆 🝆

When I awoke yet again, I felt better than I had since Monterey. My energy level was so high that I rose to sit on the edge of my cot. The bunkhouse was sparsely populated but the floor was neatly rowed with cots. I was smack in the middle and, for the life of me, could not figure how this location was chosen for me. I was obviously carried here, so why not to a cot close to the door? Was I that light?

Sleeping with her head turned away on the cot directly next to me, was my boob-fondling friend, Dahlia. That's when I uncovered the mystery of my placement. Dahlia oversaw my recovery, so placed me close to her watch.

"Dahlia," I said softly.

She turned and saw me through sleepy eyes. "You're up."

"Yeah. I'm glad you're here."

"How are ya feeling?"

"Other than some stiffness, better than ever," I enthused.

"Cheers," she said, slowly rising.

"Sorry I woke you. I was just excited."

"I was just drifting. Don't move yet." She stood and I was awed by her exquisitely healthy physique. Dahlia stretched thick, porcelain arms above her head, flexing broad shoulder. I almost started crying at the demonstration of strength and beauty. She walked around her cot and took me by the hands. "Stand slowly," she ordered.

I did so with her help. I stood eye-level with her shoulders, entranced.

"You okay?"

"Some pain," I admitted. "But my mood is great!"

"Well, that's half the battle. I'm going to hold your left hand and I want you to balance on the opposite leg."

I did with little trouble.

She switched hands and asked me to do the opposite, which I did effortlessly. "You keep yourself in pretty good shape," Dahlia commented.

"A lifetime of running from the police."

"Ah, a story for another time." Dahlia covered me with a clean, white terrycloth robe.

"Are you the house nurse?" I asked.

"I'm a doctor," Dahlia announced.

I considered this strike one in my chance to ever get with her. "Shit, I'm sorry," I offered sheepishly.

"It's okay," she said while studying my eyes. Her intense gaze was melting me from the inside out, burning in places that hadn't felt heat in a long time. "I get it all the time.

"Good for you. I hardly get it at all."

"Don't try so hard, Titmouse," Dahlia quipped, then added in a more hushed tone: "You'd nearly won me over before I ever heard your voice."

I took this as a hint to shut the hell up. The more submissive I was, the better my chances. Dr. Dahlia was probably used to going after and getting what she wanted.

She held a hand before my face. "How many fingers?"

"Auburn."

"What did I tell you?"

"Couldn't help myself... Two."

"Okay, you're going to walk with me to the bathroom. Then we'll scrounge up some food in the kitchen. Slowly..." She kept my hands in hers and walked backward as I followed, unsteadily at first.

"'Titmouse' reminds me of *Dune*," I said as I stabilized.

"Oh, a reader."

"The main character was named Maud Dib after the desert mouse from the book."

"I loved that whole series," Dahlia said. "But a titmouse is a bird."

"Oh, shit. That's strike two."

"Strike two?"

"Never mind."

Dahlia released her left hand and turned to walk forward, still holding my right hand. We started encountering more people, more curious gazes. The bathroom was shiny clean and co-gendered with many toilets, shower stalls, and urinals. "Let's not shower yet cause of that large wound, but some hygienic cleanup might make you feel better."

"Somebody sunk some money into this place," I observed as I washed up at one of the sinks.

"It was a Boy Scouts camp many years ago. Janet got it on the cheap when it was abandoned. Over time, she refurbished the place and added a couple dojos."

"It's beautiful."

"Students do the janitorial work, cooking, and whatnot. Keeps overhead down."

"So I suppose I fall under the whatnot category."

"I've cleaned my share of toilets. Speaking of which, how about walking on your own to that stall over there. I suppose you're anxious to relieve yourself."

I was and I did so successfully.

Dahlia was impressed. "I doubt you've ever been labeled just a 'whatnot,'" she said from the other side of the stall. "More likely in the 'Holy shit!' category."

I smiled to myself. I may not strikeout after all. "You're impressed because I'm shrouded in mystery." I exited the stall and Dahlia pulled the door shut behind me.

She looked down at me trapped under both her arms, hands holding the top of the door. I looked into her eyes and resisted the urge to loosen my robe.

"So what's in Canada that you can't find here?"

"You've been talking to Sensei."

"You know she does all the talking. I mostly listen."

"I have dreams in Canada."

"You're an outdoors kinda gal, eh, Iris?"

I shook at the sound of my name in Dahlia's mouth. "Well, ya know, I've been homeless for a few years now. I might as well stay outdoors."

"Let's get some food," Dahlia suggested. She lowered her chin to my cheek and whispered in my ear, "Iris…"

Chapter 19

"Twist the fist, Titmouse," Sensei ordered. "It's a corkscrew punch."

I tried again and got it.

Sensei smiled but barked, "Add power, woman. Hit hard!"

I was only hitting the air, but I knew what she meant. My previous punches had power I never thought possible. Over the weeks, I'd finally gotten involved with chores, pushups, eating correctly, and regular training, which put me in touch with my strength. I concentrated and was able to bring that same might into my corkscrew punch, though I didn't understand the function yet of twisting my fist at an opponent. I favored kicks, a bit too much, which was why Sensei brought me back to handwork.

"Women are always thought to be strong kickers, but we can swing a punch as well as any man if we realize it's possible. Learning to punch well will throw a male opponent off-guard. He won't expect it."

Across the dojo, Dahlia practiced on the edge of the mat. Out of the corner of my eye, I watched Dahlia jump six feet and do a 360° mid-air kick.

I stopped as Sensei hollered to, punch, punch, punch. I turned to her, slack-jawed. "I need to be able to do that," I said, barely able to get the words out.

Sensei glares at Dahlia, who did the same trick. "She does that for your benefit," she insisted, shaking her head. "Interrupting my teaching like a schoolboy."

"My benefit runneth over."

"Corkscrew punch, Titmouse! Punch! Punch!"

💧 💧 💧

We were enjoying a crisp, autumn mountain evening around a fire. A small group, women laughing and singing, a guy playing guitar. This happened on occasion so we could get away and enjoy our vices Sensei made a point of condemning.

Girls shared cigarettes and vodka, a joint passed around the circle occasionally. I was sitting next to Dahlia, bumming a cigarette from the guy with the guitar, when I murmured, "You wanna sneak away and find something fun to do?"

"Isn't this fun?" Dahlia answered with a question.

I slipped my arm under hers to hold her hand. I had to concentrate on our surroundings, then concluded this was pretty damn fun. I didn't answer, just playfully squeezed her hand, our fingers interlocked.

At that moment, Dahlia became my girlfriend. I wasn't sure what she considered me, my speculation was a play toy; even though she chose to warmly hold hands over the carnal fiddling I'd offered, I was a bit relieved. I was really too tired to perform. It felt good to just sit there and love who I was with. And why was the urgency of romance my first priority? Why did I feel I had to offer sex to keep Dahlia interested in me?

We spent our evening like that, hand in hand, engaging the group from the familiarity of being girlfriends, our homosexuality completely ignored. The world was changing fast, not that I was monitoring modern culture since I didn't watch TV or read magazines. I was on the trickledown end of advancements in civilization, especially during my stint in Middle America. But I knew what was acceptable on the streets, in the world of underground products and services.

The next morning, our clothes smelled of campfire and I was coughing up a bit of smoky phlegm from inhaling the burnt residue mixed with cool night air. Dahlia was a bit hungover yet cheerful because today we would have new friendly faces on the campus that would remember us as mates from the night before.

The early morning bunkhouse was smelly with karate students yet to take their showers. Even with the openness of windows and doors, the smell of skin, sweat, and nightly dreaming held to the floor where Dahlia and I slowly readied ourselves for kitchen duty.

"I have a car," Dahlia announced. "A Volkswagen Rabbit, early model."

I looked with a blasé curiosity.

"I mean, parked *here*," she reiterated. "In the lot."

I had no idea what she was getting at.

"Let's take a day trip to the village north of here."

"Oh!" Enlightenment finally sparked in my brain.

We sat on our cots in the middle of the bunkhouse, quietly relaxing. Janet worked me hard yesterday, so my muscles were extraordinarily sore. She was on a time table and wanted me ready for our trip to Alberta. I had filed Canada away in the Denial Archive of my mind and was savoring my time with Dahlia. I was motivated to do the work, though more for the sake of catching up with my girlfriend's abilities than to leave. The plan to be somewhere other than Sensei's school was fading away into a blissful fog of forgetfulness.

"There's a diner and a pizza place there. We could have lunch together."

"Wow! Something other than karate food."

Dahlia laughed. "There's some clothing boutiques, too."

"Boutiques?" I mocked with a smirk.

"You need other clothes," Dahlia said. "You have three outfits. Your gee, what we found you with, and a robe. Don't you want some shorts or a house dress to show off your twiggy limbs?"

I stood, wearing the robe. "Feel these legs," I ordered. "That's muscle, sister. I'm not the skinny softy you seduced when I first came here."

Dahlia feigned shock at how hard my legs had become, then rested her hands on my hips. "So, do we have a date? Will you go have lunch with me?" Her brown eyes looked up at me inquisitively, her chin on my sternum.

"Of course. Who else would I go on a date with?"

Dahlia swept her hand across the room, gesturing at the bunkhouse filled with women.

"Oh, I don't even think of the others that way. I'm kinda new to the whole 'objectifying' thing. I only have eyes for you, Dahlia."

"Are you asking me to go steady?"

I laughed out loud, not as a schoolgirl with a crush, but as a woman who found herself in a funny situation. "Yes," I chuckled. "I am."

"I mean, I thought so," Dahlia said with a hint of nervous laughter. "I thought we were."

I couldn't wipe the smile from my face. This goddess, a martial arts expert and medical doctor, was nervous about what Titmouse thought about their relationship. It made me feel very special. More than any relationship I'd ever had. I didn't know what I did to fool this woman and I was never going to examine why, for fear that it was nothing at all. That I wasn't fooling anyone and this person actually found some value in a relationship with me other than sex.

God, I was a therapist's dream client!

🞂 🞂 🞂

"So, I have to ask about the little joke you made this morning," Dahlia said.

"Huh?"

"About 'being new to objectifying women.'"

Shit! It was time to get to know Iris.

"I'm not that into labels," Dahlia started, "just wondering if you are gay or do you swing both ways?"

"I've been heterosexual all my life," I answered. Then I shoved a spoonful of mashed potatoes into my mouth because I knew it would be a while before I got back to lunch. "I fell in love with this girl, though."

"So you're bisexual?"

"We were partners in crime, literally. And in despair. She ended up dead, which is why I was running away to Canada when I bumped into Earl."

"So this girl was your first gay experience?"

"We never had sex or even kissed." I looked longingly at the gravy-covered beef on my plate. "We shared sleep space and such, like girls do. But nothing else."

"So she wasn't into it?"

"Oh, she was into it big-time. But completely respected me and didn't want to put me in a position I was unsure of."

"She was gay then."

"She had never been with a man, and that, along with a slew of other issues, made me hesitate."

"So how did she die? That's so sad that you never pursued your desire."

"She killed herself. Her name was Kira. She wanted me to follow along with her plan, but instead I ran."

"Oh, you poor thing." Dahlia's eyes were wide and intense in anticipation of more of this tale. "Aren't you grief-stricken?"

"Guess Earl beat the grief out of me." I managed a forkful of beef before Dahlia went further down the road.

"So you're used to boyfriends?"

"All of my male sexual encounters before Kira had been in the form of rape or something transactional. Like for shelter or not feeling alone." With that, I was done. I put my fork down, no longer hungry. This was not what I considered casual lunch conversation.

"So," Dahlia started, tears welling in her eyes. "You've never had a real relationship with a man, and you didn't have sex with this Kira, so that makes me your first actual sexual partner."

"Is this what you had in mind when you asked me out?"

Dahlia slowly shook her head, bottom lip pouting and chin quivering. "I just wanted to get to know more about you."

"Well, welcome to Iris," I said gruffly before standing and leaving Dahlia with the check.

Out on the sidewalk, I felt the desperate need for a smoke and booze. There had to be a Woolworths or something like that where I could steal a bottle of vodka and a pack of Winstons. I started toward the business district.

"Before Kira," I heard Dahlia shout after me. She ran to catch up and continued talking, out of breath. "Before Kira, you said all of your male encounters were of rape."

Dammit, I was irritated. I stopped in my tracks to hurry up and confess all my sins so I could move on. "There was a boy in Monterey. He was a bit different, the last person to speak to Kira before she died. He was trying to be helpful even though his head was loaded up with weed and coke. I needed a place to crash. So I guess that technically means I used him."

"I'm sorry, Iris. I really am." Dahlia was full on crying and talking between sobs. "We're girlfriends and I don't know any of this about you."

"I'm sorry, too. I'm sorry I needed to be so brutally honest. I'm sorry that I didn't concoct an elaborate backstory with a happy childhood and a college degree. I'm sorry I'm a piece of trash and tried to fool you into letting me be your degenerate girlfriend. I loved Kira because I had to. I loved Kira because she was a testament to everything that had gone wrong with my life that I needed to reconcile… I loved her out of necessity, but you are the first love of my life. Yes, I'm a grown up woman who didn't find love until I woke up to your hands on my tits. I'm really, really sorry that I didn't warn you about me!"

Dahlia stood, silently weeping with her hands at her sides. "You're none of those bad things, but there's no way to convince you here and now." She talked softly yet forcefully. "I live where I'm at." She shrugged and looked around. "I'm in love with you. Right here and now. The person standing in front of me is the woman I'm in love with and I want to be her girlfriend. I'm so sorry about the things that happened to you and it hurts my heart, thinking of you in any kind of pain like that. But we can go back to the school today. You can keep working and training and I'll be by your side the whole time. Whatever comes up in the future, or from the past, I'll be there with you and we'll get through it together."

"Okay," I started. My brain was reeling from the exchange but my intuition said to believe Dahlia and not be angry. "Okay, buy me a drink and it's a deal."

"Let's both have a drink," she agreed and we headed down the sidewalk, looking for an open bar.

"I'm dying for a smoke," I said while we walked.

"You're not, really. But I'll get you a pack."

There was nowhere acceptable for us to have a sit-down drink. All the bars scared us, even though we had been trained to kick everyone's ass. So we settled on liquor store gin in a brown paper bag on a park bench. I lit up and greedily inhaled before scooting over so my hip touched Dahlia.

"So, maybe after a few drinks, we could still hit the boutiques," Dahlia suggested.

"I'd like that."

"So..."

"So," I repeated back.

"Friends?"

"Sure," I answered, extending my hand to shake.

She took it lightly and leaned in to plant her lips against mine.

"I don't get you," I admitted with our lips still touching. She smelled of gin and my head was starting to slowly swirl from the alcohol and close proximity to her.

"I wish you could see you," she said, then her tongue touched my upper lip.

I pressed my tongue against hers and placed my lips against her mouth. I opened my eyes to see her gazing at me. The soft brown eyes I longed for, inviting and full of warmth. Looking into those tantalizing depths, I could almost talk myself into trusting her.

"No more prodding today," she suggested. She sat back straight and took another drink of gin. "Next time, it'll be my turn to share."

"I hope that will be boring compared to mine." I took the bottle and tipped my head for a long drink. This would have to be it with the booze. I was ready to shop with my girlfriend's money. My eyes were on Dahlia as I drank and she answered me.

"You might be surprised," she said.

💧 💧 💧

Janet kept chickens but not for meat. She was a vegetarian and only used the eggs for her residents. She didn't promote vegetarianism, so we were free to eat what we brought from home, the city, or what we could hunt from the nearby woods. Dahlia and I often chose the foraging option.

Guns were frowned upon at the school but not restricted, as Sensei believed in every option for a girl to protect herself. Hunting with a gun was taboo for being too easy, so archery was offered as an alternative. Sensei provided a fine array of bows and well-balanced arrows. For me, she suggested a lightweight recurve, assuming I would be an active hunter, running through brush and ducking under trees. Dahlia owned a compound gadget with fancy string, pulleys, and sights set to 70 pounds of pull-tension. Sensei witnessed less aptitude in Dahlia for the sport than her little Titmouse, since she proclaimed to feel sorry for any game I might miss with an arrow, as I would certainly run it down and break its neck with my bare hands. She all but stopped short of envisioning me naked and feral, sitting high in a tall tree, eating a newly downed rabbit, raw and warm, with only my machete.

♦ ♦ ♦

"When did you realize you were gay?" I asked Dahlia. We had just finished target practice in the archery range. It was still warm since winter had not settled in on the mountain yet. I wore the short, white dress Dahlia bought me when we were boutique shopping and had to constantly remind myself not to sit in the grass and stain the thin, flowing skirt.

Dahlia sat on a log cut for firewood. Her pale face was smudged with redness from the heated workout. She wore her gee and had her face pointed into the afternoon sun, eyes closed. I knew she was listening to the birds from the woodline that bordered. It was a form of meditation that quickly grounded her and settled her mind.

I cared little for chirping and tweeting about. I found it an annoying reminder of sunup when I was still not ready to wake up. My mind was clearer when I was on the move. I found peace when I had a task like a wounded deer to run down. Otherwise, I was just as likely to go to sleep.

"I don't remember not being gay," she answered.

"So you've never been with a man?"

She opened one eye and kind of tilted her head at me as I sat on a nearly identical log. "I've been with plenty of men."

"Yeah," I related.

"I understand it was never pleasant for you."

"You've had fun with men?"

"Sort of. I like men. I just don't like sex with them."

"Were you married or something?"

Dahlia lowered her head and opened both eyes toward me. "Guess it's my turn for a backstory."

"I'm not trying to pry."

"But that's what a leading question is."

"Sorry, I think I'm more bored than anything."

"How can you be bored?" Dahlia asked, gesturing to the swaying treeline with the sweep of her hand.

"How can I be bored?" I answered with a question as I gestured toward her, both hands palm-up.

She smiled and treated me to her dimples and sparkling eyes. "I just have had plenty of men as friends during school and my residency. The higher-up medical careers aren't drowning in female students. I was always broke and looking for a leg up. I knew my male friends were capable of vouching for me and opening doors, but all I had to show my gratitude for them with was my body... It's not like I was whoring myself out. Just friends with benefits. I always initiated it and got rejected plenty of times. The educated types I ran with actually valued me as a friend. I think the ones that gave in, did so out of politeness."

"Right..." I offered.

"It's a different crowd than people think. It's close-knit and we really kick in for each other. The hours are long, the work grueling, and play subdued. It was hard to find men or women not suffering from insomnia, who would be interested in some platonic kissing. I planned on passing along help to others when I was in a position to do so."

"*Platonic kissing?*" I quoted.

"It's a thing, trust me."

I was careful to keep my attitude in check. Dahlia's problems seemed small compared to those of hard knocks. I tried to take an interest in her feelings. She wasn't a traveling companion, business partner, or someone with a spare bed to get me through the night. She was my girlfriend and I needed to act accordingly and think long-term. Or at least longer term than usual. Just because her situation wasn't the same as mine didn't mean the anxiety and exhaustion weren't as bad. "So you're on a vacation or something now to be here?" I asked. "What do they call that for professional people?"

"A sabbatical," Dahlia answered. "I graduated recently and work as a grunt in the emergency room. So don't call me a professional. Let's keep our labels on an even playing field, cause we're equals, Iris. Labels don't define our relationship."

"Okay. Titmouse will be careful of labels," I teased in my favorite childlike voice.

"That's not a label, it's a love name!" Dahlia laughed.

I laughed, too. I didn't mind the pet name everyone called me. It was a nice tradeoff for the giant scar that crossed my body. "It's hard to compare myself with a doctor," I admitted. "The playing field isn't as level as I'd want it to be."

"Are you kidding? With the trip to Canada you're about to embark on? What you're trying to accomplish is just as big a deal as what I'm trying to do. We're both…" Dahlia stopped, her eyes tearing. She hung her head sadly.

I knew exactly what had just occurred to her, the same thing I had tucked away in my Denial Archive: We were going to separate. She may have never lost a relationship before, while I was used to it.

🜄 🜄 🜄

Admittedly, much our time "hunting" was spent making love. When that wasn't occurring, we had a system for flushing out prey toward each other that was pretty successful. Sensei was right that I was usually the one crashing through brush and briar, trying to drive something edible toward Dahlia. The forest around Janet's camp seemed endless. We could hike for miles in either direction without running into civilization. Except downhill one would soon find the road that led to towns with electric lights, gas heat, and cable television.

Higher elevation was said to be mostly impassable terrain covered with snow and rock. I'd gotten permission for an overnight trip up the mountain soon after I recovered from my wounds. It was a long, uphill battle for me with snow caps and rock formations I was in no shape to explore. The desolate area called to me though, and not the same way death did at one time. It was just the beauty of the howling wind and barren landscape. It was a complete isolation that I longed to follow. The extreme fierceness of nature promising me the gutting of everything I'd experienced in civilized life.

At our last hunting instance, I came upon Dahlia with a draw on a beautiful and rare white wolf. We were not supposed to shoot it for food, but the four-legged hunter had teeth bared at the object of my heart's desire. Out of fear, I drew my bow.

Dahlia's look of determination softened to curiosity, and she lowered her arrow. The wolf growled low and long, then barked once.

While Dahlia returned her arrow to its quiver, I kept a draw on the killing machine. She stared the white wolf down somberly. Something strangely existential was occurring with Dahlia and it scared me. She was mumbling something under her breath that sounded curiously like a prayer.

"I'm a medical doctor," she finally said coherently.

The animal stood like a statue.

"I'm an ER doctor," she shouted at it. "I save lives! That's my job!" Dahlia lowered her head and bow to one hand. She turned in my direction. "It's time for me to leave the school," she announced.

"Wait, what? For how long? Why now?"

"Long enough to reestablish my old life."

The wolf looked on, its nose in the air, sniffing at us.

"I don't ask this near enough," I started, "but what about me?"

"Sensei isn't finished with you."

"I want to go with you. What the hell, Dahlia? You think this dumb animal that's too lazy to attack you is some kind of sign?"

"I'll be back to fetch you when the proper time comes." Then Dahlia turned and walked downhill to the school.

I didn't even want to know what that was all about. All that concerned me about this white wolf was that it was going to cause the loss of the woman I loved. Maybe they had some strange connection that, in an instant, caused her to reconsider her life goals. Maybe its growl stirred something primal in her, a competitive thing that was missing out on up here in the wilds.

My head turned from her to the wolf who was following her progress. "Hey," I shouted.

The wolf turned its attention to me.

"Fuck you!"

The white wolf put its nose to the ground and went off, looking for some unlucky rodent to snack on.

Chapter 20

I had been back in the States for a couple weeks. I suspected as much when the night sky changed, but I knew for sure when I lowered elevation and saw the long expanse of flat forest land. I was on the wrong side of where I wanted to be. I aimed for the coast, yet what I observed was the east of the mountain range. My navigation was sophomoric at best, I should have done better and been less lazy.

The goal for my horse Narragansett and me was now Picture Rock Pass, Oregon. I'd found I could board this sweet baby in Eagle Point and keep on to California by hook or crook from Eureka back down the coast. I was still somewhat north of that. My baby reared up on his hind legs and jumped when the crash occurred. A little over three miles north and higher up, but the sound was deafening. Snow shook loose from the tree leaves as the ground rocked ever so slightly. I figured plenty of tragedy was occurring up on that mountain that I could do nothing about, but, after soothing Narragansett, we made for the smoke and flame anyway.

💧 💧 💧

I methodically started down the fuselage a second time to satisfy the pilot's dying wish, checking for survivors. Admittedly, my first pass before finding the pilot alive was quick, just looking for open eyes and conscious people. The plane was somewhat intact, at least where the passengers were. The tail was busted off and of course the cockpit smashed as it took the brunt of the impact. Everyone was fastened to their seats, for better or worse, mostly worse.

I'd checked nearly 200 passengers, only to find them all dead. Empty eyes stared into the void of their final moments and had to be closed. I patted down the corpses in search of IDs. I was eventually nauseous. Before exiting the plane, I realized I had to check the overhead compartments, maybe find something useful for myself. Another bottle of vodka would be handy. As I made for the exit to force my poor horse to watch me throw up, I remembered the bathroom.

That did not keep me from relieving my nausea outside in the snow, where Narragansett looked on, bored. He'd seen this far too often and probably assumed it to be normal human behavior. Back inside, I noticed the bathroom door read **OCCUPIED**. I couldn't open it and preposterously decided to knock. I heard a muffled shuffling inside, and the lock moved to vacant green. I took a deep breath and opened the door.

A short, ebony-skinned woman was seated on the sink, conscious, but with an obvious double leg fracture. She wore a flight attendant uniform, I assumed, since the logo on the jacket matched the one outside the plane.

"You're not okay," I observed.

"My leg is broken in a couple places." She hiked up her skirt to reveal her thigh shaped like an S, bruised and swollen. Other than her flushed face, she looked mentally okay. "I ended up here on the sink. We crashed, I'm guessing?"

"Into a mountain. My name is Iris."

"Iris, my name is Rene. I work on the plane, but was stuck in here. Guess I forgot to unlock the door. How is everyone?"

"Dead, except for you." Rene didn't take that news well. I could have been more tactful, I supposed. I assumed she was in shock. A double fracture probably hurt like a bitch.

"I need to talk to the captain."

"I already did, just before he died. You're all that's left."

"You can't be serious," Rene sobbed.

"I saw all the passengers and double-checked."

"How did you survive?"

"I was three miles away when you hit the side of the mountain."

"Shit," she quietly cursed. Her head drooped and she cried softly for a few moments.

I lightly touched her shoulder but she was unresponsive. "We're a long way from civilization, Rene. I know you're in pain but you need to pull it together for a little bit so I can get you situated. We need to wrap that leg up and get you comfortable, do something about that pain. I think there's morphine on board."

Rene lifted her head and met my eyes. Her face was tear-stained and grimy with eroding mascara. Her straight, black hair was disheveled with strands pasted to the tears. The whites of her jet black eyes were bloodshot. She tried to stop the waterworks and spoke with her chest still heaving. "We need to get to the cockpit."

"It's a gore fest up there with 200 dead people between us and the pilot. Let's just concentrate on you."

"The radio is there. We don't have to go to the cockpit. There's one in the kitchen."

"How about we get you out of the bathroom and then I'll go get it."

"You can't get it. It's in the wall. We have to use it up there. If you want me situated, do it up there."

"Okay," I agreed.

I was short but she wasn't much taller, so I was able to support her as she hopped down from the sink and out of the bathroom. When we entered the aisle of passengers, she started sobbing again. I sat her in a rear seat, away from the dead.

"Can we cover them?"

"I can, Rene. You just stay here. If you move too much, you're just going to make your leg worse."

"There are blankets in the front, the kitchen."

"Where the radio is."

"Yup."

"I'm also going out for a bit. I left the first aid kit out there, and I have to check on my horse."

"Horse?"

I didn't answer, just turned toward the opening created from the wreck. Narragansett was faithfully waiting my return. I gave him a handful of pasture grass from our supplies and made sure he was secure to a piece of wreckage. I trusted him so far not to wander away, but not beyond how long I would be with Rene. With kit in hand, I made my way back down the aisle, covering the dead as I went. The remaining white terrycloth blanket, I covered Rene with.

"We have to move up front," she protested.

"In a bit," I agreed. "You're in shock."

The morphine was in tablet form, which was good since I wasn't confident about giving a hypo to someone. I had my own canteen so was able to provide Rene a drink to swallow the pills down. I sat at her feet to wait.

"You have a horse outside?"

"I told you we're a long way from civilization. There's no roads or cars up here. We're pretty far up."

"What are you doing up here?"

"Traveling through to California. And before you continue with the 20 questions game, yes, I'm traveling on horseback. I lived in Alberta, Canada, the last two years, learning the land. It's a dream I've had since childhood. I guess I went a little native, as far as living in the wild."

"What brings you to the US?"

"I'm American. I ran away from home for a bit, but now I'm back."

"I'm feeling better. More relaxed. The drug must be working."

"Your skin looks healthier," I observed. "Less flush. Let's move you."

"Is there power?" She asked before we started off.

"Not sure. The lights aren't on."

"We need to get up there either way. Food, water and all, it's up front."

I supported Rene on my shoulder while we slowly marched up the aisle, past 100 white terrycloth tombs on either side of us. The kitchen had a fold-out bench long enough to lay her out on. It took a few minutes for her to regain her composure and catch her breath.

When Rene came to, she assessed the area. "Radio," she said, bluntly pointing to a phone receiver on the wall behind me. I picked it up and heard static. "Turn on the speaker."

There was a round speaker made up of small holes poked through a steel plate with two knobs next to it. I turned the speaker on and filled the small kitchen cabin with the familiar static of a radio receiving no transmission.

"Click the button."

I looked around dumbfounded.

"On the receiver," Rene pointed out.

I pressed the button on the hand piece. The white noise was momentarily interrupted.

"Repeat a couple times."

Nothing.

"Hold it down and say, 'SOS,' into the mouthpiece."

I did. No one answered.

"Okay, little rest." She closed her eyes.

"Maybe our reception is bad," I offered.

"We're probably being ignored. They know by now the plane's down and are listening but ignoring stupid sounding shit. They're desperate. We need to get the flight information from the cockpit so we can let them know it's us."

"I need to."

"Right."

"So we have power?"

"The radio is on a battery, so it won't last long. But it's dark in here. Try a light switch."

The lights didn't work. The gravity of the situation was setting in on me. Rene's situation, actually. I could get on Narragansett and ride off any time, but she was in a horrible state. Night would descend in a couple hours. Her pain was probably intense, no one knew where she was at the moment, and rescue was going to be difficult. My trip was indefinitely postponed.

"I'm eventually going to rummage through the carry-ons for anything that we can use," I said.

"That's a good idea." Rene closed her eyes and laid her head back to rest.

My first priority was Narragansett. Eventually, I'd have to lead him away from the plane to find something for him to munch on. I unloaded my provisions from him and brought them inside, including my machete that I attached to my belt.

I searched the cockpit after covering the pilot with a blanket. I swiped his open bottle of vodka and searched for paperwork, most of which was at the navigation station. It seemed appropriate to have a stiff snort from the late captain's bottle. The nameless copilot also required covering, his wallet went into a pack I'd designated for IDs. I searched for some sign of how to get power to the lights but gave up quickly. The room was a confusing mass of unmarked dials that would only give digital clues to their function if power was available. I did score a bright flashlight, which raised my spirits a bit.

Searching the overheads was tedious with the faceless dead present while I raided their belongings. Eventually, I would need food to feed my nausea and avoid the dry heaves. Surprisingly, I found no other flashlights or batteries. "Who travels cross country without emergency provisions?" I asked myself, suddenly fearful of getting a response. I knew the answer was everybody, all of the people not on horseback who assumed their safety and needs were met by the services they purchased.

One thoughtful soul did have a transistor radio and scented candles. I worried though that the radio would be useless here in high country. After a thorough investigation, I had a somewhat helpful haul to bring to the kitchen:

- *Various magazines and fiction books.*
- *A cassette player with headphones.*
- *One birthday layer cake.*
- *Bag of pretzels.*
- *Bottle of olive oil.*
- *A photo album.*
- *Magnifying glass.*
- *Piles of cash that might be useful when I get to Cali.*
- *A bag of balloons.*
- *Lots of makeup.*
- *An unopened fifth of 18-year-old Chivas Regal.*
- *One carton of Winston cigarettes.*

"Who the hell is Greg Brown?" I asked Rene when I returned to the kitchen.

"A passenger?"

"No, I found a cassette and tape player."

"Flight 296," Rene said softly. "We're flight 296, the pilot is Captain Strong, William Strong. Our destination was LAX."

"You remembered." I picked up the radio microphone and remembered to press the button.

"Flight 296. Captain Bill Strong to LA. LAX?"

Rene opened her eyes and watched me.

"Is that right?" I asked.

"Good enough."

Nothing returned but static. I repeated myself a few times then sat on the floor, waiting for an answer.

"You really have a horse?" Rene asked.

"Yeah. It's gonna be dark soon and I have to see to him before then."

"You're just a cute, little button. What're you doin' hiding out in the woods?"

"I'm not hiding. It's just how I live... been living lately. I haven't always been a mountain girl."

Rene didn't say anything after that, just laid quietly studying me. I studied her back and started to get the notion she may be like me, as far as romantic preferences. She was a pretty girl. Woman, actually, same age as me but I think of myself as a girl.

"You always wear that black cap?" she asked.

"It was a present, and it's wool, so it keeps my bean pretty warm."

"You have movie star features."

I smiled shyly. "I don't know what that means."

"Contoured oval face, pointed chin, intelligent almond-shaped eyes. If you styled that long, black hair, there would be no difference between you and a Hollywood starlet."

I laughed before I could stop myself. "Sorry, that's rather specific. There's not many 4'9" Hollywood starlets."

"Four-nine. Jesus Christ, you're a little person."

"I'm aware."

"No, I mean a little person. Under four-ten a person is considered disabled."

"Like a midget?"

"I don't think people say that anymore. It's a little person, and you don't seem disabled at all, but technically you're a little person."

"It's never been a handicap, mostly been a blessing."

"I bet. I wish I could fit anywhere I wanted."

"I use a lot of step stools in the civilized world," I joked.

"How do you ride a horse?"

"Narragansett? He lowers his neck," I admitted.

"That's amazing."

"My mentor, Ian, taught me how to make that happen."

"You have a horse riding mentor?"

"Oh, no. He's a conservationist in Canada. A park ranger. The parks up there have a program for student conservationists. If someone wants to do that for a career."

"And that's what you want?"

"I don't know. I like the life, but now I'm searching."

"For what?"

"Flight 296," the radio interrupted. "Flight 296 to LAX!"

"Does the cord reach over here?" Rene asked.

It did, I handed her the receiver.

She pressed the button. "296 to LAX," she announced. "Plane down. Pilot Strong unavailable."

"He's dead," I reminded.

"You never know who's listening," Rene explained.

"Won't they want to talk to him?"

"Unavailable means dead."

The radio was quiet again. I sat back on the floor since this seemed Rene's forte.

"How long have you been down?" the voice asked.

Rene looked at me questioningly.

"Over three hours?" I offered.

"Three hours. Power is unavailable and using kitchen radio."

"Am I speaking with flight attendant badge #1576?"

"Yes."

"Can you give me the numbers?"

Rene closed her eyes. When she spoke, it was halting and raspy from anxiety. "One: injured and cannot walk."

"Rene, who placed the radio call?"

"A passerby."

"Are more community people on hand?"

"Just her."

"Give us a few. Try to get us a location along the flight plan."

"Got that, radio running on battery."

"There's not much time. Turn it off for 30 minutes. Then turn it back on, key up, and we will continue."

"Situation is critical."

"Make it 15 minutes then."

"Got that..."

💧 💧 💧

I left to see Narragansett without saying a word. Something was bothering me and I needed to get a pin in it. I offered him pellets from our provisions, forgot to check the kitchen for vegetables or a piece of fruit. I'd treat Narragansett before nightfall. He needed a walk and I needed to get away from the plane to smell some fresh air.

I led Narragansett to a shallow creek we had passed on the way to the plane. While he drank, I rested my forehead against his neck. He was as used to this as my barfing. I closed my mind and Dahlia's brown eyes haunted my thoughts.

💧 💧 💧

"I'll be back," she had promised.

"Why don't I believe you?"

"Trust me, Titmouse."

I took a couple steps up the stairway so I could look her in the eye. She approached, leaving her bags piled in the foyer. Her hand reached for my cheek and I started crying uncontrollably.

"I know how long you have left in training. I'll be back."

"I have somewhere to go," I cried.

"We both do, Iris. If you're not here when I return, then I wish you the best of luck. My heart is always with you, my little Titmouse. Remember, wherever I am, that's your home."

Dahlia turned and left for her car waiting outside.

I wanted to beg her to wait for me, but I just continued crying because I knew what was going to happen: I would never see her again.

Chapter 21

Janet looked like a normal person in a dark winter jacket and blue jeans. Since she'd been here before, the story of which remained a mystery to me, she knew how to dress and what to expect. Just as she taught me to regulate my anxiety and defend my body, she instructed me on proper clothing for the northlands and what to expect from the unforgiving mountain wilderness.

"We call you Titmouse because your free spirit resembles the flight of a bird. And you're tiny, otherwise we would call you Eagle Girl or something," Janet informed.

We were on one of few stops on our journey north to Alberta. After so long eating healthy, I treated myself to a giant greasy cheeseburger and salty French fries. Janet had a salad yet insisted on stealing a number of my fries.

"Must have been a self-fulfilling prophecy," I replied. "You knew little of my spirit when you named me."

"That's not true, little one. I was the first to see the bloodied room and Earl's dead body. I saw the fierceness the world faced from you before the others did."

"So it was you who named me Titmouse!"

The dingy diner was mostly void of patrons, yet the few in proximity turned at my exclamation.

"Before I burned Earl's shack with him in it, I told Dahlia I was calling you Titmouse. So you can blame her that everyone on school grounds calls you by that name."

"Uh-uh, you don't get to pass the buck like that."

"I doubt your sincerity, Iris. I know you would defend Dahlia to the death, even against me."

"Maybe. How could I help myself, Sensei? I'm defenseless against Dahlia."

"Another untruth, Iris. You have wrought the same to Dahlia as you did to Earl. One with benevolence and the other with justice. Each equal in strength and ferocity."

"'*Wrought*' and '*ferocity*.' Don't you ever use plain words, Janet?"

"Fuck you, Titmouse."

"Ah, the language of the ancients."

"Dahlia will return to the school and you will be gone."

"I have to do this, Sensei. I need to experience Canada, for how long, I'm unsure. I hope Dahlia lands in my future though."

"She fell hard for you."

"Did she tell you this?"

"Not in words. But I know my students. I may not understand homosexuality, but I know love when I see it. And hers is bright."

I sought the colorful twilight out the window, unable to look Janet in the eye with an acceptable answer.

"I feel your time alone is short, Iris. I know more about you than you do yourself. I've instructed girls like you many times before, in one form or another. The wilds of Alberta are going to strip you naked of the blindness to your inner self."

"What do you mean, Sensei?"

"I predict, after a time in Canada, you'll be ready for a place to call home."

"Well, now I will. You just planted that seed!"

"It was already there. You've had no home all your life, growing up on the streets, and then you flourished on your little cot next to Dahlia."

"So you want me to make your school my home?"

"Home resides in the heart of your loved ones. There is not a town or structure that you can call home, but a heart and warm eyes. You call yourself 'girl,' but I see a woman before me. Women don't roam the streets like urchins, they go home."

I took a big bite of my burger and thoughtfully chewed. "You're giving me a lot to think about, Sensei. I never really planned to live this long, to be truthful. As an urchin girl, I think I was always running from that."

"I remember you telling me about wanting to die."

"It's hard to shake off old habits."

"Yet you killed a man, defending your life."

"Oh, fuck that guy. He got what he deserved!"

"So tough and defiant, Titmouse. Are you looking for an invitation? Someone to beg you to stay and play your role?"

"I seriously don't understand you."

"And that's the problem." Janet stole another fry and pointed it at me. "You're free of the mental illness symptoms that kept you from the truth. The truth of your importance in the world. I think Dahlia and I would be content strapping you to your cot and keeping you safe with us forever, but you need this. One last uncompromising adventure. You need Canada to crack open your heart."

I choked up as tears rolled from my eyes and down my chin. "I'm not hungry anymore," I announced. I left the table and went outside, wishing I'd had a cigarette to smoke.

We continued over the border and the remaining hours of the trip in silence. Janet somehow managed to drive through the night and past the morning without a hotel room. She was either desperate to get rid of me or a robot.

♦ ♦ ♦

Picturesque Jasper, Alberta, settled in the Athabasca River's rolling hills of lush green forest and a backdrop of snowy mountain peaks. It was everything I hoped when we first came on it from the higher elevations. In town, Janet found the park district building to enroll me in my wilderness adventure.

"I'm meeting a ranger tomorrow morning at this office," I informed Janet out on the sidewalk. "Guess I need a place to bunk down."

"Let's get you a hotel room then."

"Hotel? I'll just camp under the stars. It's warm."

"It's my treat, Titmouse, accept it graciously. I'll get you settled then be on my way."

"Whatever. Someplace cheap, I won't be there long."

"Someplace fucking nice, Titmouse! A comfortable room with charm and a meal. I insist."

"Wow, you take this whole debt thing seriously." I started walking quickly to the car. "Come on now, you got me here like you said. I graciously accept that and now we can part ways."

"I'm not getting you a room out of debt, Iris!"

I stopped because a flash of light flooded my senses. I turned to Janet and put my arms around her waist and settled my face in between her breasts. "I don't need an invitation," I blurted before the waterworks started.

Janet wrapped her arms around my neck and gently squeezed as her lungs filled with air and exhaled relief. She would get her wish. Canada was going to bare my soul.

She did what she needed and set me up with a room for two nights, just in case. It was nice after all, a four-post bed, television, fireplace, and a second-floor balcony. Janet called and ordered room service for me.

"Maybe watch the local news tonight," she suggested. "Get a feel for the place you'll be calling home for a while."

"I'm not sure about home."

"At least temporary."

I walked her down to her car and hugged her again. "Tell Dahlia," I started but couldn't finish.

"You will return."

"I'll try to make it back one day."

"You will return to me," she ordered.

"Yes, Sensei."

Janet started her car and drove off. I felt an emptiness I'd never experienced. Alone and sad, yet hopeful. The second-story balcony called to me. I had plans to enjoy cigarettes from there and watch the sunset. I spied a corner drug store down the street and hoped Canada sold Winstons.

Chapter 22

A tall man, short woman, two horses, and a pack mule crossed a wide, grassy field in search of a shallow stream they remembered. I understood referring to myself as short, but I was a woman by that time in age and experience—if not maturity. The horses were thirsty, and I was tired. My mentor, Ian, had put me through my paces that day, taking me from the snowy mountain forest to the dry, warm prairie lowlands in an attempt to get my horse to know me. Narragansett was a jet black Friesian whom I'd fallen madly in love with at first sight. I did not know when I applied for this internship that it would involve a horse, especially one as beautiful, intelligent, and charming as Narragansett. My hope was that my love would not go unrequited.

The pack mule was called Mal, which was short for Malady, and he was a complete asshole. Ian never explained why he kept the ghastly animal around. Mal bit me twice, the first was when we met. He also kicked me once and I never turned my back on him after that.

"Iris, back that way in the east some 300 miles, they squeeze the oil from the sand," Ian somberly informed.

"300 miles?" I looked around with renewed interest at the pristine woodlands surrounding us. That was close, too close for comfort. 300 miles from paradise, the government was allowing the total environmental shift of the Alberta countryside. The soil and plant life would never return to its indigenous existence. Animal life would be forever be altered... if it returned at all.

Ian was a blond with hair tied back in a ponytail like mine. His beard was also blond, covering a square jaw and weathered face. He was so tall, I'd have to climb a tree to talk to him without craning my neck.

"All of this is merely an illusion," Ian explained. "It may be beautiful, but it's a shadow of the past. The perimeter is surrounded by train tracks. People with too much money to spend ride those rails and take in the beauty of the shadow, believing this is what nature is and the world is still untamed."

I leaned my head against Narragansett's neck to steady myself.

"I tell you this so you can make an informed decision. I can't mentor you in the ways of these mountains, and the living and dying of these people, without you knowing if you're here with the ideal of helping, or mourning."

"Wait. This is new to me. I thought this region still held pristine natural forests. I want to be here in the cold and immersed in the natural world. It's all I ever wanted."

Ian looked around, at the trees, the sky, the shadows made by the setting sun. "This probably as good as it gets. I'm just saying it's not what it used to be, and, in years to come, it will become even less than this. The Canadian government promises it can extract the oil from the sands and return the land to its natural state. But that's impossible. It will change, and further sever our connection with the natural world. What I connect you to here will change in our lifetime. I don't want you to have any notions of living your life out here without soon encountering grief."

"I don't borrow grief myself."

"Is that what I'm doing?"

"Maybe you can't see the forest for the trees?"

"Is that supposed to be funny?"

"Do you always answer a question with a question?"

"Look, you little shit. Your comedy is a poor attempt at denial. I'm the mentor here."

"Denial is my home environment, friend. It keeps me alive." I approached the cantankerous mule to start unpacking. "I want to get camp set before dark."

"Did you realize," Ian asked, "that your hair color matches your horse?"

I did not, and my love for the horse and feeling that we were destined for each other nearly melted my heart.

Chapter 23

I'd learned during my internship in Canada that I could spend a lot of time alone, but I didn't care for it. I wasn't alone with Rene back at the plane, but she wasn't on equal footing. She was going to be dependent on me for some time. She hadn't realized that yet. A helicopter wasn't going to attempt a rescue at this steep elevation, a team on foot would take days to arrive, and I knew a storm was coming.

Rene had no way of knowing that we had tonight and tomorrow before it hit. That meant weeks held up in the damaged plane fuselage, which I had no problem with, but she would eventually succumb to infection since her fracture had broken skin.

The whole situation rested on me and I could barely carry it five feet above the ground. So I was lonely and really missed Ian. Narragansett held still as I hugged his neck and stroked his mane, allowing me some time to not be brave.

💧 💧 💧

"All you need, the woods will give to you," Ian said.
"Yeah? What do you use for tampons, pine cones?"
"Oh. Shit."
"It's okay, Ian. I come prepared. Just shining a little light on your philosophy."
"You're a tough adversary," he admitted.
"Sorry. I don't really mean to be a confrontational asshole. I really am here to learn."
"I guess I am too."
The skyline of Alberta overlooking Jasper was overwhelming and I was feeling small. "How do you get used to this?"
Ian watched the sun set between mountain peaks. "You can't. Isn't that why you're here?"
"I mean the sense of immensity. I feel so unimportant against this view and it'll only get worse when the stars show."
"That will change in time."

"I'll get used to it?"

"No, but you'll realize why you came here."

"Why might that be?"

"I'm afraid to tell you, but I will. Usually, I let a student learn on their own, but feel a sense of urgency with you."

"I'm young. I got the rest of my life. There's no hurry."

"It's not in haste, but something's coming that will take you away from me. Something important that you won't realize until you're in the thick of the shit. That's the big secret, all this wild beauty is supposed to endow you with a sense of purpose. You're important, Iris. Your life matters, more than this sunset, more than the stars in the sky. You matter more than all that."

I shed tears. Not sobbing or crying, just tears rolling down my face. "What could ever take me away from this?"

"I don't know. But it's happening. I can sense it, like a storm brewing."

"You can sense a storm brewing?"

"Yup. One coming tomorrow. Big one."

"Where? How?"

"Here and because a cold front started coming through this afternoon. You'll learn this before you go."

Chapter 24

"We're gonna be okay," Rene announced on my return. "I think..."

"That doesn't sound convincing."

"LAX radioed while you were out and a crew is coming to rescue us."

I sifted through our provisions on the kitchen floor.

"Whiskey!" Rene noticed. "Oh God, cigarettes!"

"Sounds like we share vices," I commented.

"Oh, we're gonna get along just fine."

"Maybe not like you think."

A frustrated look appeared on Rene's face. "How so? I was just warming up to you."

"LAX will be radioing back. I have bad news, not so much for me, but for you."

Rene said nothing.

"A storm is on the way. Probably will hit by tomorrow afternoon. A big one, with snow, and that equals a blizzard."

"How do you know?"

"I've been up here long enough, I know."

With that, the radio speaker made a loud cracking and a voice filled the kitchen.

"Rene, we have some bad news."

Rene took the receiver and pressed the button. "Don't tell me a storm is coming."

"That's exactly it. The rescue is postponed until it passes. This could add days to your evacuation. Do you still have a companion with you?"

"Shit," Rene cursed. "I do," she said into the mic.

"Rene, your fracture needs to be set and bandaged. We're worried about infection."

She held the mic and said nothing, closed her eyes. The gravity of the situation was just beginning to sink in. The plane lacked power and therefore lacked heat. The large opening meant we barely had shelter once the winds and snow hit. I opened a pack of Winstons and lit one up. For a few moments,

I enjoyed the smoke. I hadn't had a cigarette in what seemed like a lifetime. I inhaled and exhaled the sweet tobacco while Rene opened her eyes and looked at me, but really wasn't looking. She was lost in miserable thoughts.

"Rene?" the radio speaker asked.

"I'm here," she answered.

"It's got to be done, young lady. How equipped does your friend seem to be? Can she get the job done?"

"Oh, she's plenty equipped. She has a machete, and a horse."

The voice in California was chuckling. "Sounds like you may be in good hands. Wait…" A thought must have struck him, or somebody, he came back on after a few moments. "Can you guys travel? Get down below the storm? If she can…" The radio died.

"LAX. LAX!" Rene started to panic. "The radio's out. The battery must be dead."

"Doesn't matter," I answered. "He's right, we have to make a run for lower ground. So they wouldn't have radio contact with us anyway. They'll just have to assume we are traveling. They can't get up here but someone will meet us down there."

"I can't travel."

"You have no choice. It will be a week or more before they can get up here, and you'd most likely get infected and die by then. If you get infected or sick from the fracture, at least we will be closer to help if we head out. Maybe even at a point where they can reach us. If we hurry, we can beat the storm, or make our chances better."

"And I was just warming up to you."

I smiled at that. This wasn't about making a friend. I could leave anytime. I could get caught in the storm and be fine. But I wasn't sure I could safely transport a lame person down a mountain. "I sure as hell can get off this mountain. I've never been in a rescue situation though. My training is lacking and you probably won't be much help, especially after we set that mess of a leg."

"What if we just stay?"

"We'll die for sure."

"Both of us?"

"There's no sufficient shelter in here and there's no time to make one. The trick to surviving this is to keep moving. Thank God we have Narragansett."

"Your horse."

"Yeah, it's actually him who'll be doing the rescuing."

"You can go. I can stay and take my chances. I might make it."

"Nope. You'll die. I'm not good with that, I've already warmed up to you."

"So this is like extortion."

I laughed. "A little, sure."

Rene eyed the Chivas. "Well, let's have a drink first."

"No time. We need every minute to get ready. I need to set, bandage, and splint that leg. I think I can rig up a sled from these seats and cushions, attach it to Narragansett. Get you swaddled and situated so we can travel. You can drink all you want. Probably a good idea. Hell, wash down another morphine pill."

Rene eyed me seriously. I guessed she was gathering her courage. "Shit, we're just a couple little button beans. We can't pull this off."

"Doesn't matter. We have no choice. We have to pull this off."

"Gimme another pill," she instructed. "We'll save the bottle for flat land."

I relaxed a bit while Rene fell under the spell of morphine again. She never asked for the bottle and I didn't offer it. Somehow I became the designated nurse, so I kept the bottle and the first aid kit with me. "I'm going to use a row of seats as a sled," I informed Rene. "I have rope so, with a little adjustment, I can get you comfy and secure, then attach the whole mess to Narragansett."

"You need tools. The seats are bolted to the floor."

"A couple rows came apart in the crash. A row is three seats all one piece, so a row will be enough to carry you and everything we need. I just have to move some bodies around."

"That sounds fun… There's clothes and such in the storage compartment, but the hatch is locked."

"That's not a problem. The entire fuselage is cracked open from the impact so I have full access. That's why we have to leave soon or we'll freeze."

Rene closed her eyes, a sign I learned from before that the morphine was kicking in. I took it as a cue to get to work. Moving dead passengers stiff with riggers was not something I looked forward to, so the storage compartment was my first destination. Storage was not tall enough for me to stand so I had to crawl around with a flashlight, opening luggage and checking inside packages. We got lucky in that one of the late passengers was a mountaineer. Probably a hobbyist but all of the proper equipment was available in their pack. Including dark goggles and a parka, both large enough to suit Rene. Oversized actually, since she wasn't much larger than me. That was perfect though, I planned to swaddle her in layers.

There was a very functional and comfortable pair of boots. Those were mine since I was going to be on my feet. The mountaineer also had heat packs. Adding those to the ones already on board was going to help Rene and me if we got stuck during the blizzard. If we got caught in the storm.
I considered that and changed my thinking to when we got caught. The trick was to get as close as possible to lower altitudes, where the storm would filter off and be less lethal. After gearing up, there would be two essential items to strap to my side: my machete and the flare gun Captain Bill wanted me to have.

Further inspection of the hold turned up little else. A ceramic heater, the kind that sucked the air out of a closed tent, but might be nice in the kitchen upstairs. Junk food, and a silver camping wrap. I'd heard of those but didn't know how they worked. I found a small backpack to carry all the passenger identifications.

I was tired by the time I moved all the gear from storage to the fuselage. I was still breathing a bit heavily when I checked on Rene. She was out but we had to make a hasty exit. "Rene," I pleaded, hoping for her eyes to open.

"Little girl, are you seriously waking me up?"

"Time to set that thigh," I said.

"Oh God, no."

"We're outta time. We have a blizzard to race. Sit up." I handed her another morphine tablet and the bottle of Captain Bill's vodka. "Mouth, drink, swallow," I ordered.

I wrapped my scrawny arm around her thigh and pushed against the seat until I felt the bone fall into place.

"Oh, shit!" She screamed while kicking me with her good foot. "What the fuck, sister?"

I stood from the fall Rene inflicted on me. "That's one," I announced, brushing the dirt from my ass.

"Hell no!" Rene yelled.

"It's a double fracture, sister. So drink, swallow, and hold the back of the seat."

She sobbed, tears running down her dimpled cheeks, but relented. She knew this had to be done, heard as much from LAX over the radio.

I set my forearm higher, pushing against her pelvis while pulling on the upper fracture until I felt the familiar *click* of matching ends falling into place.

This time, Rene didn't scream, she just passed out. I took the opportunity to splint, wrap, and tape the leg. We needed a breather before swaddling in winter gear for the ride down the mountain.

💧 💧 💧

The final piece of Rene's ensemble was a rope securely tied to both of our waists, a trick Ian taught me during our first snow storm. Chances of survival doubled if we stuck together.

"Why is the sky white?" drunk Rene asked.

"Say what?" I answered, annoyed. She was completely wrapped and I was ready to roll.

"The sky."

I looked ahead, over Narragansett's ears and saw clear blue with a few hanging clouds. "Looks normal to me."

"Is something wrong?" Rene insisted. "Am I dying?"

Her face was expressionless, covered with a scarf and goggles. I looked straight up and the sky was indeed white. Completely white, it was the storm.

"Damn."

"What is it?"

"The blizzard just caught us. Shit!"

I jumped on Narragansett bareback and turned toward his rear so I could control the makeshift sled with the ropes. I had rigged the ropes so I could strap my legs onto his back rodeo-style. "Narragansett, go! Ya, boy! Hit it!"

He took off in a hurry. Narragansett was as aware of the storm as we were and wanted to catch the blue sky ahead. I held tight to the ropes to keep Rene straight while my baby broke into a full downhill gallop. I had to trust him. This was what Ian prepared me for. This was why he wanted me to have an intimate relationship with Narragansett, the same he had with his horse, Thorn. I totally gave my trust over to the animal and concentrated on Rene.

She screamed and I yelled at her to shut up as the white sky descended on us. Rene couldn't practice the trust I was committing to my horse. Narragansett was the only way we were going to get any distance in the blinding snow, and we would have to rely on him through a complete whiteout. While we traversed the mountain, I could walk along, or ride the sled with Rene, machete ready to cut the ropes if my beloved disappeared into a crevasse or over a cliff. It was heart-wrenching to consider, but I rationalized it as attempting to save Rene, an innocent victim of the mountain wilderness that I called my home.

Narragansett suddenly stopped and Rene was on the bad end of a crack-the-whip game. She didn't scream. She'd gotten used to the fast pace and settled in as we got going. Her trust in us must have taken root, she didn't say a word when the sled finally came to a stop.

"What is it, baby?" Narragansett was spooked. I saw nothing in the whiteout that engulfed us, and then I heard a loud growl and saw blood fly. Narragansett fell, almost pinning my leg under his belly. Fortunately, my size saved me from falling under him and I wiggled free. Quickly, because I knew what happened. My baby was the victim of a bear attack.

I could see Narragansett's neck had been slashed wide and just finished bleeding out. Fear kept me from guilt in that moment, but not from anger.

"What are you doing out in this storm, you son of a bitch!" I was blind, the machete found its way into my hand. The rope attached to my waist led me to Rene. I had the blade extended into the pure white around us, ready for the strike. My breath was heavy and Rene was quiet. I leaned in for a look and barely saw her blinking behind the dark goggles. She was scared shitless though I doubt as scared as me.

The lines attached to Narragansett moved, then grew taut. Rene got pulled along. I assumed the bear was dragging away the horse carcass and cut the line. It stopped moving and I knew we were in trouble. I doubted it spotted us but it certainly heard the snap of the blade against the line. My thoughts went to Rene. I'd allowed 30 feet of rope between us to hook Narragansett to the sled.

The bear was going to search until it found us. The best bet was to bring the fight to the bear. At least I would get in one surprise swing of the blade and it might be a good one. I followed the sledge line, moving my head back and forth, looking for something giant and hairy. And there he was, on all fours next to my fallen hero with a confused nose sniffing the air. I had a long moment to consider my strike and even a strike after. A quiet *suburi* to the neck might do the trick, which I did. The bear didn't know what hit it but swung both paws wildly forward. One hit from those sharp claws and I was done for. Rene would just lay there and freeze while Narragansett and I were dragged off to a cave as lunch.

A fitting end for us both, but not today. When it reared up and roared on its hind legs, I could see it was a she. Hungry cubs probably sent her out for food and she got caught like us. I didn't give a shit about those cubs. The choice between Rene and cubs was easy. I saw how to win this and kill the giant.

Being 4'9" had many advantages, because when the bear reared, I ran to her belly with my machete. She swung a massive paw down but missed because of a blind spot. I did an imperfect thrust because the sharp end of the blade was pointed toward the sky, but there was a method to this madness: Killing a large mammal with a blade, human or otherwise, was not like the movies, where a samurai sword was thrust into the gut and the victim fell over dead. Death occurred with disembowelment. So it was a thrust and slice, normally downward. But at 4'9" against a standing brown bear, the slice needed to be upward, which I achieved.

A gush of hot, wet guts spilled onto me, drenching me in the copper smell of fresh blood and the stench of shit. I removed the blade but not before I was certain the tip reached under the rib cage and unattached her heart from its arteries. Luckily, the animal fell on its spine. She was still growling, but in pain. Flush with rage, I approached her head and gave the finishing blow. The blade pointed earthward toward her skull, and, with the full force and hurt over the death of my horse, I buried the sharp end in her brain.

I must have been a smelly, angry, bloody sight when I approached Rene. "You're getting in," I announced with shallow gasps of air. "Time to warm up and ride this fucker out."

"I'm not," Rene said meekly. Her goggles were off. She had seen the whole thing.

"It's that or freeze to death. We have to ride out the worst of this storm with no horse. I can't sled you myself in horizontal, blinding snow. We can fall into any crevice or ravine. You'll take the bear and I'll take Narragansett. I'll open them both and, when it's safe, we can move on."

"I can't."

"You'll die."

"Stop saying that!"

"It's what's facing you. Death by freezing or worse. You have to do as I say."

"Why? My God, why?"

"Because I've been through this before. Narragansett and I have survived a few blizzards in our time. And he's about to help me survive this one." I cut the tape with the machete and pulled Rene free of the sled. The time for squeamishness and argument was over. I was stuffing her in that fucking bear or would die trying. She tugged at the rope like a sinner wanting to be free of the devil.

I yanked back at it. "We stay attached no matter what! If you separate from me, we'll never find each other again. And what then?"

"I die."

"Yup. You, not me, 'cause I'm making it down the mountain." I got Rene situated in the smelly mess but she wouldn't shut up.

"Wait," she pleaded.

"You gotta rest now. We both do."

"I'm small, there's room for us both."

"You want to share the bear carcass with me? That's a little weird—even for me."

"No! Don't leave me alone."

"We'll still be attached with the rope."

"That doesn't matter. Anything can happen. I need you here with me."

"I'll be in the horse!"

"Pull your horse on top and we can share the warmth. Please!"

I glared at Rene for a few moments until I felt the punishing wind. It was stranger than anything I ever thought of. Wrapped up in dead animals with another woman during a blizzard, but it actually started to make sense. "Give me a minute," I promised. Sobbing like a baby, I slit Narragansett open, butterfly-style, with the machete and struggled until he was on top of the bear, meat-side down. I slithered in between the two carcasses and settled in beside Rene. I used the machete to prop open a slit between the cadavers so we would have some fresh air.

"This is warm," Rene concluded. Her breath was shallow, clearly still nervous, most likely panicked. She laid her head on my breast and put an arm over my tummy. "I don't care if you're straight. I need a live body or I'm gonna lose my mind."

Chapter 25

I used the old-fashioned, canvas, military-green pup tent while Ian owned a more sophisticated, orange nylon, two-person dome. Base camp was wet from the melted snowfall. I broke camp, making sure I didn't lose my boots in the occasional mud puddle. We were heading to town that morning and he seemed extra excited.

"I still recommend a heater," he said.

"Haven't gotten cold yet."

"The weather will change soon. You'll get cold."

"I've heard horror stories about heaters and suffocation."

"Those stories are true, but that's why you're here, correct? To learn how to stay warm and not asphyxiate?"

"Yes, sir."

"We'll get one in town. I'm excited to do laundry. Wash my undies with soap. You should too. Undies and bras and stuff."

"I have no bras 'cause I have no tits."

"I see boobs right there," Ian pointed out. "Why do you always say *tits*? 'Boobs' is so much friendlier."

"'Cause that's what they are. Just like cows. Mammals have tits, clowns have boobs." I never owned a bra. I didn't think Ian understood the luxury of not wearing a bra, so fuck it, I took off my shirt.

"Okay, I get it."

"You take your shirt off all the time."

"I don't have boobs."

"But you do, the same size as mine."

"Is this something I have to get used to?"

"I would appreciate it."

"Fine. We're mountain people up here. So let's take off our shirts."

"Is it too much for you?"

"I guess not now that you've indoctrinated me to your boobs. Tits, that is."

"Okay then." I kept my shirt off.

"Do you need a boy?" he asked. "A little sugar on your cornflakes?"

"A boy won't sugar my breakfast cereal."

"We're headed to town. Everyone needs a little now and then."

"I don't want a boy. I need a girl. Understand?"

"Yeah, I get that. I should have realized."

"No you shouldn't have, not unless I told you. Don't assume." I wasn't shocked he was sexualizing me with my shirt off. That's why I called them tits and not boobs.

"Tough crowd tonight," he said.

"Sorry. I really mean it, I'm being too hard on you. I came here to be mentored and I'm being very resistant."

"I think you just want honesty," Ian said thoughtfully. "I did. When I first came to the mountains, I wanted my mentor to be upfront, so I was honest with him, first thing. I was young and frightened and let him know. It didn't help change his tactics, but at least he knew."

"Tactics?"

"Suffocating from improperly ventilating your tent is not a hands-on kind of lesson. I'll teach you to avoid that. But you'll learn some things on your own."

"That is frightening. What if I fail?"

"You'll go home, it's that simple."

"Can you give me an example?"

"Just now, you learned you don't need to cover your tits in the mountains. Stuff like that. It will mostly revolve around food."

I chuckled.

"Right? Food and drink will become the most important lessons. Lighting comes in a close second, especially since you're a reader."

"I have one book."

"Of course. You carry your living space around with you, so more than one book at a time is not practical. By the way, *Jane Eyre* is not what I consider nature reading. We're here to live, not brood."

"Then what does my mentor recommend?"

"Anything by Barbara Kingsolver, for starters..."

"Well, maybe I'll find some wonderful, maidenly THOT of yours while at the bookstore tomorrow."

"One can only hope."

💧 💧 💧

We ventured back into Jasper, careful not to get too close to the locals since we hadn't bathed in quite some time. Ian suddenly turned to me with a horrified look.

"What's wrong?" I asked.

"Nothing. It just dawned on me that I didn't remind you to wear a shirt into town."

"Holy shit, Ian, I know enough to dress myself in public."

"I know. I know that. It's just a thing, like leaving home and not remembering if I turned off the hot iron."

We walked on, Ian assured that I wasn't nude. The horses were stabled at a small ranch on the end of town that held a contract with the park district. They could make side cash by offering showers. The streets and parking lots still held piles of snow shoveled from the last snowfall, whereas the surrounding woodlands had already drank the runoff during the unseasonably warm day.

"I have an apartment not far up the street," Ian said.

"Really? You're a resident?"

"Some of us don't feel stable without a home to go to, little one."

Little one?

"I'm giving you a key, so you'll have a home, too."

"Wow."

"Wow?"

"Yeah, Ian, that's *very* accommodating."

He stopped in front of a short apartment building on the main street downtown. At times, I assumed he got neck pain from looking down at me so often with such stern expressions. "Are you being sarcastic?"

"I didn't mean to be. Guess I just don't take the whole 'home life' thing seriously."

"You're pushing 30, Iris. I can't really call you girl anymore. Home is important at times. Someplace safe to shelter yourself from the world. Take hot showers and eat warm meals."

"So I've heard."

"Well, if I'm echoing someone else's advice, maybe you should take it to heart." He marched up the steps and let himself in.

"No security?" I asked, following behind.

Ian laughed a bit too loud as he ascended the stairs to his floor. "This is Canada, shorty." His apartment was locked though. He opened it with a key.

"I would appreciate," I started from the hallway, having to follow him in to finish. "I'd appreciate it if you settled on a pet name for me. I'm tired of being surprised each time."

"Sorry," he answered. "I'll settle on something. It's just that you're a walking dynamo of inspiration." He opened a drawer to remove a key that he handed to me. "Home," he reminded. "Even if I'm not here, this is your home."

"So you get the key back after the internship."

"No. What I said means for anytime. Your home is wherever I am."

"Shit…" I fondled the key between my fingers.

"Two bedrooms." Ian gestured toward the back.

I opened the door to a brightly colored room with two windows facing the streets and a neatly made double-bed.

"Electric floorboard heat," Ian said from the kitchen, where he was inspecting the contents of the cupboards. I adjusted the heat to medium. The floral bedspread was inviting and I got into it, falling victim to the soft pillows. The room heated up quick and my eyes grew heavy. I hadn't experienced a real bed in so long.

"You want some mac 'n' cheese?" was the last thing I heard before the shadows of sleep overtook me.

🌢 🌢 🌢

I awoke to darkness and an empty apartment. That meant Ian had got the jump on me and probably had his laundry finished. I stumbled around, feeling along the walls until I found a light switch. The small kitchen showed a pot full of lukewarm mac 'n' cheese. Ian's bedroom was open but the room was empty. Shit.

One dirty bowl laid in the sink with a spoon, processed orange stuck to the inside. I filled it with more gooey pasta. As I ate, I thought about the difference between life here and my life with Janet. Overall, I was restless, which wasn't a concern under her tutelage. I experienced strong desires there for both Dahlia and Canada, but not this low-grade anxiety. Did I miss the school? My introduction to the wilds I wished to call home?

The clock read **10PM**. I assumed laundromats were closed. Though it was a small town, I wanted to explore. After a shower, I'd follow the scent of whisky until I reunited with Ian.

Before that was time for snooping. First were the bookshelves, which lined two walls. The first hardcover that caught my attention stood alone, face out: Linnaeus' *Systema Naturae*, which cemented my notion that Ian was a serious naturalist and full-fledged nerd. I'd heard of Linnaeus though never seen a copy. Who actually would? It was a reference book for identifying wild botany. But Ian had read it, had it on display for easy access. Then there was *Go Ask Alice* with the original cover. I remembered reading that about the mentally ill girl documenting her descent and how nervous it made me, hitting a little close to home. No Steinbeck. Ian would need an introduction, like *Cannery Row*.

I couldn't think of Steinbeck without Monterey coming to mind, and Kira. It was our hero Ed Ricketts who drove her to that specific town. All she really wanted was warmth and the Pacific beach. I never had the opportunity to share that dream with her. I closed my mind for a moment to envision those intense green eyes glaring me down, bloodshot, always yearning. Sometimes, I wish I could just give in, so engrossed in my independence.

Time for a distraction: The bedroom or bathroom? I chose the bedroom, the more taboo choice. Ian made his bed, how droll. The dresser seemed like a big no-go, but I was drawn to a photo album decorating the top. It was a 5"x7", every page a different young person, each person outside, each setting familiar to me. Past interns. I sat on the edge of Ian's bed, flipping the pages. Did he give apartment keys to all these people? There were more than 20 young, smiling faces, maybe 30, all male. Shit, I was Ian's first female protégé.

    I tossed the album on the bed and got ready to shower. I didn't care if Ian knew I had looked at it or was in his room. This was supposed to be my home, so I got comfortable. The medicine cabinet was boring: Aspirin and untouched shaving gear. The water was hot and the shower fogged the mirror. After washing, my eyes grew tired again. I hoped Ian had coffee because I really wanted to stay and catch up.

    I wiped the condensation from the mirror and looked at my brooding self. The scar across my breast still had an angry red outline, though it had healed long ago. Dahlia was right, it looked really cool. I was badass without the need for a tattoo to advertise my strength. My dark hair was growing. It had been in a ponytail and unwashed for so long that I never got a good look at the length. Tonight, I would leave it down and free. It made me look more feminine and, at the moment, I enjoyed embracing that.

    My reflection made eye contact and I didn't look away. Deep, dark eyes that matched the locks casting a shroud of secrecy. There was something about this person I was attracted to, an overall elegance I'd never noticed.

    The night was unseasonably warm but I brought my jean jacket anyway. I lit a smoke and started walking into the denser parts of downtown. It wasn't long before I came upon a sports bar playing loud rock music that spilled into the street. The sidewalk was dotted with people my age, holding drinks and smoking, so I entered, pretty sure I would find Ian. He was at a table with a group of townies drinking and telling stories. I went to the bar and ordered a beer and a shot. I wasn't carded, as usually was the case. I watched Ian in his element before making myself visible.

    He spoke and everyone laughed as he finished a drink. Ian did a quick search of his surroundings, like he was looking for me. I stepped away from the tall men I was hiding behind. When he found me, he smiled and winked. I downed my shot, grabbed my beer, and took the long way to Ian's table for a chance to peruse the rest of the decor.

Much of the bar was ornamented with sports memorabilia and Japanese weaponry I recognized from the school. The bō staff over the bar caught my attention. It was exactly the size of the one Sensei trained me with yet was adorned with green vines and various-colored dahlia petals. The weapon held me mesmerized for many minutes until I shook myself free of its spell and went to Ian's table.

"Titmouse," Ian said with a drunken loudness I'd never heard from him.

In the spirit of the occasion, I took a long swig of my beer. "That one can stick," I informed.

"Titmouse?" another blond woodsman questioned.

"Duncan, this is my protégé, Iris," Ian said by way of introduction. "This is Duncan, the proprietor of this fine establishment."

Duncan smiled and extended a paw to shake my hand. "It's called The Rusty Nickel," he explained.

"Nickels don't rust," I said.

"That's the joke," Duncan answered.

I managed a smile like maybe the joke actually worked. "I love the Eastern weaponry on the walls."

"I won each piece," Duncan said.

I finished my beer in one long gulp. "I particularly like the bō over the bar."

"Won that from a black belt in Japan in a tournament."

Tournament? Black belt? This was foreign information to me. No one at Janet's school wore belts of any color. "It's a real thing of beauty."

"You familiar with the bō then?"

"I'm well-trained with them, my weapon of choice."

Ian's eyes widened as this was news to him.

"Well, it's not for sale," Duncan informed.

"Are you interested in a wager?"

"Run it by me, young lady."

"If you set that bō out back in the snow, straight up, I can kick an olive off the top without upsetting the staff."

"How about something realistic," Duncan offered. "That staff is six foot from end to end and you barely stand five foot."

Ian was quiet during this exchange.

"You'd have to leap an unrealistic distance," Duncan ciphered.

"That's the bet." I turned to the bar and ordered another shot and beer. Downed the shot and gulped the beer while admiring the soon-to-be-mine painted bō staff.

Duncan walked up from behind. "It has to be an authentic karate kick from pavement-level. No running start."

I nodded.

"What's in it for me?"

"I'll put up my horse. Ian gave him to me, he can give you the particulars. We stabled our horses just out of town."

Duncan talked with Ian. I ordered another round while Ian approached. The liquor loosened me up enough to smile flirtatiously at the voluptuous bartender. She quickly smiled back, eyes sparkling with possibility.

"I have no idea what you're doing," Ian exclaimed.

"Getting a new bō and probably laid," I said, making serious eye contact with him. "It's a sure thing,"

"I can't get you another horse."

"Let me worry about that."

"You're gambling away a lot 'cause you can't finish my program without that horse. You'll have to leave."

"I got the horse right here," I said, pointing my thumb at my head. "His name is Paul Revere."

Ian walked back to his table and spoke to Duncan. Soon, the owner signaled for a ladder to unmount the bō. I followed as it was carried out the back door. One employee balanced the staff in a pile of snow while another approached. She was dressed in a tight fit to increase tips, almost six feet, and presumably a family member with long, blonde hair and a chubby schoolgirl smile. She placed the green olive atop the staff.

I warmed up with a couple moves from my *kata* training to ground myself. A crowd of onlookers were starting to make the excited sounds of anticipation. With little thought, I made my vertical leap, stretched my right leg up and out, and began the 360° spin Sensei made me perform until it was part of my tool box. Of course, I couldn't leap six feet off the ground, but I could leap far enough that the heel of my right foot reached that by the time I finished my spin. As I had done so many times in the past to impress my beloved Dahlia, I swiped the olive from the top of the staff with the bottom of my heel, this time to impress the barmaid. The olive flew purposefully at Duncan, who caught it single-handedly, and the bō did not even shudder from the breeze my leg produced.

    I immediately removed my new staff from the bank and went into my bō *kata*. I mimicked the very moves I watched Dahlia do so eloquently and often in my recent past. This bō reminded me so much of her. It would rest in my designated bedroom, decorating a corner and filling my dreams with fantasies of love. I stopped midway in what was supposed to be a lethal jab, but what turned into a deliberate point at the sexy barmaid who covered her heart with both hands and expelled a love-struck sigh. I turned to Ian and gave him a wink that was supposed to say, "Don't wait up for me." I marched my new staff into the bar, the tight-jeaned blonde following close behind, and worried there might not be time tomorrow to get my laundry finished.

    The bartender poured me another whisky to go with my fresh beer. It occurred to me that if I ever saw Janet again, I was going to tell her about this black belt thing because, when Duncan bowed to me with an excited smile, he mentioned I must be a third-degree to be so well-practiced.

    "Ah, sure," I answered, returning his bow. "Degree three."

Chapter 26

I laid in a bed of fallen leaves, staring up at the autumn clouds rushing between the treetops. It was a silent afternoon, more so than usual, like the quiet before the storm. The birds were songless, no woodpecker ripping off tree bark for the tasty, scurrying larva. Then the silence was broken by the familiar honking of geese overhead. I opened my eyes just in time to see the V formation fly by. Silly birds, what were they doing at this elevation? There was no lake or pond up here. One could never accuse me of thinking geese were intelligent.

I considered love and my lack of it. Love was tarnished because of Kira. I equated love with death and tragedy. I'd never had a companion to share time with and this filled me with dreaded loneliness. Kira was a partner in larceny and malicious debauchery, lasciviousness, and buggery, even without our skin enticing lust for each other. She was not the one to befriend me, hers was a mission of wanton desire. Dahlia was a dream of the past and I contemplated if she was ever even real.

Ian had loaned me a rifle. To him, survival was found down the barrel of a gun, not the handle of my trusted machete. I laid in the leaves, eyes fixed on the clear, crisp sky, holding the rifle across my chest like a toy soldier a child left on the bedroom carpet when her mother called her to dinner. It hadn't been fired yet, as Ian had wanted.

"Shoot something," he had instructed. "A rock or tree, kill a squirrel. Fire the rifle while you're out on your own."

I closed my eyes and remembered practice shots at empty tin cans at camp with his dutiful instruction on loading, releasing the safety, cocking the gun, and relaxing while pulling the trigger.

"When you're hungry, that machete won't get you any venison or pheasant."

Rustling steps broke the afternoon silence. I assumed Ian was checking on me and braced to be chastised for holding a loaded weapon. Sniffing filled my ear and I figured Narragansett was next to me instead of Ian.

"Baby boy, can't you give me a minute to meditate or take a nap?"

I was answered by a deafening roar and the spray of wetness against my face. My eyes opened to the angry face of a momma bear. I jumped up and she reared back, her two cubs looking on from behind. My hands shook while I released the safety, raised the rifle, and fired on the bear.

The gun discharged and struck the mom on the shoulder. A useless waste of ammo. I turned to Narragansett but tripped, my rifle fell out of my arms. That's when she munched a chunk of my left thigh. My face was buried in the grass and I waited for the next strike, but heard a *thump* and the angry yowl of the bear behind me. A wet nose nudged my face up and I heard Narragansett's familiar snort. He had kicked the bear a couple yards, my blood red on her snout. The sound sent chills through my soul from the coldest fury of fright I'd ever experienced. The next strike would be my back or neck. She wouldn't eat me alive, screaming and kicking at her cubs. For this, I was grateful. My body was frozen yet Narragansett nudged me again.

I managed to firmly grab his mane. He jerked up, turned, and ran. I slipped but the reins found my hand, so I wrapped my legs around his neck. With my blood splattering everywhere, Narragansett never broke stride from his sprint while I grasped the pommel with one hand. "Narragansett! Find Ian!" In one fluid movement, I swung myself into the saddle. "Take me to Ian! Ya, boy, go!"

Momma Bear was losing ground on my miraculous black stallion. Narragansett was such a magnificent animal, how Ian could part with him was beyond me. He was more than show and speed. His strength and heart were greater than any being could hold. He'd just beat down a bear! I saw Ian from far off, searching out his protégé among the firs when he caught sound of the bear. He was riding in our direction as we exited the tree line. With her falling farther behind, the shot was easy for Ian. He was nearly a quarter-mile away but nailed the bear square in the neck, dropping her with a loud tumble. The bullet broke air by my and Narragansett's head.

The momma bear roared when she regained her senses. Giving up the chase as hopeless, she returned to her cubs. Narragansett stopped upon reaching Ian, breathing heavily as he lowered his neck so I could slide off.

"Good boy, Narragansett," Ian complimented. "Up!" The horse raise his head and Ian took the reins. He placed me behind himself on Thorn and led Narragansett back to camp.

The wound was ugly but only tore my outer flesh. Ian cleaned and packed it with gauze before wrapping it with tape. One layer of surgical tape and an outer layer of duct tape.

"I'm so surprised," I explained as Ian finished dressing my hip.

"You shouldn't be. That's why it's called the wild. But I will warn you now, this won't be the last time."

"I've never fought so hard for my life. There was a day I would have accepted a bear mauling and been happy for it. That's what surprised me, that I didn't lay down and concede my fate."

"So now you've experienced it," Ian announced. He added the bloody rags to the fire.

"Experienced what, exactly? The fangs of death?"

"The edge. You just came back from the edge, from not going over into the abyss. This is what you came here for. You rationalized plenty of other reasons for coming up here. The cold Canadian nights, fresh air and water, natural beauty, but, tucked away in your subconscious, hidden by your talent for denial, you knew what the wild was all about. Everyone does, that's why we're here alone right now without a crowd of students. The untamed savagery of nature is treacherous, and you knew that going in. I told you there were lessons I could not teach you, this was one. Trust me on the lesson I can teach you though, this won't be the last time." Ian cracked his bottle of Wild Turkey and handed it to me.

I gratefully took a swig. "I could kill a bear for a cigarette," I announced.

He took the bottle back and took a drink. He stood and opened his provisions, removed a box of cigarillos.

"That will do fine," I said, relief apparent.

Ian took a piece of kindling from the fire and held it to me to light up. "Did you quit smoking?" he asked.

"No. Never really started. Tobacco is just an occasional luxury." I took a couple puffs on the mellow smoke and another draw of the Wild Turkey. "The last time I smoked was a cigarette and it was just before meeting you." I stared into the fire and remembered my trip. Hangman nooses and the ocean, hitchhiking and nights under the beach stars. The whisky was warming my belly and loosening my tongue. "Thanks for saving my life."

"All in a day's work, though I have to admit I worried about my shot. It was hard to stop my hands from shaking at the sight of you two escaping from that bear."

"Just say, 'You're welcome.'"

"You're welcome, Iris. I'm glad you got away and my shot was true."

I felt giddy, unfettered. My mind went back to pre-bear attack ruminations. "A girl died in California. She lost her fight with depression there on the Pacific beach. I was on a quest of sorts, looking for lost pieces of myself. It led me cross country to that vile end."

"So you escaped to Alberta?"

"Not because of her. I was always going to make that this trip, if I lived long enough."

Ian cast his reverie to the fire. My statement might have been too revealing. And he was a smart man who'd already learned a great deal about me. He'd experienced confusing days when I couldn't leave my sleeping bag or concentrate, refused to talk.

"I've been to the edge, Ian. It's not unfamiliar territory. It didn't involve bears as much as it did bullets and car crashes. Police, incarceration, and lots of dying. I'm not here to experience near-death, Ian. I know how to fight and about beating the odds. I want to live, Ian. Life is what I seek in Alberta, that's the real adventure. I know all about how to survive and how to die. It's being alive I have a hard time with."

"Are you ever going to stop bogarting the bottle?" was Ian's only response. So he never addressed the subject directly, but the rest of my mentorship revolved around disclosing the secrets of nature. No more about the struggle to stay alive, but those little mysteries he kept to himself and never disclosed to any other protégés. His secrets that kept life sacred in hopes of awakening new purpose in me.

💧 💧 💧

"You wanna do some platonic making out?" I pleaded back at base. The booze softened my edges and I was crashing after the adrenaline high from almost being eaten.
"Is that like friends with benefits?"
"Sure, yeah, okay."
"I thought you liked girls."
"I kiss boys sometimes. Especially when I'm lonely."
"Are you lonely?"
"Terribly, Ian."
"Well, I'm not."
"We've been up here six weeks. Don't you get lonely?"
"I get lonely when I'm *alone*, sometimes. I'm not lonely when I'm with you. I like you, Iris, and I care about you. I enjoy the time we're having together."
"Well, I am too. I just need a little closeness."
"I don't get you, Iris. I feel intimately connected to you. I consider you a friend now. I look forward to seeing you after we're apart. The last thing I feel with you is lonely."
"How do you do that?" I whispered.
"If you don't mind me being critical, the first thing that comes to mind is you might be a little self-absorbed. I told you about being in the moment. Be aware of your surroundings, listen and concentrate. Well, I do all of that with you too. I do that with most of the people I mentor, but it's different with you. You have a unique passion that moves me. My time with you is spent with you, not in my head."
"So I'm like a distraction?"
"No, Iris. You're like this really great, little bean of a person who can do amazing things and has a great outlook

that feeds me emotionally and stimulates me intellectually. I spend time on myself, my emotions, and stillness. But it's healthy to focus on other people too. Good people like you, who are led by virtue and act on powerfully felt passions. It's right, Iris, it really is healthy."

"You're not lonely all of the time? Or most of the time? You don't wake up feeling uncontrollable desire each morning?"

"I wake up with high expectations. I wake up looking forward to morning coffee, with you. Sitting by a fire and waiting for that spark in your eyes. I won't give you this platonic sex you want. We can go whoring when we get into town. All I got for you is unconditional respect and caring."

"I mean, I like you, Ian."

"It's just like any of the other practices I taught you. Be aware of your surroundings. I'm part of your surroundings. You don't lose anything by being aware of me too. That's how you cure the lonelies."

We had been passing the bottle back and forth. It was half-empty and I was drunk. I was ready to pass out and not think about the many weeks of healing I'd have to endure before Ian and I could pick up where we left off.

💧 💧 💧

The oil sands would take two days and one sleep to get to on horseback. Ian and I made trips like that weekly. It was how we make our living. So, for my furlough, I asked Ian to take me to Athabasca. He didn't answer or say a word about it for two days.

"So you're ready for the mourning," he stated finally.

"Is it that bad?"

With sad eyes, he nodded. The sun was warm as evening approached. He had a faraway expression, one he held for two silent days. We started out on a Friday dawn. I had the next week off but Ian didn't. He counted this as work and said he'd get away with it, said his bosses would understand.

We rode on another unseasonably warm day, deep into autumn with winter right around the corner. Ian was not his perky self and made for a morose companion. I offered to make this trip myself but he insisted on coming, claiming I would need the support. With a sense of foreboding, we pressed on to experience whatever it was that I would need a babysitter present for. I was sorry I'd asked him to come.

"We won't actually enter Athabasca," Ian explained. "It's a city and our horses won't be welcome."

"Oh, who wouldn't want Narragansett?" I quipped.

Ian didn't even smirk. "There will be a place to board the horses just outside Athabasca while we catch a ride to the city."

"Wow, a city. I might get laid again."

"Look, it's important for you to see this. I'm very proud of you for your concern. A student has never asked to make this trip before and I've never offered. It's just too hard on me, but you're worth the trouble. And someone like you, with your passion and wit, needs to bear witness. Someone the wild is making love to has a right to know these ailments."

💧 💧 💧

I called it the Canadian outback though I never said so to Ian. As the elevation changed from the mountainous region we called home to the flatlands between us and the oil sands, the flora changed from wind-resistant trees and rock formations to shrubs. Bird watching was different on the outback than the mountains with a greater variety of species and better environment for prey animals.

Birding was part of the job, though it wasn't an occupation I was passionate about. It was enjoyable and I learned a lot under Ian's tutelage; my notepad carried an immense amount of information about the feathered population of the Jasper, Alberta. The breeze carried much more birdsong and annoying chirping on the flatlands than I was used to. It also carried fragrances of wildflowers and prairie grass, the occasional animal droppings, and a civilized form of life from far off.

Ian preferred indigenous peoples' definition of 'civilized' that involved living with the land and not fighting nature as if she were a wild beast in need of taming. He was kind of a hippie at times, which was why many of his teachings went over the head of a girl who was more apt to steal cars and sleep under overpasses.

I often had to remind myself that I did come here. My past and civilized experiences did not necessarily fall into the category of affirmative life achievements. Canada called me for a reason, one more than the romance of a fire crackling on a winter night. Ian was the key to finding that reason so I needed to take his lessons seriously. He was the key to becoming the woman Janet saw in me.

♦ ♦ ♦

We rode slowly, letting the animals make their own pace. Ian was owned by Thorn, a tan mustang with a blond mane. He claimed a magical connection to the animal, like she was a familiar and he was a warlock of nature. He didn't believe this, as far as I knew, but said I'd be lucky if I ever experienced that with Narragansett.

"You wouldn't logically take a lover with a terminal illness," Ian explained. He turned his head to make eye contact as we rode side by side. "But that's exactly what you're doing. It's what you did when you entered this program."

"I wanted nature in the coldest possible setting. Cold nights in Canada to cleanse my soul."

Ian didn't respond. Or maybe he understood on an existential level. He could be here for the same reason, I wouldn't know, we talked so little about our pasts. Our time was spent in the present. He had a job to do, even at day's end under a clear, cool sky littered with bright stars that were never so vibrant where I came from. No stories to build comradery were shared between us. I was beginning to find it frustrating.

"The direction you're heading is different than what you wanted, Iris. You're borrowing grief, as you like to say. We could turn back to your cold Canadian nights right now and finish your internship in Iris' land of denial. Because after Athabasca, everything is going to be different."

"This sounds like a warning."

"I know you're a tough character, but how much pain do you have to endure? Why put yourself through it when we can return to the beauty of Jasper?"

"I need to see, Ian. I'm living here now, this is home. I have to know the grim truth, especially since it's so close."

We rode to past twilight and set camp in the dark. This was no great feat as I could set camp blindfolded. Ian hunted fallen branches and I set up propane cooking gear to whip up some grub. Tonight's pack mule, Malady, was indifferent to me as I dug through the provisions. Ian promised he would always be that way, but tonight Mal was uninterested in biting or kicking me.

"Whatcha cookin', wench?" Ian joked when he returned. Perhaps his mood was lightening with nightfall.

Still, I responded appropriately: "Fuck you."

"Steak, eggs, potatoes, and corn: Someone's hungry.

"You packed it."

We ate hungrily by the campfire. A owl belted its horrid noise for all of Alberta to hear. I was euphoric after eating and wondered about why I was without cigarettes. "Did you bring the Wild Turkey?"

"You don't want to reach our destination hungover."

"But I'm on vacation."

"You have an odd concept of relaxation. I have an idea."

"Platonic kissing?"

"No, 20 questions."

I thought on that for a few minutes. "How about just two questions?"

"10."

"Five, and that's my final offer."

"Deal!"

"I go first," I insisted. "Are you gay?"

"No, I'm mostly straight."

"What do you mean by mostly?"

"Is that your second question?"

"Oh. I see how you're playing. No, I've only used one question. Your turn."

"Have you ever been married?"

"No. Lesbian."

"I thought you went both ways."

"Is that *your* second question?"

"That wasn't a question. It was a statement, or an assumption. The idea of 20 questions is to invoke conversation, disclosure."

"I swing both ways but the love of my life was female. So I'll only be happy coupled with a woman. Is that a sufficient answer?"

"Yeah, sure."

"My turn. What were you before a conservationist?"

"A machinist?"

"I get to try that one again."

"Fair enough."

"What were you before becoming a conservationist and explain what that something is?"

"A machinist is what it sounds like. I worked with machines and made things out of metal. Machine tools like lathes, drills, presses, that kind of thing. I specialized in drill press, it was horrific. Grease and dirt mixed with metal shaving always on my hands, arms, and hair. Long hours on my feet in cold shops with cement floors. It was fine when I was a kid and stuck in the illusion of prosperity, but I outgrew it."

The sun had set and the fire was full blaze. Ian and I sat next to each other on a log while we ate. The owl stopped screeching. The cool evening was silent sans the crackling of the firewood. I could smell pine on the slight breeze.

"Where were you born?" Ian burned his last question.

"Florida. I was brought up in a trailer court, which makes me white trash. Though I spent my childhood in a Florida trailer court, the only ocean I've seen is the Pacific."

"Really...?"

"No, I'm fucking *lying*. How could I make that up?"

"That your third question?"

"No. Where are you from?"

"New York. Grew up in Manhattan, which makes me white skyscraper trash. My parents were well-to-do but I struck out on my own at 17 and spent my youth in financial embarrassment. I followed a machining apprenticeship into Canada. Now I'm here with you."

"So you've gone from financial embarrassment to social embarrassment." I laughed, Ian did not, which made me self-conscious.

"My turn," he said morosely. "You have parents?"

"Fuck my parents. My turn."

"No, wait. There's a story there."

"Not one I'm telling. My turn."

"So much for disclosure."

"I'm an open book except for my parents."

"I get another question 'cause that's not fair."

"Fine."

"Have you spent time in an institution because of mental illness?"

"You already know the answer to that. Talk about not being fair. I answered truthfully on all the paperwork when I signed up. You know full and well what a basket case I am."

"No, I don't. I've seen no evidence of you being mentally ill at all, and I was told to keep a look-out and report to the office if you showed signs that you wouldn't make it in the program. But there's nothing to report. You're sane as anyone else I know. Sane and brave, willing to go the distance."

"Where I come from, 'willing to go the distance' is considered insane. A young woman who is strong and decisive must be crazy. A woman, or any person, who seeks adventure must be psychotic. I seem sane to you because I'm in my element. Living in the wild with a horse and sleeping in a tent under the stars. Maybe I just finally got what I always needed."

"I think you're a superhero."

"Because I can ride a horse?"

"Because, instead of giving up, you went after what you needed. Most people settle, but that's not good enough for you. It's all or nothing and I admire that. You do what you need or you won't survive. Surviving makes you heroic."

I didn't know how to reply. When I thought about it, I did feel sane. More so than the time I spent in Illinois. "I'm pretty proud of myself," I admitted.

"You should be. I'm proud of you. Proud to take part in your life, proud to be seen with you."

"You sure you don't wanna make out?"

"Just focus on the conversation. This is working pretty good for us. Sure you don't wanna go for 20?"

"Is that your fifth question?"

"Only if you answer yes."

"Let's see how I'm doing at five. My turn. What's been your best relationship?"

"Thorn, of course."

"I should have guessed."

"You'll say the same of Narragansett one day. If he survives you."

I made a face that was supposed to clue Ian into telling me more without burning one of my questions.

"I stole her," he added. "Passing through Ontario. I mean, she was loose but somebody obviously owned her. I didn't try to find her home, which is technically stealing."

"Finders keepers."

"Well, okay, but they used to hang horse thieves. Some of these mountain folk still might."

"We're a long way from Ontario."

"Exactly. My turn. You have any artistic talents?"

"I sing like an angel."

"Seriously?"

"Yup, but you'll never hear it. No one ever does."

"That's not fair."

"Only if you've ever heard me sing. Until then, you don't know what you're missing, so it doesn't matter. I've been trained as a classical dancer though. I'm good at that so I don't mind showing off. I dance jazz too. I can dance most anything."

"I'm intrigued."

"If we're together long, you'll eventually see me dance."

"So your parents had you trained?"

"That's an extra question and I already told you about my parents. I started dance at eight is all I can say, that and fuck my parents. I'll let you get away with that question but you really gotta answer the next one well."

"Oh shit, I'm anxious. Go ahead..."

The fire was slowly dying and I wished I had made coffee. Ian had become a shadow in the dance of orange light flickering from the fire. I was aware of him because we sat close enough that we were touching. With our parkas on though it hardly counted. It wasn't a friendly closeness as much as it was a huddle for warmth.

"What are you afraid of?"

"At the moment, you."

"Ha! I'm pretty little, Ian."

"You're fierce. I don't do fierce very well."

"Maybe I am, but I'm still too small to have any effect."

"No you're not. You're big. You're the biggest thing on the mountain. You fill the entire space with your presence. It's scary, and it makes me afraid."

"That's crazy talk, what are you really afraid of?"

"You think I'm not serious? I'm your mentor and *you're* supposed to pay attention to *me*. Everyone notices you when you enter a room. Teeny tiny Iris is the largest influence everywhere she goes… You gotta get in touch with yourself and be responsible for how you affect the world around you. You're a fucking celestial dynamo and right now you're like a kid with a box of fireworks, looking for a match. You came here to learn about the wild but the wild is you."

"If only I would use my powers for good."

The shadow of Ian's hood turned away at my sarcasm. I was a little pissed at his misdirection.

"You ever heard of the term gas lighting?" I asked.

"I answered you. I'm afraid of more existential things but I answered you with what was on my mind. My turn."

"Your turn? I might let you get away with that."

"Have you ever been in love? Or more like who do you love? 'Cause it certainly isn't yourself."

"Yes."

"Yes? That's your answer? It was a leading question."

"Her name was Dahlia. 'Was' cause she left me. And I know your big presence bullshit is false 'cause she was the celestial dynamo you described. If you see that in me, it's 'cause I'm a walking testament to her. She's the reason I'm here now. Otherwise, well, I don't know. I can't even imagine…

I'm done. No more 20 questions. I need to go to sleep." I promised myself that kidding about platonic kissing was over.

Sleep was haunted by dreams of my former love. Her dark eyes, glorious smile, soft lips, and protective embrace caused me to toss and turn, entangle myself in my sleeping bag so that I had a hard time unwrapping myself at sunrise. It led me to a morning filled with regret and a poor attitude toward my vacation companion.

Hours on horseback without a word. I broke camp without breakfast, not caring what Ian thought of that. He was merely along for the ride. This was my vacation and it had turned glum due to his choice of 20 questions over alcohol. He may have planned this on the outset of the trip.

As lunch approached, I had to act. It was up to me to pull myself out of my doldrums. Ian probably didn't care, maybe he did this to all his protégés. I was hungry, which would require discussion, stopping and measuring our progress, making plans for arriving at our destination. "It's time for food," I announced.

"We have an hour yet."

"The sun looks like noon."

"You really need a watch," Ian admonished.

"I've sworn off watches."

"Did you get a rash?"

"My last watch was really nice and was stolen."

"So get a not-so-nice one."

"There's more sentiment to the story."

"Look, I'm sorry. I bummed out your trip and now I'm lecturing, even though that's my job, but this *is* your vacation."

"I'm sorry too. I'm hard to get close to."

"Is it actually going to require physical contact, Iris?"

"I'll try harder. I'm warning you, emotional intimacy with me is not always pleasant. I did, however, give you the choice between the two."

"I'm intrigued enough to try anything. I don't usually give this much of a shit about my students. But there's something about you..."

"Are we on schedule?"

"I believe so. We'll get there early evening."

"Woods to the right. Rocks to the left."
"It's your vacation."
I chose rocks.

🌢 🌢 🌢

Athabasca in the orange sunset was a sight to behold. From our vantage point, we could take in the river running along the surface mine. The river that ran southwest, to Jasper.

"Is this fucking up the river?"

"You know the answer to that," Ian snarked. "The tar sand is a gift from the glaciers, and so is the Athabasca River. What they've done here is unforgivable."

"Pretty harsh, Ian…"

The machinery to extract oil from the sands was enormously impressive. The buildings billowing smoke into the sky, connected by a complicated pipe system, was the size of a small town. Nearly the size of Jasper. The mining itself, as I saw it through Ian's binoculars, was performed with even more impressive machines and trucks. Bulldozers pushed the tar downward into a pit, where it was collected by a machine resembling a downtown office building in size and scope. The smell was putrid. The hot sands and burnt diesel wafted up to our position. How we never caught a whiff of this repugnance in Jasper was beyond me. I couldn't say this to Ian without a lecture on distance and prevailing winds. He had a habit of completely bailing on the spirit of conversion with literalism. Perhaps a natural defense, I knew I had mine.

People were hard to spot. It was as though giants walked the earth in Canada, wreaking havoc as they raped the sands and poisoned the Athabascan waters. It was truly otherworldly and I was having trouble with disassociation. This place was entirely different than our mountain home in Jasper, so different than what I came for.

I turned to Ian for grounding and handed him back his spectacles. He turned and sat on the permafrost.

"It is over isn't it?" I asked my mentor.

"'Fraid so. Nature is gone. At least the one we were taught about. The idea of nature is dead, soon to be a distant memory. God made an Eden for us and He kicked us out. Now see what we've done?"

"God? He? No wonder this fucks you up in the head."

"You don't believe in God? That must be nice."

"I don't know what to believe. I do know if God exists as you see Him, then He doesn't believe in me! He calls me a faggot and spits in my face!"

"That's not true."

"Oh, really? Have you lived my life? When was the last time you visited Florida?"

"I don't know about Florida," Ian admitted. "I know the story though. This was all created by God or the Oversoul or whatever you want to call it. We were put here and we destroyed it. There's barely enough nature for the next generation to survive on."

I walked up to where he was sitting cross-legged, facing away from Athabasca. My anger gave me the strength to grab his collar and raise him to his knees. "I wasn't put here. I came from here." I grabbed up a handful of dry dirt and showed it to him. "I came from this. This is me, and the air, and the water, and whatever falls from comets. That's me. I'm nature. From this dust the god you believe in raised me and, to this dust, I'll go back. And that dust will be used to create another, and another, and trees, fishes, fucking raccoons. I'm nature, Ian. I am! I'm Nature's queer child. I believe in what I can hold in my hand." I let the dirt sift through my fingers and onto the ground. "I believe in what I can stand on and see. I believe in what I can hold, feel, and burn in my heart. I believe in the stars and the wind. I wasn't put here. I'm the wind, the rivers and oceans; I'm the mountain we live on. It's me, Ian, I'm Nature!"

I don't know if Ian understood my perspective, or my disappointment with him at the moment. He just stared slack-jawed at me. Sometimes, trying to discuss belief systems with people became a pointless endeavor, all wrapped up in personal buzzwords and meanings that had nothing to do with the English language as a form of communication. I felt disillusioned that he would miss my point that I, as a human, could have a direct impact on what was happening below us. Because I was nature, it affects me and I can affect it.

"Mercy," Ian barely let escape. "God has mercy."

I didn't—couldn't—answer.

"May God have mercy."

"What?"

"On you, Iris." He averted his eyes from my confused gaze. "May God have mercy on you, Iris."

"On *me*!" I was flabbergasted. Hurt, angry, and about to cry. "Fuck you, Ian."

In one swift motion, I mounted Narragansett and set off back to Jasper alone. "Come on, baby," I pleaded with my horse. "Get me out of here."

Narragansett dutifully set off to home without my guidance. I was useless until the tears cleared. The landscape rushed by in a blur. Something about the two of us was connected, I learned that after the bear attack. I hoped I could live up to what Narragansett saw in me. In any case, he knew something was up between Ian and me, and his loyalty and care for my safety showed in his quick pace.

We rode through the night, which was against the rules. I didn't care about Ian's rules. I had no idea where we were headed, I hoped Jasper, and this wouldn't be the last time I put my blind trust into Narragansett. After 10 hours, my baby stopped at a slow mountain stream, glimmering in the light of the rising morning star. I knew we had been moving up in elevation by the way I breathed and how my sinuses and ears were feeling. Higher elevations were something my body could not grow accustomed to. The symptoms were a sign that Narragansett was heading in the right direction. As he drank, I slid off his back only to land on wobbly legs.

"Sorry, boy," I apologized. He had been pushed too hard and I could expect no more from him today.

I stopped at the slow-moving freeze to wash my teary face. My reflection looked back: wind-chapped white skin and black hair pulled into a ponytail. My brown eyes seemed to decorate the bottom of the stream like a pair of darting minnows. I removed my shirt to feel the exhilarating cold. My face was sad and my expression empty. I pulled my hair loose and shook it out. It was longer than I'd expected, flowing around my shoulders and breasts, shiny and reflecting the sun. Narragansett snorted and I remembered to look around for bears or cougars. When I looked back, a nervous smile appeared on my face. It was cute. I was cute. I looked childlike, naïve once again.

Was that me? Was I still just a child whistling in the dark, believing in monsters? Or was I the morose woman I believed I'd become? Wise and tortured with emotionless expressions. I caught myself, didn't I? Caught how I must look to others like Ian. No matter how I felt inside, the child would still shine through. That smirk didn't look standoffish. It was meant to, but instead looked inviting. I looked damn friendly.

Shit.

The landscape appeared somewhat familiar though it wasn't our usual stomping grounds. In angry haste, I'd run off, leaving everything packed onto Malady, who was still with Ian. My coat, provisions, and sleep gear were strapped to the side of that evil beast while I was yet a day from base camp, babysitting an exhausted horse.

My plan was to scout the immediate area in daylight for a safe place to make camp. A fire was required. Food would be nice but we would survive without it for one day, sleep tonight, and start the next morning. My machete was at its permanent location: strapped to my thigh. Maybe we would come across an angry badger I could best with the sharp end of my blade.

Luck was in our favor as I found an abandoned shack. Obviously, someone's hunting camp further along the stream and in good repair. I knocked on the one door to no avail. I peeked in the one front window and saw nothing in the dark, single room. A brick chimney built into the back was promising. I was going to get in and apologize later. First, Narragansett needed to be retrieved from downstream. He would be proud of my find.

With Narragansett by my side, I turned the antique door knob to get a feel for the locking mechanism, but there was none. The door was unlocked! My baby stood in the doorway as I entered to explore.

"Hellooo," I swooned into the darkness.

The lack of an answer was my invitation to enter.

"We're in luck, horse. There's firewood."

Narragansett snorted in reply. He was shy to come inside and I knew he wouldn't unless I led him, which I would before nightfall. Attached to the wall was a wooden bench, which probably doubled as a daybed. There was no traditional bedding, which made sense since it would eventually wind up a nest for vermin. That was fine with me, I'd find a way to get comfortable. The fireplace was clean and equipped for cooking: a dry pile of wood was stacked next to it. The kitchen area had a small pail for water and two cupboards in which I found canned and packaged goods.

"We eat tonight, Narragansett," I shouted, but he lost interest long ago and went back to drinking from the stream. "Spam, mustard sardines, instant *au gratin* potatoes," I informed, holding the items up outside the door for him to see. I was talking to my horse and didn't know whether to consider myself lucky to have a horse to talk to or sad that I *only* had my horse to talk to. The cupboard was actually filled with items more suited to my palate than mustard sardines, but I was excited and wanted to show my horse our luck.

My copy of *Jane Eyre* was also packed away on Malady but I found myself busy enough starting the fire and preparing food to fill most of the day. Narragansett had a couple sacks of provisions that had matches packed away. I wasn't in the mood for hunting up flint stones, though Ian did proficiently teach me to start a fire that way. Matches, a deck of cards, a flashlight, and a fresh pack of Winstons I was unaware I possessed. In fact, I was sure they were not mine. They must have been placed there by a tobacco benefactor, and that benefactor had to be Ian.

I sat on the bench in the cabin and thought, *Why couldn't I just be like everyone else?* I really didn't care what Ian's beliefs were until he invoked this weird spellcraft on me. I could have been more sensitive to his sensibilities. He probably was aware of my pagany notions so I didn't need to smash him over the head with them.

From past therapy, I knew at the moment I was only sad, not depressed. My depression was in remission, but sadness often resembled depression so it made me anxious that I was slipping again. If I was more like Ian, maybe I'd be happy. To be like Ian was to be like everyone else, and what would be wrong with that?

🜂 🜂 🜂

"You are not running *from* but *toward*," a haunt from the not-too-distant past echoed in my head. Memories of Sensei came to mind. We were practicing with the bō and she was carrying on a conversation during, like she was prone to do. It was either meant to enhance my concentration or hers. "So, your friend was buried in a potter's grave?" she asked.

"I don't know what that is."

She stepped back into defensive mode as I assumed a power attack, just as she had taught me: to not just go through the motions, but have intent to kill, maim, and render my opponent defenseless. Her eyes opened wide as I fiercely and repeatedly thrust the end of my bō at her, then backed off out of curiosity over the whole "potter's grave" thing.

"A potter's grave is where people are buried who died with no money, family, or friends. It's a state burial. The local government pays for it, sometimes for a headstone, especially if the corpse had identification on it. So, I can assume you did not visit her grave." Sensei went on the offensive. She'd thrown me psychologically and put her best moves toward me to see if I would break down. Her rationale to teaching me the bō was that I could find a big stick anywhere if I truly was to live in the woods. I might lose my machete or have no rifle at hand, but a long staff was always made available by Mother Nature.

"No," I answered breathlessly. "I left under adverse circumstances."

She stood at rest, bō at her side. I clipped Sensei at her kneepads and brought her down, then stood over her, ready to deliver the death blow. Her eyes bugged, not expecting me to take advantage of her relaxed stance. It was supposed to mark the end of the session, but, on the battlefield there were no

Darkness was about to descend when I was surprised by a *knock* on the door. Narragansett had given no warning, so I knew it was Ian.

"I'm naked," I lied.

"You're in my hunting cabin," Ian announced.

"Thanks for the smokes."

"Please don't smoke in my cabin."

I made no noise for a spell before opening the unlocked door.

"I thought you were naked."

"My shirt's off."

"Your shirt's always off."

"I didn't know this was your cabin. I smoked in it."

"That's okay."

"Why is there so much fresh food in here?"

"For you. I stocked up before vacation, just in case"

"You were planning a fight?"

"No. But anything could happen. This is halfway to Jasper."

"So, this is a cache."

"Exactly."

"You smell kinda like liquor. Are you drunk?"

"Sorta?"

"How are you 'sorta'? You got booze?"

"I have winter apples from a storage facility in Athabasca."

"That sounds gross."

"Only the first one." Ian opened a leather satchel and produced a shriveled apple that had obviously been frozen. "They ferment on the tree, some like these are picked and stored. Eating them is like drinking apple Jack. Try it before you knock it. They are a gift from the horse stable. I think I impressed them with my tale of losing my protégé to the evils of Protestant ideology."

I did and found it surprisingly euphoric. It tasted good with only a hint of fermentation. "How many you got?"

"Plenty enough," Ian replied with a smirk. Winter apples and forgiveness were just added to my list for the night's activities, right under a warm fire, food, and napping. I took another apple before I stoked the fire.

Thorn whinnied at Narragansett on the other side of the door while Ian poked around inside the cabin, checking supplies, probably planning the evening meal. "So I have to ask about that large scar across your boob. It doesn't look old."

I felt naked. "Well, you witnessed my karate."

"Third-degree black belt. Very impressive."

I laughed. "Sometimes you bite the blade, sometimes the blade bites you." I motioned across my body, hand following the scar.

"Story for another day?"

"It will take more than frozen apples to pry this story from my lips."

"I brought you some pressies from Athabasca."

"Oh, Christmas time!"

"First, you have to hand over *Jane Eyre*."

"Fine. I've read it twice anyway. Malady has it right now. Along with my parka, flashlight, all my survival gear."

Ian took my book from Malady's pack, returned to the cabin, and handed me a copy of *Walden*.

"Thoreau?"

"Yeah. Read about being alive instead of how to be a zombie."

"Okay. What else did you bring me?"

"Skis. Malady has those too. A pair for each of us."

"You want me to ski?" I asked wearily. Breaking my head open on a pine tree at 60mph didn't sound so appealing.

"Cross country," Ian explained. "It's more fun than it sounds. 'Tis the season. I thought about snowshoes at first but they don't make a size small enough for you to negotiate. You're the perfect build for skis though! It'll be fun, you'll see. It's a great alternative to cabin fever."

"Cabin fever?"

"Yeah, Iris. The snow is coming and when it gets too deep for the horses, there's nothing else to do. With skis, we can stay out and about."

I smiled. This was what I came to Canada for. This was why I left Monterey and my "redemption" behind. If I was going to choose to be alive, I actually wanted to live. "Cabin fever doesn't sound like fun," I presumed.

"It's more of a saying than an actual thing. It's another way to describe boredom or even winter blues."

"Whew! I was scared. I don't need any more neuroses in my collection."

"I know your deal," Ian informed.

"I didn't know I had a deal."

"It took me awhile, but I got you figured out."

"Oh, do tell…"

"You're like a shark." Ian sat at the round, wooden dining table in the middle of the room. "A shark has to keep moving, or it dies. Like the shark, you need high adventure or you'll die. If I had my way, I'd spend the rest of my days in this cabin with you eating winter apples. But that wouldn't work for you. You'd die eventually. Most people's contentment is a death sentence for you."

"I've been content," I answered defiantly. "I don't die, I become delusional. So, in a way, you're right. I'm more alive under stress, or I suppose 'high adventure.' If I'm not right on that edge, in the moment, I disappear."

"I've told you how to be in the moment, girl."

"Don't call me 'girl.'" I smiled because I was giving him grief. Deflection and denial, that's where my head lived. Yet I couldn't think back on my short life and disagree with Ian's assessment. I never changed, I just substituted running from angry bears and casual sex for larceny and heavy drug use. "Never mind," I said to him. "I can see your point. I was in a place to study meditation in the recent past but learned how to use a katana instead. Movement is my meditation. Adventure is how I focus on the present."

"One more," Ian said. He produced a Polaroid camera from behind his back.

"Oh, cool! I love Polaroids."

"I thought you might want a picture survey of your new home. I get the first one." He surprised me with a click and flash, the fire burning in the background behind me. He waved the picture in the air to dry while handing me the camera.

"Thanks, Ian," I said and meant it. I really loved this.

"I have extra film, too," he said, watching the picture develop. He turned it to me, showing me that stupid friendly smile, the fire out of focus, and my tits standing at attention like Hollywood stars on the red carpet.

"Pornographer."

He flipped the picture around and looked surprised. "Oh, shit. Guess I'm too used to your *ladies* being present. Nothing I can't fix with a pair of scissors."

I crowded him to glance at it again. "Don't you dare," I ordered. I liked the idea of being in Ian's photo album, all those boys and then me with my itty bitties on display.

♦ ♦ ♦

We sat in front of the fire with our bellies full, wrapped in the same blanket. The fire crackled and the burning logs hissed as trapped moisture escaped into the flame. Our bodies leaned against each other. Forgiveness filled my heart and warmed my spirit.

"We took platonic kissing off the table?" I quipped.

"Yes, Iris. That doesn't mean I don't love you. I'm just not going to become physically engaged with someone who will drop me for the first barkeep that crosses her path."

"Fair enough."

"Besides, your internship nearly is finished."

"I know."

"I can get you work."

"I'm not staying," I informed him.

"Going civilized?"

"Not on your life. Just going back to the States. The hard way, though down the mountain range."

"That's not so hard for folks like us. That's home."

"The mountains are my home but this isn't my country. I'm American and I'm borrowing grief by lingering here."

"Don't go back there," Ian said softly. "Don't go back to what you escaped from. You've arrived. Stay in that, whether here or in America."

Chapter 27

The storm passed quicker than I thought. Rene and I spent the hours quietly huddled together, holding on to each other as the gales blew against the carcasses. Though I had no fear of wolves *during* the storm, it returned after. The winds were settling and the smell of fresh-cut meat would soon permeate the forest, attracting every form of scavenger.

"We have to be moving," I announced, struggling against the dead weight of Narragansett to get ree. That managed, I rigged the reins to myself and got Rene settled.

"What's the hurry?" Rene asked. "The storm is over."

"The wolves will be here soon, attracted by the smell, the smell we are covered in."

"Shit, how are we getting away?"

"Me, Rene. I'm the horse now."

"You're too small, Iris. The horse was huge."

"It's downhill on fresh, dry snow. All we got to do is get the sledge moving. Physics will do the rest."

"Physics?" She was crying when she passed me. I couldn't stop the sledge but I ran behind and guided it with the lines. The weight before me packed the snow so I was able to run. If I tripped up, I'd be dragged by the weight of a sledge avalanche made of broken airplane seats.

This went on until I could barely keep up, out of breath. I wasn't a marathon runner, but the distance wasn't 26 miles either. The temperature was rising and my ears were popping. I took this as a good sign that we were hitting the lower elevations. I was right, the angle of descent widened and we slowed our pace. The snow disappeared suddenly and we stopped. This was something I failed to consider.

"What now?" Rene asked.

"Now I catch my breath."

"Listen, little sister. This is enough. You've done enough. It's over and you're finished."

"What are you talking about? Were so close," I insisted between deep breaths, hands on my knees.

"You may think you're Wonder Woman but this is enough. You killed a brown bear in a blizzard and just ran downhill for what felt like forever on a near vertical angle. You're fucking done. Your heart's about to explode. You've gone above and beyond and I can't take it anymore. If wolves or an owl or something eats me here, that's fine. It's nice here. The sun is out and warm. The breeze smells nice and the birds are singing. This is enough fuss over me. We made it, you're done, and it's up to them now. So, move along now and get some dinner. I'll be fine."

Rene was right, I was finished, plain done. I fell to my knees. The only option was to carry her and I wasn't fit for the task. My immediate concern was that I was dying, based on my continuing loss of energy and blurring, darkening eyesight. Rene was going to have to pull on her big girl panties and watch me die at her side because I couldn't move. I heard voices just beyond the tree-line. If there was a search party hunting for us, that was them. My last act of consciousness was to fire Captain Bill's flare gun at the crystal sky.

💧 💧 💧

I was skiing on cloud like snow, up high on white summits, following Ian down and into the forest below. The sun was bright like a nuclear bomb going off. The sky was without the constantly blowing winds I'd become accustomed to in higher altitudes. Ian disappeared among the dark trees, became nothing more than a memory. A dream I'd once had of carefree days and the deep sleep of night.

He left me alone. If only I'd reached out, maybe we'd be together with my bō in the corner of my room, sleeping off the last party. Then, I wouldn't have made the poor decisions leading to my death. I'd be home in Canada even though that wasn't home.

A home looked for me though, with eyes sadly wondering about my well-being. Home was lonely without me. I was the missing puzzle piece that put it all together, made everything whole again. Home was functional but lacking, looking out the window and hoping for my return.

Chapter 28

My memory was unclear. I had visions of a sterile hospital room, the smell of antiseptic, and a woman's face making eye contact with me. Waking with my wrists and ankles restrained, not able to rise and use the bathroom. Machines next to me and in me, attached through my mouth and down my throat. Rubber lines in my nose and veins. Tears running down my face.

The woman's face was unfamiliar and she kept repeating that I was okay. I was safe and so was Rene.

"Rene? Who the hell was Rene? I was supposed to be dead," I tried to tell the worried face, but no words escaped my throat.

"Iris, you're in a hospital." Another unfamiliar face. A man with dark, compassionate eyes and slicked-back black hair. His skin was brown like Rene's but he spoke with an accent. "Everything is okay. You're okay, Iris."

I was not okay, I was part machine and the mechanical noises were driving me insane. Whoever those people were, they were keeping me from Kira by keeping me alive. Turning me into a cyborg so I could be in Hell, never to touch those soft lips and lose myself in the brightness of her green eyes. What went wrong? I knew all about how to kill myself and should have been successful! I promised her. I promised I would!

They made me a cyborg but didn't fix that thing in my head that made me want to sleep my life away. Did that mean I had to stay in the hospital again? Stay until they ran out of money and had to let me free. Iris the cyborg, fighting crime and saving lives, doing good with tears in her eyes.

More faces of young women and men wearing scrubs. The dark-skinned man with worried looks in his eyes. People with needles and food syringes keeping me alive for their own purposes, never once asking what I wanted.

"We need you, Iris!"
"Wake up, Iris!"
"Please, Iris…"

◆ ◆ ◆

The doc had a curious look on his face. "So, Iris, a crew from the airline went to survey the crash scene and retrieve lost passengers and the black box."

"I don't think any of the passengers got lost," I said sardonically. He was a young, brown-skinned man of Middle Eastern descent. His bedside manner was soothing and slow, smile reassuring. I loved his dark, cropped hair mostly because it perfectly matched mine.

"You know what I mean," Dr. Agarwal proclaimed.

"The wolves didn't get to them first?"

"Apparently not, or I'm not sure, they didn't say."

"What did they say?"

We were alone. He made sure of that by clearing my room. I felt uneasy, like I was going to be interrogated.

I wasn't wrong.

"A team decided to follow your path down the mountain."

"That seems like a waste."

"Iris, they found a dead bear."

I hadn't forgotten about the bear, or the time I'd spent dead. I just never thought I'd have to explain it to anyone. I had nothing ready to say, no speech prepared to make myself look good. And by good I meant normal. I didn't want to be Ian's shark, I wanted to be acceptable.

"Look, man, it was him or me! Besides, that bear killed my horse. I hate that bear. I'm sure it's illegal or immoral or some shit, but fuck that bear."

"So, you just killed a brown bear by yourself."

"I fucking hated that bear."

He looked confused and more than a bit inquisitive. I knew I didn't look like much, but a sharp machete in the right hands was no match for any mammal. Especially in the hands of a rage potato like myself. Sensei made sure I was clear on that. Confidence was the strongest weapon in any warriors' arsenal. I folded the hospital blanket over, exposing my left side and hiked the hospital gown up enough to expose the thigh that had been victim to the attack in Alberta. The wound had long healed but the bite marks were still visible and an ugly chunk of meat was missing on the left side.

"Sometimes you bite the bear, sometimes the bear bites you," I informed.

The doctor grimaced and shook his head, but it was really none of his business. By the sorrowful look in his eyes, I surmised he cared more than he ought to. "You're going to have to stick around for a while. I'm worried about your health, Iris, and I want to run a few tests. You'll need to return for follow-up visits."

"Fine," I said with the impertinence of a 15-year-old.

"Is there somewhere you can stay for about a couple weeks? I know you and Rene are not from the area."

"I can get a hotel room. I have cash with my gear." I gave in easily. Caring people were hard to come by, and I was collecting a small fan club. I could've used the relaxation and adoration right about then.

"My family has a small ranch near town. You are welcome there if you need a place. If not, we would still love to have you over."

"Is that a bit irregular for your profession, Doc?"

"It is but not unprofessional. Especially in the case of a homeless bear hunter."

"Oh, don't say that, Doc. I don't hunt bears. I love bears, from a distance."

"My three children bother me every night about you and I say I cannot tell them because I'm a doctor. My wife also pesters me about you."

"I feel like a superstar," I joked.

"You should, after what you went through. At least be proud of yourself."

I blushed. "Make you a deal, Doc: Keep this on the down-low and I'll come visit your ranch and see your family."

"I can't do that," he apologized. "The press has already been to the hospital, asking about your condition. We have to keep quiet about our patients, but your friend Rene has family here who already spilled the beans. I have to give a press conference almost every day. So does the airline company."

That was a bit of a shock. My life didn't require press coverage.

"Well then, protect this for me, please." I made a gesture so he knew I wanted my face kept private. I already knew they didn't have my name. Rene would remember that I'm Iris but absolutely no one except the Canadian Forestry Service knew my last name. I never gave it out and never had to. As long as I paid cash, no one cared one hoot.

"Deal," Dr. Agarwal said, extending his hand. I shook it and couldn't help but smile. "You're a unique woman, Iris."

Unique. "I bet you say that to all the gals, Doc."

He winked and chuckled, "Don't tell my wife."

💧 💧 💧

Rene had a mother. I found that odd somehow. To me, Rene had no past or family and no prior relationships. It was because I was finished with my mission concerning her. Like Bugs Bunny did so often before me, I stumbled into a situation and had to deal with it. Part of that was to get her ass out of a blizzard and down the mountain, then I was finished and ready to move on, hide in my hole again and eat carrots. But she wasn't finished with me.

Her name was Audrey and she was just as tall as her daughter but not as thick. Somewhere along the line, Rene had started a program or played a sport that beefed her up and hardened her muscles. All of them. The girl may have had soft skin but her body was hard as a rock. I noted that when I set her fractures.

I was told her whole family was here but the hospital wouldn't let them all into my room, a father, brothers, and sisters. The exact number of siblings, I wasn't sure, but it seemed like quite a crowd for a small room where I was trying to rest. I tried to imagine someone saving a loved one very close to me and how grateful that might make me feel. I could imagine, but it just didn't click that someone might feel that way about me.

"You gave your life for my daughter," Audrey proclaimed before everyone in my hospital room.

The doctor, his nurse, a couple aides, I studied them all before answering. "But I didn't. I mean, I'm not dead, right? Should I be having an existential crisis?"

"Not at all," Dr. Agarwal said.

"There you have it," I said to Rene's mother. "I'm quite alive, scientifically speaking."

"You died for five minutes," she retorted. "Technically, you died to save my daughter. If professionals weren't close at hand to revive you, it would have been your end."

"Don't do that shit to me. I didn't intentionally die for Rene."

"Well," the doctor intervened, "you kinda did. You took on responsibility for her well-being, on top of a mountain during a blizzard. You fought off a brown bear for her. These are not activities people expect to live through."

"I fucking did. I don't go into situations expecting to die and had every expectation of getting to flatland alive. It's what I do, every day. That's how I live and I'm damn good at it. I joined an internship!"

"Well, aren't you the hard-ass?" Audrey replied.

I didn't need an invitation...

"Look," the doctor continued, "the thing is that she's still in trouble. Rene hasn't slept in over a week. Nothing we've tried has helped. In another couple days, we will have to put her in a chemically induced coma just to keep her alive."

"The last sleep she had was with you," the doctor added, filled with implications.

"Just give her a pill," I said. "She'll sleep."

"They tried that," Rene's mom explained. "She's scared, that's why nothing works. She's experiencing major anxiety after the plane crash and maybe if she were with you, that might subside."

"That's fine," I said. "Bring her in. Got room for her right here." I patted the mattress I was lying on.

A nurse clarified, "In bed, next to you, against you, with your arms around her and heart beating against her skin."

"That's rather specific."

"It's worth a try," the doctor answered.

"She could die," the mom warned. "I've tried myself, she just shakes and sweats in the bed next to me. You might not grasp how hard this is on all us or just how powerless I feel."

"It won't work. Doc, you're a scientist, you know this is fairytale bullshit. After all we went through, I'm not fond of the idea of her dying next to me in bed."

"As a scientist, I'm always aware that there is much we don't know or understand. A warm body and firm grip can be more powerful than any pharmaceutical in this instance. And it's true, she could die from this, even in a coma. Her bodily functions need natural sleep. She watched you struggle to get through great lengths to save her life. If she knows anyone who cares for her life, she knows it's you."

I was quiet for a long time while contemplating all this. I did say it was okay, and it was. I'd share my bed and skin with her. They didn't have to convince me. Still, I searched for the source of my annoying reservation. "What about me?"

"I'll be here for you," Audrey said softly. "If you do this, however it turns out, I'll see you through it."

"That's a big promise."

"I'm good for it. If it goes poorly, I'll make it good for you by my own hands. But like you coming down from that mountain alive, I fully expect this to work."

"Deal..."

🝆 🝆 🝆

They brought Rene to my room and plopped her into bed, next to me. Rene was shaking with anxiety, breathing heavy and sweating profusely. I found it hard to believe that a sedative wouldn't be the best thing for her as I wrapped my arms around her and pulled myself against her. "We got this," I whispered into her ear. Rene whimpered softly and took some deep breaths before her shaking stopped.

Soon, her breathing regulated and I assumed her eyes had closed because Audrey held up a stopwatch for me to see. It read, **37 seconds**. She smiled a sarcastic I-told-you-so and left the room. Everyone was satisfied and followed her out, except my nurse, who pulled a chair up and opened a magazine. I guessed she was in for the long haul, but she was there for my benefit.

I was awake for six fucking hours, because I'd drank a couple cups of coffee before, yet was afraid to move for fear of waking Rene. When I did fall off, it was only two hours before she was poking me awake.

"Hey, little person," she said far too loudly.
"What the hell, Rene?"
"Who's in California you're traveling so far to see?"
"No one who's alive," I whispered.
She laid next to me, face to face. "Seriously?"
"I made friends with my demon there."

Her palms rested on my belly. She moved them up to my breasts and I lightly held her forearms. I searched for my nurse to see her reaction to this molestation but she was nowhere to be found.

"And you're going back for a visit?"
"Something like that."
"Is this demon friend a top or a bottom?"
I giggled. "Oh, she's a top, there's no doubt about that."

Rene slid her hands to my shoulders and rolled over on top of me. Her leg cast landed beside my waist with a *thud* against the mattress. "So, answer me this, what's in California that you can't find here?"

"Redemption?"

"Does redemption have skin as soft as mine?" She leaned in and kissed me. Raised up to smile at me, she continued to kiss me with no indication of letting up.

I put my arms around her, my hands on her back. Her skin was indeed damn soft. I pulled her against me a bit more firmly.

She melted into me like gooey marmalade.

Chapter 29

I had horrible dreams of blood and gore. They were recurring nightmares, though only on limited occasions. They weren't anxiety dreams, they could happen any time, no matter my mental state. So, I couldn't blame it on the hospital or the pain all over my body, or near-death experience. There was only one person I ever blamed for this recurrence: Lisa.

Yet another person who felt obligated to me but couldn't wait to get some distance between the two of us. Though I had to admit I was very high-maintenance for her, she could have left me at the psych hospital and I would never had been the wiser. But she didn't. She was a pain in my ass, but that was Lisa. For better or worse, she cared enough about me to stick it out.

Her agony at that time was more than I could take and she was my first experience with saving a life under duress. Lisa left a bad taste in my mouth and a delusion in my head that made the hospital my home for years. When I saw her bloody and dying, all I could think about was Kira in the same position. I had no ability to help Kira, but my help was the only thing available to save Lisa.

It was more than I could take. There was just too much blood and responsibility. Her screams still haunted my nights. I was lucky with Rene; it was my turn to die in that episode. So, when I awoke from yet another dream of Lisa dying, I nearly had a breakdown seeing her lurking over my bed. "Am I still asleep?" I asked no one in particular.

"Iris! It's me, Lisa."

"I know, I was just having a nightmare about you."

Lisa frowned. Her forehead wrinkled, the characteristic sparkle was missing from her baby blue eyes, and she had cut her blonde locks in a pixie style. "You're not dreaming. I came to see you."

"You're different," I noticed. "Your eyes, you've aged, your hair is short."

"Gee, thanks. I was just about to say you still look like a 12-year-old boy."

"Sorry, trying to convince myself you're really here. You know my past."

"It's me, for sure."

"Gimme back my watch."

"No…"

"Where's my fucking money?"

"That, I have," she announced with a smile.

"What?"

"Seriously. I got your money."

"I don't believe this. How the hell did you know I was here?"

"Everyone knows you're here, silly. It's all over the news. Haven't you watched TV?"

"TV gives me anxiety and newspapers, well, come on. Are there pictures of me?"

"No one has pictures or film from the mountain. Just a story about you and a stewardess named Rene. But when they reported on a tiny ball of fierceness named Iris, I knew who it was. You were in a plane crash?"

"I've never been on a plane. I was up in the mountains when the plane went down. Just me and my horse."

"Horse?" Lisa looked bewildered. "Mountains?"

"We have a lot of catching up to do," I explained. "What brings you here, other than the money? I've been in a hospital twice and you've been at my bedside both times."

"I live here. In Portland. Got married and moved here."

"I'm in Portland?"

"No, dear, but close."

"How did you get the money?"

"My piece-of-shit ex is in prison, so I made the trip to Illinois and confronted him during visitation. He just gave it to me. Well, not *there*. He didn't have a pile of gangster funds in prison, but he had it in a safe deposit box and told me how to get the key."

"That's amazing!"

"You know why that asshole left me there to fend for myself? Left all of us, actually."

"I don't really care," I said. And I really didn't. I was so past that life and would probably have a complete nervous breakdown if I had to continue it. "Everything changed after, you know? What happened between us changed me. I went on a completely different path."

"But you haven't stopped being a superhero," Lisa said with a serious face.

"Whatcha mean?"

"This is your second round with this shit and the second time in the hospital. I think it's time to retire from saving people."

"I'm not flying around like Supergirl. This shit happens to me, I don't go looking for it."

"Medication time," said a voice from across the room.

"Holy shit! How long have you been here?"

"The whole time," my nurse answered flatly.

"Can a gal get some privacy, please?"

"Well, no. This is a hospital. There's no privacy."

"Can you keep what you heard under your little hat, Nurse Ratched?"

"No. This woman is right. This is the second time you've done this to the detriment of your health and safety. It's time to retire from the life-saving business."

"My detriment is fine, and it ain't a business. I've just been in the wrong place at the wrong time." I held up two fingers to emphasize the insignificant number of times.

"If you're so fine then go outside and have a cigarette."

I stood, and it hurt like hell. "Ouch, shit!"

"Are you okay?" Lisa asked, overly concerned.

"I will be if I start walking. Help my detriment to the door, please. I need some distance from Nurse Ratched."

"That's a fictional character," the nurse said. "My name's Julie. I'm a real nurse in a real hospital."

"Kiss my ass," I said under my breath from the hall.

"If you see any buildings on fire out there, keep walking," Nurse Julie shouted.

"She heard you," Lisa giggled.

"I need to find cigarettes."

"This is a hospital. They don't sell cigarettes."

sessions. Then she smiled. "You have no proof that this woman is dead," she announced.

I took a relaxed stance then, Sensei still flat on the dojo mat. "I saw the death certificate."

"A piece of paper," she said as she regained footing.

"It was shown to me at the town hall. In the records department."

"Death certificates are kept at the hospital."

"This guy, Zach, told me he found her dead. Knew the exact spot."

Sensei stood. "Some guy you fucked told you she was dead so you believe him. He got you drugged up maybe? Made you feel good?"

"I trusted him."

"Trust no one when a cadaver is not present. People, especially young women, have plenty of reasons to fake their death. I've done it myself."

"She had no reason to deceive me. I, on the other hand, did not keep my part in our pact."

"Pact?"

"We had a suicide pact. She did her part, and well, I stand before you now."

"Suicide? You wanted to die?"

"I wanted to be with her."

"Do you still?"

"Sometimes," I carefully answered. I didn't want to lie, but I didn't want to give a complete answer either.

"I'm teaching you to defend your life so that you can just throw it away?"

"I'm worth a fighting chance," I argued. "At any given moment, my spirit may heal, but I have always fought for autonomy. My life is no person's to decide one way or another. When I die, it will be my choice. I will go by my own hand."

"So be it," was all sensei would say. She turned and walked away, leaving me to my make-believe autonomy.

🜂 🜂 🜂

"What's happened to the world while I was away?" I lamented. I was hobbling down the hallway with Lisa holding my arm for support. My legs were stiff and wobbly from overextending myself on the mountain with Rene.

"I have about half a pack of Marlboros you can have."

"You're a godsend, Lisa. When did you start smoking?"

"I always have, guess not in front of you though. Your ass is hanging out of your hospital gown."

I twisted my neck to see the back of my gown and immediately regretted it. Sharp pains shot through sore muscles and caused me to yelp. "That hurt! I don't know why I looked. I don't really care. My ass is like my tits: nonexistent."

"Sorry, just wanted you to know."

"All the other patients have their ass hanging out," I observed. "Let's find a place to smoke."

"Outside then. We have to take the elevator."

The inside of the stainless-steel box was confining. I never suffered from claustrophobia, but I was used to the expanse of the outside world. "I gotta get out of here," I said when we were finally smoking. The hospital grounds had a garden area and benches, which Lisa and I were occupying.

"Just do what the doctor says," Lisa said.

"Why aren't you smoking with me?"

"I don't smoke in front of people."

"I'm not people."

"It's just a weird quirk. Ignore it."

"Don't you want one?"

"Shut up."

I took my lit cigarette and held it up to her mouth. She gave me a guarded, sidelong glance. I winked at her and she went ahead and took a drag, her soft lips touching my fingers and making me feel tingly, straight down to my toes.

"So have you heard from Kira?" Lisa asked.

"Heard she was dead."

"Oh no!"

"Don't get too excited. Upon further critical ciphering, I may be convinced to have a second look at that situation."

"She faked her death?"

"She may have faked a suicide to dupe me. To dupe everyone."

"That sounds about right. I know a couple women who did that."

"Really? I was told it was a thing girls do but I wasn't sure."

"I don't understand why she would want to fool you."

"You never met her, not in the physical sense. She's kind of a shit, and I wasn't putting out at that time."

"There's something different about you," Lisa noticed. I held the cigarette up and she took another puff. "I mean, you're the same, just... more girly."

I laughed out loud.

🌢 🌢 🌢

I was sitting on a log along a clear pond, trying to land a trout with my new fishing pole. The sky was bright blue and the air crisp. Just what I wanted, what I loved. If Ian hadn't been with me, I might have cried for joy.

"Are you sure about this bait?" I asked. The morning was slipping by without so much as a nibble.

"I've had really good luck with fish eggs in the past," he explained. "Some days they just aren't interested, kid."

"I thought you were going to come up with a standard pet name for me. 'Kid' is demeaning."

"You're a kid to me."

"We're the same age!"

"I mean as a naturalist. You're just starting, but you're right. You're no kid, Iris. You're a full-grown woman."

"You think so? I still see myself as a little girl."

"That'll change."

"How do you know?"

"Because you've changed since coming here. You've softened. Somehow, the wilds of nature have made you womanlier, more, feminine."

I giggled at that just as my bobber went down and I felt the tug of my first ever lake trout.

Currently, on the hospital bench, I said, "I don't know if 'girly' is how to describe me, Lisa. Something has changed. I've become soft inside, mellowed. I want different things for myself."

"Says the woman who killed a brown bear with a machete."

"That's on the news, too?!"

"Forget it. What things do you want? Are you living in a material world now?"

"Like goals... Maybe I want a home."

"You're welcome to come stay with us a while."

"Thanks. There's this girl though..."

Lisa nodded and giggled. "There always is."

"The doctor here has taken an interest in my recovery. I can get him to release me early if I stick close. At a hotel, or with this girl--if I can talk her into it."

Lisa reached into her purse and withdrew a thick envelope. "This is 10,000 dollars. That squares us, but it doesn't make you a stranger."

"Wow, Lisa! You didn't have to do this."

"Guess I've also gotten a little soft."

"Can you hold onto it for me? I have nowhere to put it but up my ass."

"So, are you going to investigate Kira's passing?"

We talked in the elevator back up to my room.

"That's where I was heading when the plane went down."

"But now you're reconsidering?"

"I really want to know, but I really want to stick around here. Everyone is so nice to me. And I have cash. Even without your envelope, I made a good chunk of change in Canada during my internship."

"Internship? Does this have to do with the horse?"

The elevator opened at our floor.

"It does," I laughed.

Nurse Julie was no longer camped in my room. I sat my bare ass on the bed and told my story to Lisa. She listened intently and her only comment was not to return to Monterey. She removed the envelope of cash again and put it in my lap.

"Just relax a bit. Learn to enjoy who you are now the way everyone else is, the way I am."

I smiled and hid my eyes from her.

"At least come visit me. I'd so love to have you. I always knew you could be happy like this. It would be fun."

"I'm happy?"

"It shows, Iris. You're on fire from the inside out. I'd hate to see that flame put out by someone selfish enough to fake their suicide."

At that point Rene wheeled herself into my room followed by my doctor.

"We're gonna be roommates," Rene announced.

Lisa and I raised a single eyebrow at the same time.

"That's interesting news," I said.

"The doctor wants me to stay the same way he wants you to. I live outside of L.A. by the way, by myself."

"No cats?" Lisa asked.

It was Rene's turn to raise a brow. "Do I look like a cat person?"

"Sorry," Lisa said. "Don't mean to offend you. But, yes?"

"This is my friend and associate, Lisa," I introduced Rene and Dr. Agarwal.

"Associate?" Rene asked. "What kinda business you two into?"

"If I told you," Lisa said with a slicing her throat, "I'd have to kill you."

"Ah. Well, that's some pretty shady sounding shit. Anyway, my leg is in too bad a shape to travel home, where I would have dogs, if I wasn't a flight attendant. The doc feels that since you and I are pretty chummy, maybe we could bunk together until he releases us to our own recognizance."

Lisa gave a sidelong glance and I gave her a thumbs up.

"So it's okay with blondie here," Rene quipped.

"Lisa here," I began, "is a stray I rescued in the past, not unlike yourself." I laughed though no one else did.

"But we're retiring from the lifesaving career," came Julie Ratched's voice from behind the group.

"You're still here?" I asked, not able to see her.

"You've done this before?" Rene asked.

"Not on purpose," I answered.

"Great way to pick up women though…" Rene accused.

"I'll be driving home to my husband tonight," Lisa informed. "As cute as Iris may be, I'm afraid that without a penis, we are destined to stay close friends."

"So it's like that?" I asked.

Lisa bent down and hugged me. "I'm making a coffee run. Can I get anyone something?"

"A bottle of beer," Rene said.

Lisa kissed me long and hard just to spite Rene before standing again and leaving.

"Is that supposed to make me jealous?" Rene asked me.

I shrugged, still a bit delirious from Lisa's lips.

"You two are lesbians," Dr. Agarwal said excitedly.

"Look who's joined the party," Rene snarked while rolling her eyes.

"That's such a coincidence that a lesbian saved another lesbian's life," the doctor observed.

"Well, I'm a gold star lesbian," Rene said. "Iris here hasn't announced a side. For all I know, she's just a pervert."

Nurse Julie spoke from across the room: "You two, stop with the labels. It's no one's business who or how Iris falls in love or whether she has golden stars. This is too much, my patient needs rest. Now shoo, all of you."

The doctor quickly obeyed, wheeling Rene out of the room. She made a signal with her thumb and pinky finger that she would call later.

"Thanks, Julie," I said. "That was a little too much."

"Just doing my job. My graduating class from nursing school was, well, close. But we didn't like when people threw the term 'lesbian' at us. Back then, it was a very clinical label. I suppose today it may not carry the same stigma, yet we didn't want what was considered a deviant diagnosis following us around all our lives. We all wanted jobs and husbands."

"Oh, it carries a lot of luggage still," I assured. "You don't seem very old, Nurse Julie."

"I'm not." She was checking my vitals and tucking in my sheets around me. "It wasn't all that long ago. But still…"

"But still…"

It was at that moment Lisa decided to return, a coffee in one hand and two bottles of cold beer in the other. "Shit," she said when she looked around for Rene.

"Beer?" I asked with amazement. "For real?"

"Of course. It's a Catholic hospital."

"Hand me one," I ordered, not understanding what Catholicism had to do with it.

Chapter 30

The airline company didn't dare stop giving Rene a paycheck after all she'd been through, even though she wasn't returning to work for a long time. I was discharged from the Sisters of the Order of Some Saint Hospital much earlier than she was. With my own cash stash, I rented a cabin in Summer Lake. It wasn't exactly Rene's cup of tea since she was a city girl, but the Oregon outback kept me sane. While I was losing my habit for vagrancy, the wide open spaces relaxed me.

Alone with the quiet, I spent some time mourning Narragansett. I doubted ever returning to Alberta, so part of my grieving process was to pen a letter to Ian, explaining the heroic loss of my loving companion. He did wonder if the sweet beauty would survive me, and the answer was apparently not.

So I stayed a few days, eating and getting my coffee at the restaurant. The cabin had a full kitchen but I had no transportation into town. A taxi brought me there and a taxi would have to return me when Rene was released. I was sure the hospital would get us back with their own transportation, but we were going to need a vehicle. For better or worse, I was no longer alone and had to consider Rene's healing process over the next few months. I wasn't just taking care of myself, getting around on horseback, my machete my main tool, and foraging the wilderness for food. Adapting to the civilized world would be a necessity I never needed before. It was going to be a more complicated adventure.

There was time to kill before Rene would be released. Days or maybe weeks. I eventually stopped going to the restaurant, enjoying fresh coffee, and stayed in bed—for how long, I lost track. Regular updates came from the phone in my bedroom. I had cigarettes and kept the windows open so the smoke could escape. I tried reading *Walden* but couldn't concentrate. The cabin was fully equipped but the TV stayed off and I had no motivation to find music on the radio.

It was just one of my times I spent down. Ian had experienced this but Rene was ignorant to my depression episodes. I guessed I just bottomed out. There was so much excitement all at once when all I wanted was to be left alone. Rene was great, and the sex we stole in our hospital rooms was fantastic, but there was always the nagging idea that she felt she owed me. If she thought that, then it was a debt she would never be square with in her head. She reassured me but I was skeptical.

"What's for dinner?" Rene asked on one of her phone updates.

"Uh," I answered. "Cigarettes."

"You on some diet?"

"Just too comfy to scrounge up food."

"Your voice sounds sleepy. Are you still in bed?"

"Just a little nap," I reassured.

"It's noon, Iris. Get up and get some breakfast."

"Yes, *Mom*," I replied while yawning.

"So tell me more about the cabin and pond. You catch any fish yet?" Rene was probing. She may have been on to me.

I wasn't hiding my condition and I wasn't ashamed that the blue cloud settled on me from time to time. I just wasn't going to explain over the phone. "I'm okay, Rene. Just need a little down time. This is normal for me, honey." My voice was trailing off as sleep started to make another pass at me.

"'Honey'?"

"Yeah, baby. You're my honey bear. I miss you."

"You gotta give me something to go on here, Iris. Are you drinking?"

"No, probably a good idea though. But that will require a shower and getting pants on to go buy a bottle. Better off here in bed."

"Gimme something, sweetheart, or I'm sending an ambulance."

"Seriously? You can just order up an ambulance and the doctor will say, 'Oh, okay, let's send one'?"

"Cut it out. You're scaring me."

"I had friends once, a whole shit ton of them, and they all called me Titmouse." I attempted to change the subject.

"Titmouse?"

"Yeah. True story. You haven't seen me totally naked yet or I would have told you the story."

"Is it a tattoo you have that says **Titmouse**? You white folks and your damn tattoos."

"No, it's something else. Something for you to look forward to. See, I gave you something. I don't know shit about you but I gave you Titmouse. That's how negotiation works. Someone has to give in first and be the bigger person."

"Honey, there's nothing to me. You know it all. I fly around the country all week, I live in L.A., and I have no cats. You, on the other hand, are buried under complicated layers of history and experience. Titmouse is just the tip of the iceberg."

"It's not so complicated being a degenerate."

"I don't like that talk. I'd bust anyone in the chops who talked that way about you."

"Sorry. That was childish."

"I'm gonna talk to the doc today about getting out of this joint. I'm going stir crazy and I'm worried about you. If he won't release me, I'll just leave."

"The airline won't cover your hospital expenses if you leave without the doctor's release. Just hold tight and I'll make it over there for a visit."

"What do you know about it? The Airline will throw piles of cash at me to keep me from suing. You worry about you, I can take care of myself. You've done enough for me."

"I'm gettin' up."

"Don't call a taxi."

"Headin' for the shower…"

"I'm hanging up now."

I didn't get up at all. And I wasn't going to answer the phone for the rest of the day. Luckily, it never rang.

💧 💧 💧

The next morning, I was woken by the television. I roused, anxious someone was in the living room. When I walked out, I found Dr. Agarwal sitting on the modern sofa, watching a sitcom and laughing like a giddy teenager. "I love this show," he exclaimed, shaking his head and chuckling.

"What's up, Doc?"

He pointed at me and laughed some more. "Ah, just like Bugs Bunny. I'm watching this *Gilligan's Island* I seen before."

"Seriously? I was sleeping."

"You look like shit and you sleep too much." Somehow, I didn't think that was deemed good bedside manner.

"I don't care what I look like 'cause I wasn't expecting company. If I knew you were coming, I'd have baked a cake!"

"Come sit by me if you don't smell too badly." He patted the cushion next to him.

I obeyed. This show is all slapstick," I observed.

"I know, it's funny!"

"No, it's not. Don't they let you watch this shit in the doctor's lounge?"

Dr. Agarwal became serious. "Everyone has made me in charge of your well-being."

"Well, that's not fair."

"The hospital describes you as 'high profile.' A case everyone is scrutinizing. I came to see if you're depressed."

"Rene sent you."

"She did. But no one else knows. If they did, you would go back to the hospital."

"Because I'm high profile."

"Yes. So I'm giving you a chance for some help before they do that. Rene can be quiet but her family seems to have a lot of emotional investment in you. And they can't shut their mouths in front of a TV camera."

"They think they owe me something. I hate that. Now I'm more like a possession than a person to them."

"*Aaie*," Agarwal waved that off with a sour face. "Let's just get you out of bed. Come see my ranch, right now."

"Is that how you plan to fix my depression? Look, Doc, this just happens to me about twice a year. Rene just didn't know about it. All I gotta do is ride it out for a few days."

"You do not have a few days, I warned you already. They will come for you."

"Oh yeah, 'high profile.' So what do you recommend?"

"I have something for you at my ranch to give you a purpose for getting out of bed."

"What could be *so grand* that I'd leave this paradise?"

"I have a horse for you."

"Say what?"

"A horse. A youth Palomino mare."

"My god, Doctor, that's a little too much!"

"I didn't buy it. The town did. They asked for donations on television and acquired a horse for the one you lost."

"What town?"

"This town, Summer Lake, and Silver Lake, and Paisley. All the surrounding area."

"What could possess those people to do that for me?"

"You're joking, Iris."

I shook my head, then tears formed and rolled down my cheeks.

"It's okay, Iris," Dr. Agarwal reassured. "They all pitched in a little and the ranch it came from gave them a deal so it would be easy. It's a common horse so it's not like they bought you a Maserati."

"You have this animal?" I asked softly, trying not to sob.

"Of course."

"I'll get in the shower."

Dr. Agarwal was a seriously careful driver.

My excitement rose with every mile. I needed distraction. "May I ask about Rene's recovery?"

"All you have to do is read the papers, Iris."

"Let's just pretend I haven't been. Any chance she can get out soon?"

"Rene just received her walking boot yesterday and has been in physical therapy today. If she does as well as expected, she can leave the next day."

"Tomorrow?"

"Yes, tomorrow. Will she be staying with you?"

"Yup."

"Then tomorrow."

"What's a walking boot?"

"Rene needs support so she can walk with crutches. Her fracture was bad and surgery complicated. Without the boot, she could reinjure the fracture even with her muscles developed so strongly."

"So no wheelchair?"

"If the physical therapist says so."

"I need to get my shit together, I guess."

"You need this horse, Iris. She's a beauty!" Dr. Agarwal leaned close to the steering wheel, driving like a grandma with eyes on the hood of the car. He turned slowly. It was a nice late model BMW he drove and I believed he didn't want it hurt more than he was concerned about his own safety. Though, on his own property, he drove it like a race car. Instead of introducing his family, he went directly to the stables.

The doctor spoke after exiting the car. "Iris, everyone is aware of your desire for privacy. I did as you asked. So this is an anonymous gift just in appreciation of your strength, courage, and what you did for Rene."

There came the tears again.

"Follow me," Dr. Agarwal said as he entered the barn. He closed the door and led me to a nondescript center stall.

I was overwhelmed with the people who did this, and then the beauty of the young animal Dr. Agarwal presented. "Oh my god," I said, looking into the soft, knowing eyes of the blond-maned animal. I reached out to touch her nose and she didn't flinch. It seemed she was making eye contact with me. "What's her name?" I asked.

"That's for you to decide."

I felt her neck, then stroked her mane. Her only reaction was to nudge my shoulder with her nose and snort. "Her name is Thorn," I announced through the tears.

"Beautiful name for a beautiful horse," Agarwal remarked. He talked softly and deliberately. "Take as long as you like, Iris. This is your beauty. She can stay here as long as you need while I keep track of you and your girlfriend. I don't know your plan but, if you wish, they can include Thorn, free and clear. A gift from the people of this land, all its lakes, and forests. In honor of your anonymity, they too wish to be anonymous."

"Do they know she's here?" I asked with skepticism.

"They honor your wishes, Iris, which is just as well. If they were to see you in your strength and confidence, they may fall to the ground and worship you."

I finally laughed, long and hard. Thorn was smaller than Narragansett and still it was going to be a jump to ever mount her. "That's my saddle," I exclaimed, just noticing the pile of gear outside of Thorn's stable door.

"Right, Iris. Everything from the crash site was recovered. This was brought to me, um, in awe."

"In reverence?"

"Right, Iris. That's it."

I fought hard to remain in good humor and not let the tears flow again. What was the deal with these people? "Do they have any idea how tiny and insignificant I am?"

"Some of the contributors did some snooping and know exactly how small your height is but how large your heart is. They think you are a great reference after returning from Canada."

"Resource?"

"Yes, Iris, that's right."

"Do they expect me to work for them?"

"No." He did that swiping thing again with his hand. "Anywhere you are, anywhere you and Thorn go, you will be a resource for this country. You are American?"

"I am. Just had a little trouble getting home."

"I'm going to my family now." He pointed out the barn door. "When you are finished, come up and meet them and have some lunch. Take all the time you need." He smiled that smile that was so reassuring in the hospital. The intelligent smile that let me know he had a handle on things and all would be well.

After he left, I approached Thorn again. I raised my hand and lightly stroked her neck. She felt muscular. Thorn nodded her head up and sounded off a bit with a loud sneeze. I stepped in and rested my head against her neck and stroked her mane. She bopped me a couple times on my back with her snout and then was still. It was almost like being with Narragansett again, a bittersweet feeling, a reunion of sorts with a majestic animal. I hugged harder and heard the noises inside, felt her heartbeat and breathing. "I promise," I said. "Another woman will never come between us."

Soon, I would saddle Thorn and ride her for the first time. The rest of the night though, I was required to devote to Dr. Agarwal's family of adoring fans. This would be my first and only time to tell the tale of how I came into their father's care. I hoped I could remember to exclude the curse words.

At least, I thought, I'm out of bed.

Chapter 31

"Where have you been?" Rene asked as I pushed the front door open with one foot.

I was heavily laden with fishing gear, making for the back door and shore's edge of our backyard pond. "I went to the sports store," I answered.

"It's seven in the morning!"

"Early bird catches the worm."

Rene hobbled on her big boot, following me to the dock.

"I got a rod and reel, tackle box with hooks and shit, a folding chair, and catfish dip." I was overly excited. I quickly set up my line with a treble hook and slip bobber, covered the hook with dip, and cast a short distance from the dock while Rene patiently watched. The sun had risen hours before but hung low in the sky, reflecting yellow light off the still water. It was serene but I had other plans than to relax. "Catfish are fun to catch 'cause they fight and roll hard, all under the surface so you don't really know what you're up against until it surfaces at the shore," I explained.

"Catfish," Rene repeated.

"Yeah, they're ugly but super strong. All these man-made ponds have catfish to reduce the population. Otherwise, the water would be overrun with little, useless sunfish. Most folks let the hook lay on the bottom but I like a bobber. The big fellas will rise to chomp a tasty morsel while the little guys feed off the mud."

"You sure are the outdoors type."

"All my life. Canada gave me the chance to learn how to live with the outdoors. How to thrive and eat instead of steal and hide." With that, my bobber went down and I spent the next ten minutes adjusting my reel's drag and fighting something strong on the end of my line.

"That was quick," Rene observed. Her voice resounded the same excitement I was feeling in my chest.

I got the fish out of the water and nearly to the dock before it shook and the line snapped. "Did you see that? Did that really happen?!"

"That was a big, ugly fish."

"I bet it was over ten pounds. I guess I'll need to go back for a net. Didn't think I'd need one but a big fish above the surface is different than a big one below the surface." I rigged my line up to try again, figuring Rene would lose interest and go back in, and so I tempted her with information from town: "There's a van for sale in the parking lot of the sports store."

"A van?"

"A white utility van someone used for work. It's a thousand bucks but looks like it's in good shape. The guy in the store said he can call the seller for a test drive."

"White utility van. You mean a serial killer van."

"A what?"

"Haven't you seen *Silence of the Lambs*?"

"A movie?"

"Yeah, everyone's seen it."

"I've been kinda out of touch with what's playing the past few years." Just then, my replacement bobber went down.

💧 💧 💧

An older gentleman responded to the phone call and arrived in the parking lot to show us the van. He immediately took a liking to Rene, but who wouldn't? Her compact, muscular body had curves in all the right places, and her red lipstick smile was genuine. To a lonely old guy with silver whiskers, she was just Rene who everyone wanted to know and dote up to.

Rene explained to the old timer the reason for the crutches, cast, and walking boot. He recognized the story from TV news so now she was not just a young, gorgeous flesh snack, but also a local celebrity. She was careful of my wishes for ambiguity and did not point me out as her mountain girl savior but explained I was a roommate who would have to do all the driving while Rene's leg bones healed.

"We're losing a small fortune to the taxi company," Rene explained.

This shifted the owner's attention to me as he sized me up to determine how such short legs would reach the gas pedal. "I think you're just tall enough of a young woman to drive this. It's a three-speed manual shift though. Gear handle behind the wheel, clutch pedal and all."

"I can drive a stick," I informed.

"Let's give her a whirl then," he suggested.

The beast bucked like Narragansett spooked by a skunk until I got used to the shifting. After that, I noticed how well the engine ran. "This thing is in good shape," I reported. The back of the van had shelving and small, built-in cabinets with doors. A steel-mesh divider and door separated the front cab from the rear. The owner had used it for contracting work of some sort. "Are you a plumber?" I asked.

"Electrician," he answered. "Retired. I can't wait to get rid of this thing. It was my prison cell on wheels."

I pulled back into the parking lot and glanced in Rene's direction. "I think we'll take it."

"Well, I'll be damned," he exclaimed, "I didn't think this would sell so quick. We can get a transfer inside!"

As he headed for the store, I took Rene aside to explain to her that I wasn't street legal, as a license was not required to ride a horse. "You'll have to buy the van. I'll give you cash to cover your check."

"I understand. But I really do need you to drive me around. You gotta get legal."

"Shouldn't be a problem."

"Understatement of the year…"

💧 💧 💧

My days became filled with fishing, visiting Thorn, exploring the surrounding outback, and sex with Rene. She cooked and I cleaned, we were a regular, domesticated pair. I drove her to physical therapy and the sights and shops she wanted. Sometimes, we had a nice meal out. After a week, I was bored out of my mind. That's when the questioning started flowing in my head. One thing I knew was that L.A. could not be in my future. I wouldn't survive in a city like that. Rene and I wouldn't last and then I'd find myself back on the streets, doing exactly what I had before. Separated from myself, separated from Thorn.

My main flow of thoughts were drifting back to Kira. But I'd tasted the love of good women, I didn't need to unlock that mystery. Or did I? She was the one who got away, the love I let slip through my fingers at a time I was most vulnerable. I had longed and dreamt of her for so long that perhaps I just developed this larger-than-life version of her, wanted to worship at her feet.

I was a selfish little shit, talking myself into taking the van and leaving Rene stranded. It would only be for a bit before she got help from the hospital and the airline getting her back home to sunny L.A.. I didn't really want to lose her, but she was a sure thing and my monster heart longed for the final conquest. My chance to redeem myself in Kira's eyes, a girl who'd done nothing for me except give me a mad ride to a psych ward. *If*, that was, she was alive.

I had to know.

Chapter 32

It was time to do my ghost imitation. Slip out in the dark of night unnoticed and never to be seen again. I had my backpack road-ready and the front door open, about to leave this all behind me: Rene, Thorn, the doctors, and my fan club.

"How often has this ever really worked for you?" a voice asked from outside the house. It was Rene, sitting on the porch bench, accusingly pointing a crutch at me.

"How did you know?" I was caught but confused.

"You packed last night like I wouldn't find out. It was almost like a cry for help."

I thought about her question. The answer was no, ghosting never worked for me. I always justified it that everyone would be better off without me. In most cases though, I'd return to the scene of the crime.

"I know where you're going," Rene accused. "Back to Monterey. Were you hoping I'd make you stop? Fucking stop. Don't go!"

All I could answer was, "I have to know."

"That girl's dead, Iris."

"I need proof."

"You still love her?"

"Of course. I mean, not like I love you. We had a pact."

"You broke it."

"Yeah, but outright. How fucked up is it if she faked her end. What if I had gone through with the bargain, thinking she had gone ahead of me?"

"That's a lot of cloak and dagger for that girl to go through. Supposedly a girl who wanted you in the first place. The whole story you told me couldn't have been an act. I want you and I wouldn't go through all that just for some weird death pact. I'd make a weird sex pact instead because I want you. She's no girl anymore, by the way, and neither are you. You're a grown woman who needs to think like one."

This made some sense. Yet so did Sensei's argument. If she did fake her death, I might never know the circumstances that would lead her to deceive me.

"What if she had to?"

"Fine. Go find your lost love. I'll wait if I have to. I'm not going to disappear. I'll be right here."

I glared into those dark eyes. If Rene was coy or manipulative, those eyes would be mysterious and enticing. But she wasn't. She was honest. Made no bones about how she felt and how she wanted the same in return, emotionally and physically. Kira was similar though. When she couldn't have me in life, she wanted me in death. Same mentality with a suicidal twist. "Come with me," I offered, begged actually. That was the only solution. "We could take the van, like a *Scooby Doo* adventure. It's not that far. We drive through the pass to California, down the coast, and *wham bam*. Unless maybe you're too gimpy."

"I have a walking boot and crutches and I can still out run your scrawny, white ass," Rene boasted.

"So?"

"It's a long way. Don't try to fool me with your bullshit *Scooby Doo* stories."

"It won't take that long if we do it together. By the end, it won't feel long enough."

"No fucking blizzards."

"No blizzards."

"No horses."

"Thorn will stay here."

"No bears."

"I can't make that promise."

"Well, two outta three. That's pretty good odds."

"Six to two, pick 'em."

"What?"

"An old joke, sorry."

🔥 🔥 🔥

I loved atlases since I could remember. I sat with the map on my lap in the parking lot of a fast food burger joint, chomping my food and looking ahead. Maybe that was it, I felt like I could see into the future by following the route we would take to Monterey.

"You should stop eating that shit," Rene suggested.

"It's horrible, I know. I love this though." Grease and mayonnaise dripped from my chin as I took another bite. I chewed and swallowed. "I spent so much time eating karate food that I just go nuts eating this garbage."

"What's karate food?"

"Leaves, twigs, and dirt," I joked. "I did feel great though."

"No one's asking you to stop, just do it occasionally. I'm getting sick of this crap. I need a sit-down dinner."

"Gotta keep on rollin'," I pointed out.

"No, we don't. We're on a *Scooby Doo* adventure. Remember?"

"Right, we got a mystery to solve."

"Wonder who will be underneath the mask?"

"That's a scary thought," I laughed. "Okay, slowin' things down and looking for fun. We'll find a Denny's or something for dinner."

"That's close to what I want."

"Yeah, we can do better." I handed Rene the atlas and began driving. The back of the van was loaded with packed clothes and some sleeping gear. On a nice night, we could sleep in the van if we wanted. "Ever slept on a beach?" I asked.

"I live in L.A.."

"So that's supposed to be a yes?"

"Well, I've passed out on a beach, but not purposefully slept. Have you?"

"I hate the ocean but wouldn't mind sex on the sand."

"Little critters in the sand."

"Little critters in our butts!"

"That's pretty gross."

"We'll use a blanket, silly. Roll out the sleeping bags."

"That doesn't sound all bad," Rene admitted.

"Not bad at all. We can get further south, where it's warmer, and find a beach where we can have a fire. Roast hot dogs and marshmallows."

"Okay, I'm in. Until then, I look forward to Denny's."

"Your wish is my command."

That's how it went for the remainder of the trip. We made it as fun as possible, stopping for wayside apples and followed billboards to Bigfoot hideouts. Anything for a distraction, as far as I was concerned. I did want to get to Monterey, but, at the same time, dreaded it. I knew it would be a significant event with consequences. What I didn't know was if these consequences had to do with Kira, or Rene. There was something about our relationship that didn't fit together. We were barely in sync and I was afraid that was my fault. I couldn't get past her gratitude.

Rene never came right out and said she was grateful, I know she thought of me as foolish for wasting so much energy on her well-being. It may not have come out in words, but shown in our love-making. She was relentlessly generous and considerate. Or was secretly angry at me for forcing her into sledding down a mountain when all she really wanted was to be left there in the dark freeze of the airplane fuselage. I did die trying and that probably really pissed her off. That was where the pin dropped, I guessed, unresolved issues between us. I mean, could she express her feelings with her family, the hospital, and news stations making such a fuss about her? I was clueless on a good time to broach the subject.

Rene was not. "I think I'm holding a grudge," Rene said as we closed in on Monterey. We'd just slept on the beach for the third time, falling asleep naked in each other's arms under the stars.

"Against me?"

"Yup."

"I was afraid of that."

"I don't like owing anyone, and I feel like I owe you."

"I thought we were past that."

"I love you. And thanks for saving my life. You did a lot for me. I guess I just don't understand."

"You have the same self-perception problem I have."

"That so?"

"It is, Rene. You don't understand that you're worth it. You're worth my best attempt. And I can't help but think you would do the same for me. You would have given anything to keep those passengers alive and me safe. It sucks being powerless because of an illness or injury. I can't imagine the helpless feeling you must have had."

"I don't get it. You could have got on your horse and rode away, it would have cost you nothing."

"Ha! Nothing but my soul."

"You believe in God?"

"Not really, but I know I have a soul, and if I can't keep myself clean, I can keep my soul clean."

"I don't believe in God. I don't believe I have a soul. You maybe, but not me."

"It's a thing you have to build yourself," I informed her.

"Don't understand."

"I don't have the literature on hand to back me up, but it's out there. God doesn't give us fully intact souls, we make them from the ground up. We give birth to our own souls."

"Enough," Rene ordered.

"Would you have left me?"

Rene looked at me. I stole a glance from the highway to see the tears in her eyes. *No*, she mouthed.

"Let's leave it at that," I suggested. "I've been a good girl. Time for burgers and milkshakes."

"I agree," Rene answered with an unsteady voice.

I didn't really care if Rene would have left me on a mountain or not. I didn't leave her, and that was my thing. Whatever others did was their shit to deal with as long as I was true to myself. And "myself" was on the way to the very destination when the plane crash interrupted my travels. It was a trip I would have eventually finished with or without Rene, though I was glad she was with me.

"What are you hoping to find in Monterey?" Rene asked after regaining her composure. She stared at the passing landscape as she talked.

I stole a glance of her thoughtful look, set jawline, long hair curling back. "Thought I told you that story…"

"You talk about souls and demons without giving away purpose. I've heard the story you tell but not the true purpose that matches your *spiritual* purpose."

I laughed without any regret. "I have no spiritual purpose. I talk about souls and demons philosophically. Kira was my demon, if she killed herself... She represented what I struggled against because she was so open and committed. No doubt in her mind about dying, not like me... I had the desire, but it matched my desire for her."

"And if she's alive?"

"Then she's a real piece of shit, ain't she?" I laughed.

"So no purpose?"

"I told you before what my purpose was."

Rene continued looking out the window until the flash of remembrance struck her. "Redemption?"

I nodded.

"My God, from what?"

"Survivor's guilt. Not just surviving, but finding a way to live. Kira wasn't a coward, but neither was I, and now I'm alive and feel better... In our own ways, we had the courage to change the toxic lives we were muddled in, to cure ourselves of our illness. If I find her body, where it rests, I mean proof of death, I'll feel finally relieved."

"And if she's alive," Rene continued, "you have serious unresolved issues. Remember that if she killed herself, it was her choice."

"Just the same as it was yours to get on that plane to L.A.," I answered as I turned into Whataburger.

Chapter 33

We ebb smokey bright
when the warm rains diminish.
Demolition moonlight water dancing
with the muddy river monsters lumbering up stream.

She laughs without making a sound,
eyes sparkling - deepening dark.
And denies having intimacy
with the fingernail of God,
about healing old wounds
wet - and fiery red.

When the bathroom tiles
flood with plundered crimson memories,
when the smell of copper
fills the air,
wait for the monsters
heading upstream
and the smoke rising
from friendly shores.

Short denim skirt
and deep-set grave eyes.
She misses the monsters
and their emotional distance.
Knee-high leather fuck-me pumps
and a smile that reminds me of home.

Happy junkie giggles echo in the dark,
black eyeliner – half-moon eyes.
Ruby red lips utter pilfered promises,
lingering when she's gone,
in the fragrance trailing after
of a cold mountain sunrise.

Zach was no longer the superintendent of the apartment building in Monterey. The current super suggested I try him at his current residence, the Monterey county jail. The apartment building had a bittersweet feel, looking at it from the outside. The landscaping was kept up and it looked a bit better than I remembered. I knew the window from the street, the one Kira was looking out when she died. A shiver hit me and I figured Rene would not be thrilled about the news concerning Zach. She hated prisons, especially the pat-down and searches involved with visiting an inmate. All this was relayed to me as an excuse she used to stop visiting her cousin, since released, who was not enthusiastic about making the trip over the mountains when she was laid up in the hospital.

He was the family member with the biggest mouth, sounding off to the press about his brave sister who survived the plane crash by the grace of God who used the tiny, white girl as an instrument of His divine design. Likening me to David downing a giant Philistine with a single stone from his slingshot. This was what happened in prison. Women gained weight while men found the Lord.

Zach, on the other hand, became a bitter soul who hadn't been high or gotten laid in a couple years. To him, I represented a plain target for his bitter disposition and sober mind. The knowledge that he was a piece of shit and a liar did not deter my quest.

"Well, if it ain't the little lost girl?" Zach said from behind a Plexiglas window. He wasn't smiling. In fact, he looked annoyed and I feared I'd lose his attention quickly.

"Glad to see I'm so memorable," I chided.

"I thought for sure you'd be dead by now."

"Like Kira?"

"Ya know you gotta lay off that girl," Zach informed me.

So Kira was alive. No fanfare or romantic reunion. Just Zach looking at me through Plexiglas at the visitation center.

"You told me she was dead."

"That chick is bad news and she knows it, that's why she cooked up an elaborate *Hogan's Heroes* plan to shake you."

Rene waited for me in the lobby, hating these visits. She didn't want an encore performance for some idiot she didn't know.

"What if it didn't work out?" I asked. "What if I kept my end of the bargain?"

"I was there the whole time, you zombie," he disclosed.

"I don't remember."

"That's 'cause I was in the closet, hiding. You were too fucked up to notice. God, you focus hard on a single thing."

"You saw everything?"

"Ya, you little psycho. You're no less crazy than your girlfriend."

"Where is she?"

"I don't give that kinda information out for free. I need a hundred bucks in my canteen account."

"That's not worth a hundred. How about $20?"

"Tell ya what, since you were such a good little fuck, I'll give ya a half-off discount."

"You were a bit better of a person last time I saw you."

"Jail does things to a guy's attitude."

The place was pretty rundown and smelly. I didn't know county jails were so secure; I'd envisioned a face to face meeting at a table. Something more open where I could buy him lunch or treats. Hard to be charming, talking into a telephone receiver. "You're in for drugs, I suppose."

"Burglary. But I was stealing drugs, so ya. Look, Iris, I'll give you a taste. Kira ain't in the country no more."

"That doesn't intrigue me in the least."

"No?"

"No, Zach, 'cause now I know exactly where she is." I stood to leave. "I'll drop a $20 in your account for old times' sake."

Zach said nothing as I turned. He lied to my face and told me Kira was dead after I traveled across most of the country to find her. I did likewise about the double sawbuck.

Rene was outside. I marched up to her and stopped short. "She's alive," I said.

"No shit?" Rene was shocked.

"I shit you not."

"Tell me more, tell me more."

"I'm about to fall over dead. Let's talk over coffee, I hate the smell of the ocean out here."

◆ ◆ ◆

"So you're not crying," Rene pointed out.

"Over Kira? Guess I'm madder than anything. She staged this whole thing to get me off her trail. It was dangerous. I could have died."

"Died for love, how tragic. Don't you feel any kind of relief? You love her!"

We held up in a small, greasy diner. I hadn't been introduced to the coffee house scene yet so I still thought coffee came from a Bunn brewing machine. The place was close to the jail and reminded me of that place. Grimy with almost the same smell.

"I'm here with you, Rene. I love you. I bamboozled you into making this trip 'cause I didn't want to be away from you."

"Well, did he say where she is?"

"She's not in the country is all I could get from him and stay in my budget."

"What a dick!"

"I know she didn't go to Canada and I know she loves the Pacific coast."

"Baja."

"Kira will be easy to find. She sticks in people's memory."

"Well, I'm not going to Mexico," Rene announced.

"Neither am I. I found out what I needed to know. Let's get out of this one-horse town."

Rene was thoughtful. Her dark eyes searching the diner for some kind of clarity I wasn't giving her. She had been putting distance between us since our arrival. I just assumed

Monterey did that to people. "You know I'd do anything for you," she finally said.

"Why?"

"Why do you think?"

"You think you still owe me for the sloppy rescue?"

"Because I love you, you little shit."

"Hey now, watch the sensitivity. I'm a little person."

"Bitch, I'm a black woman who had to live through Reaganomics."

"Oh, right."

"You forgot? What do you see when you look at me?"

"Sex!"

"And there's the thing. I'd do a lot for you and that's why I'm leaving you here."

"What the fuck?"

"With the van! I'm taking a bus back home and you're going to work this Kira thing out, because what you're telling me is pure bullshit. This is an epiphany right from a cheap romance novel and you just want to run off with your play thing girl."

"It's not like that!"

"Well, I want to find out. And you do what you have to do, if that ends up knocking on my front door in the near future, I'll open it and you'll be welcome forever. But right now we have to part ways."

"Don't leave me," I pleaded.

"I'll never leave you, Iris. But I am taking a different way home." Rene stood. "I looked it up and the bus is not far from here. I can use my crutches to get there. I have cash that I took from your wallet while you were talking to Zach. I realize you're at a crossroad in your life. You have many choices and I'm just one option. I need you to make this decision alone, so that I know for sure. If you don't, curiosity will get the best of you. We'll be all settled in and domesticated with a schedule and fun life together, and then *boom*, you'll be off to Mexico to find this demon girl. Hustlin' your way across the border and leaving me with a sad, depressed horse. But let me make one final pitch, Iris: Choose me. After all you've been through, and all the great possibilities you have ahead, don't go find this girl who may or may not be in Mexico. Pick a path that includes love and safety for a change. Choose stability over chaos. Choose me. Of all that's available to you in the whole big, wide universe, why not me?" Rene smiled and winked, a single tear rolling down her face to rest on her chin. Then she turned and left the diner, just like that.

    Leaving me alone to cry in my coffee.

Chapter 34: Kira

The gig was gravy as far as smuggling gigs went, and it got Kira to Monterey a couple times a week. It was a day-long boat trip from El Sauzal, then an overnight stay. She navigated an aged fishing vessel along the coast, which was in sound shape mechanically, but the weathered appearance gave the sense of a professional fishing boat. There was no hiding 300 to 600 pounds of weed in the fish holds, so the subterfuge was needed to deter boarding in the first place.

She named her boat El Dorian Grey. The cartel grunts who loaded the fish holds before her trips never paid any attention to the name, and catching the attention of the Coast Guard was a chance she was willing to take, but it never happened once during her years on the route.

Kira moored her boat at Ensenada and hired a taxi. She was tired and could use a drink but the ride was short and her bar at home was well-stocked. She lit a cigarette to calm the nausea caused by landing.

Home was a tiny, yellow, Americanized house just outside of town, with a backdoor view of the ocean. The front was decorated like a suburban Midwest home with a roofed porch to keep lawn chairs on. The windows were accented with bargain store curtains she'd bought in the States. A cement sidewalk led the way to her door from the gravel street. The yard was dotted with flowers and blooming shrubs, both native and smuggled back from California. What she loved the most about the house was how her nearest neighbor was a half mile away. She found that a note had been slid under her door, instructing her to take a meeting tomorrow for lunch at the Las Rosas Hotel. She loved that place for the food and a large pool designed to melt into the ocean horizon.

Kira pulled an unopened bottle of vodka from the freezer and poured a drink. The sliding backdoor filled the room with a spectacular orange sunset over the Pacific Ocean that always left her awestruck. This place was all she ever wanted. It was furnished with what 1970s stores thought were futuristic pieces, but it was what was available to her in the Mexican shops. Orange, squared-off couch with a couple matching, sharply contoured chairs. Abstract end tables with Hawaiian lamps on each. She would be considered the queen of kitsch if anyone ever visited.

The next morning, Kira went early to the La Rosas to meet her boss, Tino. Business with Tino required copious amounts of tequila and she wanted her belly full before. She was just finishing a four-course meal when her boss made himself at home at her table. She was barefoot and wearing a green bikini with a sheer top. On her head was a lavish straw hat to keep the sun out of her eyes. If Tino didn't get her too drunk, she was going to spend some time luxuriating poolside.

"You're gaining weight, my dear," he opened the dialogue.

"Gee *thanks*."

"Oh, *bebita*, I meant no disrespect. You look good this way. You're a successful business woman." Tino was an older, dark-skinned gentleman with a kind face. His tiny, dark eyes were covered by Ray-Bans. He was obese compared to the people who lived here. Always well-kempt, always drunk.

"What did you want, other than to drink me stupid with your expensive tequila?"

Staff produced a bottle immediately as he was a regular and tipped well. He opened it and poured a shooter for them both. Kira drank heartily and went back to her dessert. Her glass was filled before she could shovel a piece of cake into her mouth.

"*Bebita*, it's time we upped the ante."

"I knew this was coming."

"You object to higher stakes? More money?"

She pointed her fork in his direction. "Not one bit. I'm invisible on the water. I actually do some fishing for myself."

Tino laughed and slid the drink in her direction.

Kira swallowed and motioned for more, which he was happy to do. "We talking about a heavier load?" she asked. "Less green in color?"

Tino smiled and nodded. "Plus the usual."

"I'm game."

"You will have to carry weapons," Tino ordered.

"I don't have any."

"You'll get some, and my son will teach you to shoot or else I'll have to put a guard on board El Dorian Grey."

"I know how to shoot."

"We have to know you can shoot," Tino said, filling her glass. "Shoot your way out of any trouble and get away completely clean. It's an art form to be precise about. Hard to learn, your mind must be set to purpose."

"Gotcha." She drank again. "I'm totally onboard."

"Totally?"

"I wish to follow your orders, enthusiastically."

"You really should learn the language. You live here."

"I should but everyone understands me. Mostly, everyone knows my habits. Taxi drivers and liquor store owners."

"That is not good, *bebita*. Maybe you dock El Dorian Grey north of El Sauzal."

"I like where she's docked now."

"You'll like up north too. You can alternate, maybe three or four places."

Kira nodded in agreement.

"And get a car."

"God, I hate driving."

"Then get a motorcycle. Get a car and a motorcycle."

"I like that idea."

"And you have to get a gun."

"I have no idea where."

"My son is where. When he teaches you to shoot, he will bring a gun and you have to buy it. It's a big fucking gun, you will not know how to shoot it, trust me."

"Okay, still on board."

"Totally." Tino smiled. He was still pouring drinks.

"That's right," Kira answered. "Hey, slow down. I may have gained some weight, but I'm still not half your size."

"I've seen you keep up before." Tino snuck a little bump of white powder on the back of his hand and held it in Kira's direction.

She snorted it all in one sniff. "That helps," she said.

"Good, now let's eat, *bebita*."

"Oh yeah, I could eat more."

Darkness settled by the time Kira returned home. She clicked the house lights on and pulled her vodka from the freezer. The back curtains were drawn and she left them that way. She sat in the front room and opened the curtain on the small, front window, poured a drink, and watched. Sometimes, if she was stoned enough, she could stare out the window all night. Every headlight that passed down the street would make her hopeful. The occasional pedestrian would be scrutinized in case it was someone lost, someone searching, maybe for her. She was lonely but only for one person.

"I made a mistake," Kira whispered into the darkness. "It was a mistake."

The weather looked bad for Thursday. Tomorrow, she could sleep off all this booze, but Thursday meant work. Kira had endured some pretty fierce storms in the past, always with success. The engines on El Dorian Grey were much newer than the outer hull let on. Shit, that boat would take her to Hawaii if need be.

Occasionally, she looked in on Zach when in Monterey. He was such a pissant, breaking into her hotel room to steal her stash. She felt no remorse having the police cart his ass away. A couple times a month, she visited to drop off some cash. He did, after all, take part in the big con of letting little Iris off the hook.

On nights like this, Kira watched out her little window and drank, hoping one day Iris would figure out she was duped and come looking for a fight. The stage was set in Kira's bungalow. After all, Iris was under a bad influence. Suicide pacts were stupid and only delusional patients of Riverside fell for those. It was a ploy to get sex. Her plan was, *You're here now, so you must want me on some level*. Kira was up for that fight, and taking off each other's clothes after. So, in a way, she was using Zach as bait since he was the first person she'd go to.

All of Kira's activities were centered on this proposed meeting with Iris. Whether she was aware of it or not, she was in love with Iris, and built this life around her for that meeting.

In a way, she was trying to be the provider, a husband. She could take care of that little bean, give her everything she desired until finally Kira would taste her soft lips and see adoration in her dark eyes.

What was wrong with that girl anyway? People bent over backwards in view of Kira's green eyes, brown hair, and voluptuous sashay. No matter how much weight she gained, she knocked them dead in their tracks.

"I'm sorry," Kira prayed into the darkness outside her window. "Come home, little bean. I'll make it good on you."

💧 💧 💧

El Dorian Grey set off early Thursday just as the coastal storm was bearing down with full force. Kira doubled down on her checklist, making sure the radio was in working order, checking the fuel supply, and safety provisions. She donned her boots and a black slicker that had been so hard to find. Why some things were so important to her, she did not attempt to guess, but her hunt for a slicker other than yellow obsessively went on for months early in her smuggling career.

This wasn't going to be an autopilot trip. Kira's fear was of smashing into shore and losing her cargo. Being blown out to sea wasn't a concern, she had the equipment and sea savvy to get back on course, but the quickest route was as the crow flew, following the shore and avoiding islands along the way. So she stayed awake, sober, and at the helm for the duration of her journey, only taking short breaks to grab another soda and candy bar.

The same way she was going to learn how to shoot big automatic weapons, she had learned to handle El Dorian Grey from Tino's son. Tino, born and raised and still residing in Mexico, had named his son Larry. It still made Kira chuckle. She knew the story of how Tino wanted his boy to study in the U.S. and work there to establish safe smuggling routes. To do so, Larry needed to be proficient in English and lay of the land. She understood this but nothing justified the name Larry in her mind.

Whether his name was American or Mexican, Larry was an alright guy in Kira's mind. She did have to explain to him that homosexuality was a real thing, and, no, she's never been with a man and didn't expect doing so would change anything. Besides, Larry was married, with a pair of fine sons.

Despite Tino's intensive training to make traversing the storm easy, Kira was tired after 15 hours. The boat could sink for any unforeseen reason, and she would make for shore, but not home 'cause Larry and his big guns would be waiting. Her life hedged on 500 pounds of dried plants arriving on American soil. So she only stopped by the county jail long enough to drop a hundred bucks into Zach's canteen account and leave to recuperate her body and senses quick as possible.

She relaxed that evening at the hotel. The same hotel she always used, often the same room if she arrived on a weekday. Everyone knew her: the concierge, the night manager, even the owner. So this was like another marina. A habit she would have to alter. Tino would be asking for reports from his American counterparts on her behavior. If it was predictable, it would mean another meeting and bottle of tequila, another sick day of depression, looking out her window at the empty street in front of her house.

Kira needed familiarity to survive. But that was how mistakes were made. Habits created patterns that could be followed if anybody ever gave a shit, which was something she couldn't fathom. Who cared about a little weed making its way to California's shores once in a while? People the government gave blocks of money to in the name of the war on drugs, that was who.

The next morning, on the way through the lobby, Kira noticed a black-wool stocking cap on the floor. It looked so much like the one she owned during her stint in the Midwest, that it took her by surprise. It would be nice to have this for sentimental purposes, but El Sauzal was not a suitable climate for wool caps. She handed it to the concierge at the desk.

"Someone must have dropped this," she said.

"Ah," the concierge stated, "I recognize this."

Kira smiled at him and walked out the door, heading for El Dorian Grey.

Chapter 35

I was alone in Monterey, again. I broke a serious promise to myself. I was too old for this shit and Janet was right, I need a home, and I knew where it was. But night had fallen and the air stank of salt water, so tonight was for hunkering down and making a plan. It was not so bad, breaking my promise. I had a long history of doing so and decided, from now on, no more promises. At least this time, I had a wad of cash and transportation.

I treated myself to a Janet-style hotel room as a reward of sorts, not for breaking my promise, but in preparation for my journey. Nice bed, a full shower, fireplace, and a fourth-floor balcony overlooking the ocean for me to smoke cigs. I called room service and ordered a big cheeseburger and fries.

Kira went to Mexico while I went to Canada. We are polar opposites. I wasn't angry with her now that I know she had a felonious benefactor watching over me. Still, she was probably betting on me not keeping my end of the pact, since she didn't keep hers. So the next leg of my journey would take some research.

When I bought my Winstons, I also purchased another atlas. I sat at my hotel desk, planning the route. This was different than hitchhiking on a freeway in the cold dark, hoping to not be raped. It would require a phone to find an address. The concierge recommended that I use the Ethernet in my room to access the Internet, whatever the hell that was.

I chewed greasy burger while studying. There was going to be a library trip tomorrow to search out-of-town phonebooks. I wrote the names of cities on hotel stationery. The next morning, I made phone calls from my room while munching potato chips, in denial of my ever-expanding tummy. A couple charming lies told into the telephone to hospitals gave me all the information I needed. It was easier than I thought.

I checked out with the concierge late the next morning. "You dropped this the other day," he said, holding up the black-wool stocking cap I'd worn for many years. The cap Kira gifted me a lifetime ago.

"Thanks," I said softly. If he hadn't given it to me, would I have missed it? I was unable to release myself from thoughtfully gazing at Kira's long-past gift.

"Don't forget to keep your head warm," the concierge reminded.

I smiled and looked up to meet his eyes. "That's right," I replied. I covered my bean with the familiar fabric and walked out to the street. The sun was warm and bright and the van was visible in the parking lot. I found the keys in my jeans and started on my trip.

My drive was uneventful and I liked it that way for a change. I didn't need to pull my machete for defense or try desperately to stay alive. I was just driving. I may have turned a corner in my life. Maybe my circumstances changed, or I had. I felt more in control of my destiny than I ever had.

There was a light shining in me and I didn't know the source. I guessed it had something to do with Janet first, then Ian. I felt endowed with confidence and virility I'd never known. Was this what it took? Teachers to show the way? Obviously, I had missed this in my traumatic upbringing. Whatever the source, the light was in me, a part of me, and I would do whatever it took for it to stay unextinguished.

My constitution, tiny as it was, was growing tired of junk snacks. I needed real calories and decided to get back on the karate food. The lessons Janet taught me were not temporary while I learned to defend myself. She meant for my life to change for the better. The people in her school were not the type to be picked up hitchhiking by a serial killer. They practiced living in a meaningful way, which was Janet's main role as Sensei. She knew getting me to Alberta would open an entirely new world for me. Strengthen my resolve to be prepared for the bigger adventure ahead.

💧 💧 💧

One of my many excursions to Dr. Agarwal's ranch involved getting to know my beautiful new sweetheart by riding bareback. Thorn had gotten used to my saddle but I wanted to get used to her, and her to know me. To feel me, a woman who loved her, riding free on her back and grasping her with thigh and arm muscle.

I was in love with Thorn. She may've been plain and young compared to others of her breed, but she was perfect to me. What I need after the tragic loss of Narragansett. My lost love who gave himself for my survival, and for Rene, who I suspected had a hand in bringing Thorn into my life.

Another trust bond with a horse was important to me. She seemed to take it all in stride as we strutted the perimeter of the good doctor's ranch. The land was a hilly and picturesque part of the Oregon outback I had become familiar with at the cabin. The property line was guarded with dense woods, not as wild and sturdy as the Canadian mountain region Narragansett and I explored so often, but thick with foliage offering a few trails.

Whether we were supposed to or not, I led Thorn into that so we could enjoy the forest as an entity and languish under the thick enclosure of the canopy. Her awareness of me included avoiding low branches that might topple me from her back. If a horse didn't want me on them, they knew how to remove me, and this sweet girl was taking precautions.

We pressed on deeper until the thicket would no longer allow us to pass and I was completely lost. The sun was hidden from view, making it impossible to get my bearings. I allowed this on purpose while I took in the sights and smells of the deep woods. I closed my eyes at times and just felt Thorn's slow pace beneath, actually unbothered by the songs of the bird species around me.

Everything joyous ran out of time and ends. I had plans to fulfill: a short trip south in search of redemption. I hugged Thorn's neck and whispered in her ear, "Take me home, girl…"

💧 💧 💧

After days traveling alone in the van, I found myself on the dark porch of a tiny, isolated, yellow-sided house on the outskirts of town along a gravel road. The sidewalk leading to the front door looked out of place for this wild edge of town, as well as the landscaping and trimmed brush. This was the address I sought and yet I couldn't bring myself to ring the bell. My final fear of rejection, having the door slammed in my face. I could continue homeless, I supposed, but I'd so much rather be here. I shuffled about a bit, trying to see behind the curtains. I had a sudden urge to smoke. I could still leave since I hadn't passed the point of no return. I, as the tiny urchin, could shun womanhood, hurry and jump into the van, light up, and drive on to a different adventure.

"Is someone out there?" came from behind the door.

"It's me," I muttered far too softly.

The porch bulb shone on me like a spotlight. "Hellooo?" I announced louder.

"Oh, my God," the voice said. "Is that really you?" The door shook and jimmied in its frame. "I can't get the fucking door unlocked!"

"Take a breath," I offered.

I heard a deep exhale from the house.

The lock clicked and the door opened. She stood in the threshold, both hands covering her mouth and tears welling in her eyes.

"Titmouse," Dahlia shouted. "You came home!"

Thanks for reading! Find more transgressive fiction (poems, novels, anthologies) at: Outcast-Press.com

Twitter & Instagram: @OutcastPress

Facebook.com/ThePoliticiansDaughter

GoFund.Me/074605e9 (Outcast-Press: Short Story Collection)

Email proof of your review on Amazon, Kindle, or GoodReads to OutcastPressSubmissions@gmail.com & we'll mail you a free bookmark!

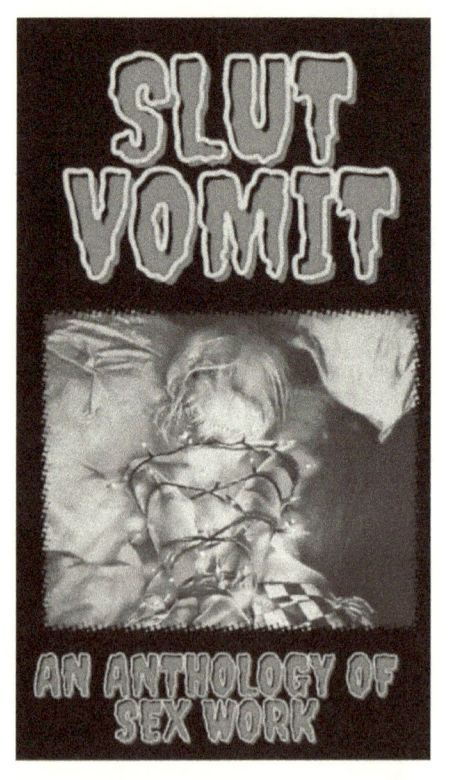

20 stories that explore the ironic side of the adult entertainment industry. Compensated cuddle bunnies to cross-dressing diplomats. Explores the world of p!ss boys and pantie sellers, every echelon of erotic entertainer from scag-seeking street-walkers to doted-upon sugar babies. Every shade of prostitution and fetishism finds a home here, as vividly represented as the LGBT spectrum.

More from Outcast Press

Loaded guns, lesbian love, inverted expectations, and lecherous mafia-types make this a novella not to forget. Kika was a map of bruises. She was a cicatrix of vengeance, the scar of a wounded mind, the fetid and gangrenous lesion of a town's malevolent psyche. And she's come back to Carbon, Georgia, to find her missing sister.

Available on Amazon, Kindle, Barnes & Nobel, Target, and more!

About the Author

I.L. Green is a certified mental illness specialist. While writing fun adventures, she incorporates what she's learned over the years recovering from borderline personality disorder that often causes symptoms of depression and anxiety. Her English degree from Bradley University is temporarily on hold as she cares for her elderly, widower father and learns more about life, love, and loss than she ever considered possible.

CPSIA information can be obtained
at www.ICGtesting.com
Printed in the USA
BVHW052259010822
643541BV00004B/323

9 781737 982951